The Soul's Glass Slipper

A Novel

ROBERTO CABRAL

Copyright © 2014 Roberto Cabral

All rights reserved.

ISBN-10: 1514254980
ISBN-13: 978-1514254981

Library of Congress:
TXu 1-941-117
Sep. 13, 2014

Revision:
Molly McKitterick
Amy Cabral

Cover design:
Roberto Cabral

Find more at:
www.robertocabral-author.com

This is a work of fiction.

Names, characters, places, and incidents either are the product of the author's imagination or are used factiously. Any resemblance to actual persons, living or dead, events, or places is entirely coincidental, except the facts related to the Great Flood of 1955, which was mentioned as a tribute to the town of Danbury, which experienced a big change after the devastating tragedy.

Printed in the United States of America

"I don't believe any of us were born as skeptics or pessimists. I believe we all have a series of events that broke our hearts and shut down those curious and excited parts of ourselves."

Sandra Champlain (We Don't Die)

Once upon a time, there was a soul…
Wait a minute; this story is not a fairy tale.
Rather, it is about life as it is, an amazing reality, which most of us are not able to perceive in our daily lives—it is incredible how we can live ignoring or not considering this reality as part of the game called life.
Yes, life is so amazing that maybe I can keep this first line. Once upon a time, there was a soul…

Chapter 1

Connecticut, Spring of 1940

An unexpected evening wind snatched the hat off his head, which rolled away on the ground almost to the other side of the street. The wind had started all of a sudden, as if nature's intention was to hold him back, prevent him from reaching home, and save him from bad news. "Damn it! This only happens when I'm in a hurry," he grumbled. He crossed the street to catch the hat. Holding, his schoolbooks beneath his arm, he used his hand to dust off the gray Homburg, he'd just bought. It wasn't his first hat. The previous one came as an obvious inheritance when his father died; he was the only son. He wore it for a while with pride when he was only sixteen, too young for a hat. People mocked him, calling him *Scarface*, the gangster. Then he decided to wear his baseball cap instead, until he was finally man enough to wear a hat.

Now that he had a part-time job in the office at The Mallory Hat Company, he had finally bought his own—a sort of diploma or a passport to adulthood, because he had recently become a father himself. Then he realized the role a hat played in a man's self-esteem.

He entered the house and found his mother dividing her attention between a book and the news broadcast about the war spreading in Europe on the radio. His baby sister was by her side, taking her regular nap. He threw his books on the couch, distracting his mom's attention from the hat with a kiss on her forehead, hiding the headwear behind his back.

"It's late Charlie, where did you go?" she said, raising her eyes from her book.

"Nowhere, Mom," he said with a sly smile, while heading upstairs to the bedroom. He wanted Georgia to be the first one to see the hat.

He knocked lightly upon the door, just in case the baby was sleeping.

A soft female voice answered, "Come in."

He put the hat on, and opened the door slowly. Sitting in bed, Georgia had reddish eyes; her face awash in tears.

His face grew pale, his smile faded, and he took off the hat, as a man was supposed to do before a woman in tears. His eyes scanned the room. Marty, his four-month-old son was sleeping peacefully in the crib. Scattered baby's clothes lay over the bed, organized by size around a small piece of luggage. Two big-sized suitcases rested on the floor near the wardrobe.

He knew the feeling growing inside well. "*No! Not again,*" he thought. The ghost was back! The same ghost that had lurking in the darkness as if waiting until the time was right.

"Where are you going?" he asked in disbelief.

She wiped her face and stared at him wordlessly. He rested the hat on the dresser near the door and came to sit by her side on the bed. "You promised you'd try," he said in a low, inquisitive voice.

She nodded. "But I can't Charlie, I'm sorry." Her gaze was tender, but her voice sounded decisive.

"Did something happen? My mom—"

"No, no..." she glanced at the baby to make sure their voices did not disturb his sleep. "Let's talk outside."

They left the house and headed into the backyard. The sun was setting down behind the houses, and the mid-spring temperature was pleasant. The wind had become only a breeze caressing their faces. They stood near the tree on which Charlie had carved their names a year ago.

"What is it now?" Charlie asked, taking control of his emotions. "Look, I know this is not a dream—having a room in my mom's house—but I can't do any better for now, making thirty cents an hour part-time. I just need a couple of years to finish college, get a full-time job, and we'll get married and have our own place with flowers in the windows and a nice Ford in the garage, as I promised." His voice became soft as he stroked her hair.

"I can't stay, Charlie. I'm not happy here," she said, her gaze revealing her anguish. "I can't pretend any longer."

Thwarted, Charlie removed his hand from her hair. "You knew, it wouldn't be easy," he said, "and three months is not enough time to make this decision."

"I have a future waiting for me, Charlie," she was emphatic. "You know how much I've dreamed about it. An actress must live in a big city where the real opportunities are; it has always been part of the plan."

"It was before," Charlie protested, "but now you have me, and we have a baby."

"I know, I know. I'm lucky that I have you and the baby," she softened her voice, touching his face gently, which helped Charlie to even his breath. His skin was warm and she sensed his effort to manage his emotions.

"Look, Charlie," she inhaled deeply. "I believe in fate and what happened to me..." she paused. "When my father got this offer to build scenery for show business in LA, it felt like fate to me. You know, my father gets chummy easily with everyone. He met influential people, doors started to open for me. I was onstage after only a couple of months of living there. Do you know what that means?

Charlie opened his mouth to protest, but she cut him off. "I was taking classes with experienced actors." She looked deep into his eyes. "If I had stayed there, I'd soon have the opportunity of my dreams: being onstage with professional actors. If I stay here..." she hesitated. She didn't want to hurt his feelings. "I feel like I'm fighting against fate."

Charlie felt like an undesirable stone in her path. Her

dreams did not include him.

"There's one more thing." Georgia's gaze transformed into sadness. "There's something wrong with my father's health. Since my mom died, he's wilting like a dying flower. He's not the same man you met, Charlie, and I'm his only family. He spent his whole life working to provide the best for me and my mom when she was alive. I'd never forgive myself if something happens to him while I'm here."

"I'm sorry about your father." Charlie thought about his own father. "I wish I could do something..."Charlie's face changed with hope. "Maybe you can bring him back to Connecticut; I could help you to take care of him."

"You know he's an old dog from the South; he never liked the cold. Why don't you come with me instead?"

"I'm in college, Georgia. I can't just move now. I'm the only man in the house; my mom and my sister need me here. "

"See, we're in the same boat." Her voice softened. "We're only eighteen, Charlie. "We both had plans. We had dreams before Marty was born. It was an accident... I'm not complaining, I love him," she quickly amended, noticing his disappointment. "But still, we need to keep our dreams alive."

"I wish you were just like the other girls," he grew impatient, turning his gaze away from her.

"What girls?" she frowned. "The kind that just want to marry, to be a wife? You had plenty of choices in this matter. But you chose me because I was different."

"I chose you because... I loved you." Eyes aflame, Charlie looked into the distance.

Georgia sighed impatiently. "I planned this conversation for days, Charlie, only to find that there wasn't an easy way out. I found though, that there are things we can do to make it work." She wished they could skip the dramatics and go straight to the plans. "I can write one letter a day; we can take turns traveling to see each other, and for you to see Marty, until you graduate and come to stay with us for good.

It won't be as easy, but it's something—"

"California is not around the corner, Georgia!" He cut her off. "We're talking about thousands of miles." Charlie instantly regretted raising his voice; it wasn't his way. He slammed his hand down on the tree trunk as if it was a door that hid an answer. Then he continued, holding back his temper. "My mom hasn't been so happy since my father died," he said, glancing around. "It has been two years already, but it still feels like yesterday. My sister was only three, and I saw my mother drawing strength from faith, so as not to give up. After you moved to LA, my mom seemed to read my soul. She told me you were just a spoiled girl and I should forget you. When you came with Marty, she fell in love right way with her grandson." He paused and gave her a pleading look. "My little sister is in love with the baby, too. We feel like we have a family again. If you take Marty away now..." he raised his eyebrows, "it's not only me that you'll hurt this time."

Georgia's eyes welled with new tears. She never meant to hurt anyone. She had tried to put herself in his shoes, and for that, she had cried all day long.

Charlie continued, his eyes revealing stored resentment. "You left once; you moved with your father to the other side of the country. Fair! You stopped writing me when you found out you were pregnant, afraid that I'd ask you to come back. I wasn't even there when my son was born. I forgave you because I love you." His gaze became overcast. "I don't know if I'll be able to forgive you again if you take my son away from me."

His last words caused her tears to fall. Charlie stared at her for a moment before heading back to the house. "Take the night to think," he said, without looking back.

A big blue moon, hanging serenely in the sky as a silent witness, revealed the earnest gaze of Charlie's mom in the window on the second floor, and Georgia wondered if coming back to Connecticut had been a mistake.

That night, Georgia could not sleep a wink. All considerations about her decision came to a dramatic ending with people getting hurt and a trace of hatred left in her wake. She lay awake in bed until the baby cried in the crib. It was 3:00 a.m. She took the baby in her arms and brought him to the kitchen so as not to disturb Charlie. She tried to breastfeed the baby, but the baby's crankiness was a sign that her milk was drying up. It was happening often lately, and she had a spare bottle of formula in the refrigerator.

She put a pot of water on the stovetop and brought it to a boil, then placed the bottle in the water to warm it up. After a few minutes, she took the bottle, squirted some formula on her wrist, and gave it to the baby. Marty sucked it eagerly for awhile before falling asleep. She brought him to the living room and settled on the couch. She would hold the baby in her arms—a breathing, warm bundle—for the rest of the night to ease the cold within her tormented soul, to feel that she had someone who she could count on. She wondered if there was a more appropriate choice to be made and tried to foresee a different future. She knew what she wanted, but a feeling of guilt was throbbing in her mind, and she felt alone, like a ghost wandering on a dark road, with a cold, threatening loneliness spreading in her soul. She missed the time when she could just lie down on her mother's lap and cry, listening to her singing, the magical power of her mother's voice relieving her childish soul. Georgia wished she could still be there to tell her what to do.

Steps on the squeaky wooden floor brought Georgia back to the present. Looking over the back of the couch, she saw Lucy Baker, Charlie's mom, in her light green nightgown. The matron had woken up when the baby first cried, and was coming to check on the light in the kitchen. Mrs. Baker glanced at Georgia in the half-light and came to join her at the other end of the sofa. She stared at Georgia with the same earnest look that Georgia had seen when she caught her in the window, and it caused the cold in Georgia's soul to grow.

"I heard you're leaving," Mrs. Baker said in a low voice.

Georgia nodded, meeting Mrs. Baker's gaze.

"You know that love comes only once in life," Mrs. Baker's said. "Maybe twice, if luck smiles upon you... but I never met a soul who was that lucky."

Georgia sense the apocalyptic tone on her voice, like a prophecy from someone who had experienced the recent loss of her loved one, and could not foresee love happening again in her life. Yet, she had barely reached middle age.

"I don't want anyone else; I will always love Charlie," Georgia replied with a tone of apology.

"You're leaving him. It sounds very contradictory to me."

"I'll come often... until he graduates and—"

"You know this will never happen."

Georgia turned her wet eyes to the baby and removed the nipple of the empty bottle from his lips. She wished Charlie's mom could be more sensitive and have good words to offer, but it seemed that she had come only to torture Georgia's stricken soul further.

"First time you left, you shattered him," Mrs. Baker said. "Charlie was still grieving his father's death. Although this is not a war that someone really wins, he overcame it with admirable courage. If you leave again, it'll be quite overwhelming for him. I'm not sure he'll be able to forgive you again. My son is a brave man, but even brave men have a limit." Mrs. Baker's voice was plain and slow-paced, her gaze, straight and deep.

"Love is powerful, Mrs. Baker," Georgia confronted her.

"But the line between love and hate is thin."

The word "hate" made Georgia shiver all over.

"I know it's a hard decision. I'm a woman too," Mrs. Baker continued in a friendly tone, although Georgia could perceive the cunningness behind it. "Charlie told me that your father needs you. It's understandable that family should always come first." She moved her gaze to the baby, then back to Georgia. "You also have dreams. Dreams are the identity of your soul, they say. But one can waste her life following impossible dreams." Mrs. Baker smoothed the flannel of her green nightgown. "Maybe fate has really opened its moody door for you, but a child requires lots of time and attention," she continued in the same tone. "Some dreams are incompatible with parenthood, you know, especially if you're a single mom: doctor appointments, nights of lost sleep... If you don't have a good night of sleep you don't function well during the day, and yours is quite a sweeping dream, isn't it?"

Mrs. Baker stared at Georgia silently. Georgia said nothing in response, hit by the raw reality Mrs. Baker was picturing for her.

The matron put a hand on the armrest as if preparing to stand up, but froze in this position. "If you'll accept advice... You won't be able to make it if you have to raise a child. Do you understand me?"

Georgia stared at her, processing the intention behind her words. Mrs. Baker gave her an enigmatic friendly smile before she stood up and headed back to bed.

Behind Mrs. Baker's apparent insensitive behavior, Georgia could see her worries for Charlie and her interest in her grandson.

"Did she really mean that?" she whispered to the baby. "Would you forgive me some day, my dear?" A tear rolled down her face and she planted a lingering kiss on the baby's forehead. Words, intentions, thoughts, and emotions: everything was so confusing at this point, but hate, this word, burned through.

In the morning, Charlie was the first to wake up, and it was very early, before sunrise. He worked in the garden in the backyard, as usual. This year, he had decided to try different techniques to grow vegetables and was curious if they were working. He loved his garden and he was very patient. He stayed there for an hour or so before returning to the bedroom.

He opened the door carefully, but could not prevent the door hinges from creaking. He was relieved to see that Georgia had already awoken. She was transferring the baby's clothes from the suitcase back into the dresser. Her eyes were bloated from the sleepless night.

"You staying?" He felt his face light up.

She looked at him for a moment then took his hand and led him to sit on the edge of the bed.

"I made a decision that's not going to be easy for me, but..." She dropped her head rather than look in Charlie's expectant eyes. "I'm leaving, Charlie, but Marty will stay," she finally turned back, her eyes meeting his. "Can you please take care of him for me?"

Charlie felt the light drain from his face. "This is madness!" He protested, but she stopped him with a finger on his lips and then kissed him. Charlie felt her warm tears on his lips. The kiss stole all words from his mouth, and he sensed that he should enjoy it with all his soul because it could possibly be the last one.

"I'm sorry," she cried, caressing his face. "This is the best I can do. But I promise you, Charlie... I promise that I'll come back."

Charlie stared deep into her eyes for a moment, as if trying to find a justification that would compel a mother to renounce her own child. Then, he realized the practical effect that her decision would have on his own life. "How do you think that I can possibly take care of him without you?" He protested. "My mom won't—"

"She spoke with me," she cut him off. "I mean, we had a conversation last night. She encouraged me to consider this. She'll help you, and I trust her. She made you a good man;

she can make him one too, though I'm not planning to be gone that long."

First, Charlie was angry with his mother. Then he considered her wisdom. The night before when he went to bed, he had faced double grief, but now he at least had something to hold onto. He made a brief calculation: he still would have his son with him, and Marty was a strong reason for Georgia to come back.

He knew well the woman he loved. When he met her in high school, she had been a feathered bird who had always found comfort in landing on his palm, but she was apt to fly away at any time. She had held her dreams above all else. But she always came back, and this time wouldn't be different. His love was still a safe nest where she could rest and be.

Charlie wiped the tears from her face fondly with deep compassion. *You'll come back to me*, he thought. *Now we'll be two waiting for you; you're not that strong.*

On Saturday morning, Charlie went out and got a taxicab to take Georgia to the bus station. He put her luggage in the trunk and waited for her in front of the house. Leaning on the side of the vehicle, he distracted his anguish with his hat, flipping it through the air onto his head.

When Georgia was leaving the house, Charlie was unexpectedly caught off guard by her beauty. *Damn, she's gorgeous!* He thought, his heart tightening. She often pinned up her black, curly hair, which was very charming, but when she let it loose, cascading over her shoulders just like now, she knocked him over. Her warm, dark brown eyes revealed her free spirit, in perfect contrast with her porcelain skin. She had long lashes, carefully lined eyebrows, like the goddesses of the movies, and dimples as a bonus to her smile that easily shined out from her sensual well-shaped lips. The belted, form-fitting, tailored yellow dress showed how fast her slim body had recovered from pregnancy. High heels and a small hat further brightened up her appearance. *If she becomes a star, I'll never see her again*, Charlie mused, his heart filling with despair.

Little Ellie, Charlie's sister, ran out from the porch and clutched at Georgia's hip. Georgia crouched to give her a real hug. "Hey, Ruby Cheek. Take care of that baby for me, okay?"

Ellie nodded with sadness shadowing her angelic face.

Georgia stood up, striving to hold back her tears, and gave a last glance at the baby sleeping in Mrs. Baker's arms at the front door. Charlie's mom gave her a reassuring smile.

When Georgia stood in front of Charlie, the tears finally fell down her face. "At least I'm the only one crying," she said.

"I got something for you," he said.

He reached into his pocket, and pulled out a present that he had bought for her on the same day he bought the hat. Her news had prevented him from giving it to her. "I didn't know why I bought it, but I guess it makes sense now."

He opened his hand with his palm facing down and a shiny glass charm dangling on a delicate chain, unfolded downwards, suspended between his fingers. She released her breath with a smile of satisfaction.

"I want you to keep this," he said, "and bring it to me whenever you come back, so I'll know that you never forgot me."

She took the chain in her hand. At the end was a tiny glass slipper, meticulously designed. "In the tale, the prince goes after her..." she smiled.

"But in the tale, she didn't leave a baby behind."

Her smile faded. She looked once again at the glass slipper and squeezed it in her hand, bringing it to her heart. "I promise. I will," she said.

She hugged Charlie one last time and entered the car that soon disappeared at the end of the street.

Chapter 2

Anna Dawson was a young woman who didn't feel good in her own skin. As far as looks were concerned, a well-qualified sperm had won the race and she had been awarded with the best genes of her parents. Her discomfort wasn't because of bad decisions she had made or because she was the unfortunate one. Actually, she couldn't remember having any major issue in life so far. Dates, or even sex, were never a priority in her youth, but she liked to flirt with guys, the sharp-minded ones. She got married—when she wanted—to a good man. Then she had a baby and her marriage slid to the background. This is how things had worked in her world so far, one thing replacing another. Yet, her unsettled spirit roamed beyond in search of something that she couldn't exactly figure out.

Back in 2000, she saw the new-agers making predictions about the new world they envisioned, but she felt that they were far more lost than she was. She thought that enlightenment could never be sold in the form of colored stones or incense or mantras or whatever comes from the outside. Those were only apparatus, which the wise monks from the East used with a purpose. The new believers in the West had misinterpreted them. For some other believers—those who wait for major catastrophic changes—the big surprise was that the year 2000 had come and gone and the world was still revolving with no change.

Her world was open as well as her mind, but nothing had really captured her soul yet. For Anna, the heart and the mind should walk side by side, faith and reason working together as a team, though people often rejected one for the other. She felt like she didn't *belong to this planet*, just like many others. She wasn't the only one, this she knew. But where were they? Where were the people who had no narrow boundaries and didn't sell their souls for the comfort of some orthodox rules?

In 2002, Anna felt like she was reaching her limits. She was tired of being a stranger in her own house. One day, she came across an article on the internet by German researchers, originally published in the *US Journal of Science*. The article stated: *"The act of exploring helps shape the brain and adventuring is what makes each individual different."* Then, she thought that writing down her feelings and thoughts, dreams and fears in a diary could be a good starting point on the adventure of exploring her own inner mysterious world. She wanted to feel alive and *different*, with a strong sense of "being special"—a sensation that had only belonged to her dreams, which everyday seemed to slide farther away.

She had made good friends in her lifetime, and among them, she could count good listeners, but, at this point, she agreed with Anne Frank: *"Paper is more patient than man."* The young Jewish girl, in the time of World War II, had been feeling alone, trapped in a house packed with refugees, and believing that nobody would want to listen to what she had to say—not even herself.

At least a little girl can be forgiven for feeling lost. Would a grown woman be forgiven by change for feeling the same way? Would someone really listen to her? Anna wondered, with Miss Frank's diary in hand, reviewing some thoughts she highlightted with a marker. *What if someone would? Would this grown woman really know what to say?*

She felt discouraged. Doubts leading to procrastination had always been a barrier in her way out of the maze. Digging into her feelings sounded like going to an old basement, full of relics covered with ancient dust. She knew she needed a big chunk of motivation to start blowing off the dust in order to assess how valuable what remained beneath was. Then, something that the young Anne wrote jumped from the pages to encourage her: "When I write all my sadness goes away."

The idea was to register on the paper whatever came to mind. Not needing to be neat or stylish, it shouldn't sound like a memoir, since she had no intention of ever showing it to anyone. It would be scattered thoughts, spontaneously expressed as they arose. She remembered her mom saying, "The beauty of a flower is that it blossoms in its perfect time." So would her writing, thoughts would bloom like flowers. Over time, she could reread her notes and look at them as if seeing herself in a mirror.

When she finally grabbed a journal and settled on the kitchen table to start her adventure, she found that the first line was challenging. She'd never been good at speaking her mind, though this was supposed to be easier since she had no audience to impress. She bit the tip of the pen (just as she used to do in school when she was anxious to start a test) and then, decided to let it run freely on the paper.

"*Sometimes I see life as mathematics, although I remember math was one of the subjects that had fewer admirers in my school days—and it's still so, I guess.*

"*I'd say: those who like math love it, and those who do not, hate it.*"

She paused. *So, maybe it's nonsense starting to talk about such a divergence*, she thought. She got upset with this unexpected problem, but this time she decided to confront it on paper. "*Why did God invent math? No, this definitely cannot be God's creation. I guess someone who wanted to make things complicated did it: Babylonians, Egyptians, Greeks... Maybe life was boring and predictable in their times.*"

She let her mind wander for a moment before resuming

her writing. *"Anyway, mathematically speaking, I can see how the universe works. My theory is simple, I'm not a genius, but as I see it, there are two different categories of people in the world: those who consider the math of life to be simple—like addition, subtraction, multiplication, division—and those who are open to exploring life through complex equations, which they sometimes spend their whole lives trying to solve. Maybe I could use the logic of math to conclude that those who make life simpler suffer less, and by consequence, they are happier; and those who experience life as explorers, are more emotionally intelligent and therefore wiser.*

"These two possibilities have their own advantages, but my conclusion is that these two types of personalities would never match. However, I see that there are couples who are seemingly opposite, even though they spend their entire lives together. Is it convenience or heroism, stubbornness or redemption, maturity or insistence? There is no way to judge them. The fact is that it's not even rare that relationships of this kind exist and last long. My guess is that we live in a dual human dimension, where each pole needs its opposite to exist, as light cannot be without darkness."

As she concluded, she realized that her writing had sent her straight to the core of her main issue at this moment: her marriage, which was exactly as she just described on the paper. The problems she and Larry had weren't because of lack of love or respect or whatever. She and Larry were different! And it was more evident every day. Their connection was loosening, as her demands for fulfillment increased.

She took a moment to focus on Larry. He was definitely the one who always wanted to make things look simpler than they actually were, and his mathematics were always predictable, though they did not always bring the results he expected.

His most recent attempt to bring joy back to their lives was the purchase of a house, the house they just moved in to. She remembered it well. It was late September. The summer had been left behind, and with it, vacation and weekends at the beach. It was time to take the warmer clothes out of the closet.

Autumn used to be her favorite season. Every meaningful event in her life had happened in fall. She was born in fall, met Larry in fall, and got married in fall. For her, fall delivered a beautiful lesson: nature knew that it must bid farewell to the glory of the warm and bright days, and retire itself to the endless cold. And it did so with majestic dignity, charming humans with the spectacle of its unusual colors. In her mid-thirties, this was the way she envisioned the verge of the winter of her age, when her grayish hair would match the beauty that experience would carve on her face. But fall had been like any other season in recent years, and this one felt unpromising, without any exciting plans, besides enjoying the treats of the new season—pies and cakes made out of pumpkins, and apples picked at the local orchard with her son—or the predictable dinner celebration of their anniversary and her birthday a week apart, which often were merged into a single event, if not blended into Thanksgiving in a combo celebration.

Fortunately, in spite of her mood, the new season painted the natural world yellow and red, orange and brown, turning the streets and hills of Western Connecticut into postcards. It was a propitious moment to buy a property. Larry's dream was that the new season in a new house could be a turning point in their lives. Anna, though, could not foresee any change from the fact that they'd be surrounded by different walls, but she did not express her feelings. She didn't want to be accused of not trying. So she agreed, and they decided to see what was available on the market. Ultimately, they weren't seeking a house, but a new formula to solve their life's equation.

Larry had outlined in his mind what he wanted, and it had

been relatively easy for him to find the perfect property: cozy, safe, and ready for them to move in. Only a month had passed since the day they went to the open house, and Anna could still hear the sound of the gravel cracking under the wheels of the car, a sound that competed only with the flapping of the leaves in the wind when they crossed the long driveway. As soon as they pulled up the car, six-year-old Marvin, their only child, slid from his booster seat, and was the first to open the vehicle door. He ran across the front lawn. They followed him from a distance, enjoying his excitement. The lawn wrapped around the left side of the house and ended in a gorgeous backyard with a wide variety of flowers and some well-shaped boxwoods, showing the care of the previous owners. The house, a split-level style, relatively new construction with a charming brick finish facade, felt like happiness.

Anna was on the deck at the back of the house staring at a delicate wind chime and enjoying its relaxing performance when Larry approached and embraced her around the waist, seeking her approval.

"Just say 'yes' and this will be our home sweet home, before you close and open your eyes again," he said with an affectionate confidence.

Anna glanced at her excited son chasing a butterfly, which was practically an endorsement for the cozy property.

"Marvin has already given his approval," she said, diverting her gaze, fabricating some joy on her face and offering her cheek for a kiss that Larry was aiming elsewhere. He accepted, and kissed her, tenderly.

He was excited, but Anna feared that it could be one more unsuccessful and disappointing try, which would ultimately lead to the failure of their marriage. She wasn't prepared to consider that as a possibility. For her, marriage was for life, and she couldn't believe that after such a perfect beginning, all joy and happiness was now slipping through her fingers.

Larry and Anna married when they still lived in their

hometown, in Pennsylvania, and they had their son there. Larry Dawson, a successful insurance executive, was chosen by the company, in which he had served for thirteen years, to inspect the franchised agencies in the state of Connecticut. He spent almost a year making weekly trips between the two states, being promoted in the end to the position of regional manager. Then he decided to settle in the town of Danbury, mostly due to its easy access to highways and airports, but also because of its privileged location at the exact midpoint between the capital of the state, Hartford, and New York City. He had been in the City many times with Anna, even before they got married, and their fascination for Broadway shows was a shared delight, which played a big role in their connection when they started dating. What he had in mind for their home, however, resembled anything but the excitement of the City. After dwelling in several hotels by himself, and later on, living in a rented condo in a central area with Anna and Marvin, Larry was looking forward to making his dream come true: living in a peaceful house, in an area where the chirping of birds and the sound of the wind in the leaves were the only songs heard, rocking the sweet dream of a perfect life: kids, beautiful house, nice car, excellent income.

Anna, the daughter of Brazilian immigrants, worked after college and during the first years of her marriage as a teacher in a daycare facility. After Larry had been promoted—which represented a considerable raise in his salary—she quit her job to devote time to homeschooling her child. It was something that she had wanted since he was born. Marvin seemed to be her partner in life, and she didn't want to be away from him, even for an hour or so.

Everything had seemed so incredibly perfect, that she couldn't pinpoint when or why things started to change. Strangely enough, when she evaluated her innermost feelings, she could see no major changes. She still felt affection for Larry. She admired him, wanted to protect his feelings, and strived not to show the drama as long as she could when it started to grow in her soul. It was a personal issue, she considered, because Larry had been always a good man, a great father, a sweet husband. How could she not love this man fully? Why couldn't she feel just as before, when love was like a party, sparks floating around every time she saw the love of her life? These thoughts had occasionally pushed her to the brink of the abyss of depression—and she had learned that depression is an emotional reaction when you don't accept a situation that you cannot change. But how could she accept what she could not understand? For her, at least the math of marriage should be simple, like man + woman + love = happiness. But life presented a new equation man + woman + daily duties = X. This "X" had taken her sleep away.

She saw some friends getting divorced without even trying to fix whatever was wrong, and she never considered it as a choice for herself. She never felt like leaving Larry. This idea terrified her. It was as if life had chosen her fate and that was it.

She could still count the good moments of family and coziness. There was even room for some romance in their lives. On those romantic nights, when flowers, soft music, and a glass or two of wine took her away from her emotional whirlwind (it had become common for Larry to use all his talents to bring her closer), she could sleep in heaven again. But, when the sun rose, the ghosts came back to stalk her helpless heart.

She had been pushing herself harder lately to find a solution to her existential conflict. She was still young, but it'd better happen sooner than later, because life was passing quickly through her. Moreover, there was no someone else, which for many couples is a main ingredient of a marital crisis. So, the best was to occupy her mind and strive to be a good wife, good mother, just perfect, as perfect as the man she had chosen.

All these memories and conjectures, she tried to translate into words in her diary: *"I have everything that I need here, but I can't understand this feeling. It's as if my body is here, but my soul is somewhere else, stuck in another dimension or forgotten time."*

When she expressed all her anguish on paper, she seemed to open a door. It triggered a series of events, as though the gods had heard her silent appeal and decided to unveil the big picture behind her reality.

Chapter 3

Since the notebook had become her best friend, the kitchen table was Anna's favorite spot to unload the heavy weight from her soul. Out of habit, she first sat with her chin in her hands and let her thoughts wander, while watching, through the window, squirrels stealing seeds she put out for the birds on the deck. Then, she drew inspiration from looking at the majestic deciduous trees beyond the long-grassy backyard, their colored leaves in contrast with the white clouds and the blue sky.

On this Sunday afternoon, though, her attention steered to Larry crouched on the deck, finishing a gorgeous, diamond-shaped yellow kite with a green tail, a model he had learned how to build in Brazil. Marvin's curious eyes were taking account of each movement of his father's not too skilled hands.

"These are the colors of Brazil, remember?" he said to his son, pouring one extra dot of glue on the edges of the kite, and then reinforcing the attachment of the sheet paper to the bamboo skewers with insulation tape. He had chosen to use the exact materials called for by the instructions, and had not given up until he found them on the market. He wanted to make sure that Marvin would have an authentic Brazilian kite, similar to the one Marvin fell in love with in Brazil.

"I know." Marvin's face contorted with annoyance. He knew the colors of Brazil well. "The blue is missing," Marvin warned.

"Good catch! Maybe we can mix up the tail with green and blue, and make it longer. What about that?"

"Okay." Marvin sounded not excited. Larry seemed to be the only one having fun with the kite.

Larry had been with Anna in Brazil and Marvin a couple of times, and learned much about his wife's parents' homeland. He went to Rio de Janeiro, witnessed the jaw-dropping view from Christ the Redeemer, and enjoyed the beaches. He had gone to Maracanã for a soccer match and felt the power the game had in Brazil. But it was in Bahia where he had seen Brazil in its most dazzling colors, the colors on walls, clothes, craftworks, and especially in the souls of the people. Then he fell in love with Brazil, and welcomed the lively and interesting Brazilian culture to be part of their lives. He knew that Marvin would grow up in his own culture and language. Adding another culture to his life starting in childhood would be very enriching. Though this would also be a hard and constant process of seeding—which obviously would mainly be Anna's job.

Marvin had never showed any problem expressing himself in both languages or enjoying the richness of both cultures. At his age, he couldn't really see the difference. This afternoon he had chosen to wear the yellow Brazilian national soccer team jersey, with the number nine and the name of a famous soccer player on the back, a gift from his grandfather.

It had been a gorgeous day so far, but by late afternoon, the wind began to blow stronger, announcing coming rain. Larry was focused on the last adjustments when raindrops began to fall on the kite's silk sheet. Frustrated, he decided to tell Marvin that they had to postpone the adventure. When he looked around though, he did not find his son. He took the kite back to the house, expecting to find the child with his mother.

"Did you see Marvin coming in?" he asked, managing to avoid bumping the fragile kite on the furniture while dealing with its long tail.

Anna had been distracted with her diary and had not seen

Marvin leave his father. At that, Larry turned the house upside down in an unsuccessful search and then went back outside, shouting Marvin's name.

In a blink of an eye, the weather had changed drastically. The day had become darker, and the rain had started to fall heavily. Anna was worried, and began to search for Marvin in every unusual corner of the house—inside closets, under beds, in the bathtub—when she noticed the door that led to attic half open. She followed her maternal instinct and went up there. The attic was a sort of camping area for her son, with a tent and some scattered toys. The light bulb had burned out, as Anna found when she tried to turn it on. She called for her son in a soft voice. A bolt of lightning lit up the room, displaying Marvin hiding inside the tent, terrified, as if he had seen a ghost. His startled eyes were flooded with tears. Anna gathered up her son. Marvin clung to his mother's lap, and only grew calmer after she repeatedly assured him in a whispered voice that everything was well, hugging him tight, stroking his black hair gently.

When Larry came back into the house, Anna was in the living room with the child in her arms, still comforting him. Larry watched them from the door, and Anna gave him an assured look to prevent him to come closer and flood the carpet with his soaked clothes.

Later that night, Anna stayed with Marvin in his bedroom until he fell asleep. The rain had given up a little, but it still fell.

When Anna finally went to bed, Larry was still awake, reading a book and waiting for her.

She went straight to the dresser to comb her wavy black hair, a habit she had since she was young. "He fell asleep," she reported, anticipating Larry's thoughts.

"Why was he so scared?"

"The storm. Just like happened in Cape May?"

"But that day he was upset because we went to the beach

instead of the water park."

"No!" She was surprised with his short memory. "We already had this conversation. It was because of the rain. Don't you remember that he slept in our bed that night?"

"So..." he trailed hesitantly. "Maybe it's because we just moved in. He will get used to the house, eventually." He was trying to make things simple.

Anna gazed at him in disbelief. He was supposed to remember those relevant events in their child's life.

Larry slid through the bed and reached out to her. He positioned himself behind her back and started to gently rub her shoulders.

"How did you know that was exactly what I wanted?" she said, relaxing with the touch of his warm hands.

"I used my super-powers. By the way, is there any time when you don't want it?"

"You're right," she smiled.

He kept moving his hand gently from the back of her neck to her shoulders then to her shoulder blades, slightly rotating her shoulders back and forth. She loved when he did that and wished he would never stop.

"Today we've lived one month in this house," he said. "You think that it was a good choice?"

Anna sensed the intention behind his question. "The house is wonderful." she pretended naivety.

"Is that it?"

"Marvin seems happy here."

"And ..."

Anna became silent, sensing the expectation of this man by her side, so dedicated, so caring, so patient. She'd been sliding from an open conversation since they moved in, afraid that it could only make things harder, though it was becoming almost impossible to avoid further. In fact, she wished that she had something new to say, something romantic and spontaneous to enchant him. "I see what you want to know, Larry. I see everything you're doing for us," she finally said. "You've always been unbelievably wonderful, trying to fill in for the lack of interaction with my family since we moved to Connecticut. But, I guess, I need more time. I just need to thread it into my head. Marvin and I will adapt. Things will fall into place at their own pace. Just be patient, okay?"

"It sounds like you're blaming me for moving us away from Philadelphia..." he cocked his eyebrow.

"No, I'm not," she assured.

"I want you to tell me if something is not right, okay?"

"You did the right thing. The problem is not you. It's me, and I'll settle myself up."

He looked at her reflected in the mirror, wondering how to enter her world, which seemed every day more impenetrable. He'd been trying his best, and still could not find words or gestures to bring her closer, to become the one to whom she could open her heart. He could listen to life, every day, telling himself that to love meant to give even more, to wait a little longer, to push acceptance farther and, sometimes—or often—not think much of himself.

I don't think I can bear it for as long as you want. I'm just human..., he thought, but didn't say it.

The rain picked up during the night, and Anna got up more than once to check on Marvin, but he was sleeping quietly. She forced herself to relax and finally fell into a deep sleep for a couple of hours. In the middle of the night, the thunder returned in successive bangs. Marvin's crying awoke her with a gasp. She sat straight up in bed disturbed, wondering whether she dreamt it. She lit up the bedside light and noticed that Larry was also awake.

"Did you hear that?" she said.

"Yes," he replied, jumping out of bed, followed by Anna.

When they got to Marvin's bedroom, they found he sitting in bed terrified. Larry hugged his son tightly. Marvin cried inconsolably. "Stop the rain... Please, don't leave me alone! I don't want to die." He repeatedly said as if still caught up in a nightmare.

Anna and Larry grew worried and tried to calm him in turn for almost an hour before they decided to bring him to their bed. Once Marvin felt safe, snug between his parents, he became quiet and slept the remainder of the night.

The day dawned optimistically with a clear sky, and a big, bright sun, as if the entire storm had been only a bad dream.

When Larry came to the kitchen for breakfast, dressed for work, Anna was talking to a friend over the phone and Marvin was absorbed in his drawing, surrounded by sheets of paper and crayons on the kitchen floor.

"How's my champ?" Larry kissed his son.

"Look, Daddy!" Marvin showed his work. "I'm drawing my dream."

Larry gazed at the paper, praised him briefly, but didn't give much importance to Marvin's artwork. Anna, on the phone, had caught his attention. She was disheveled and her eyelids were bloated after the sleepless night, but, even so, he was attracted to her.

He stared at her, noticing the way she spoke and expressed herself. There was light in her, the same light that made him fall in love with her ten years ago. He was intrigued that she didn't sound as confused and faded as she had been lately. Larry believed that her problems were associated exclusively with him, although she always denied it.

"Why don't you come over this morning?" Anna said to her friend, at the end of the conversation. "Then you can see the house."

Before she hung up the phone, she caught Larry staring at her with those melting eyes and raised her eyebrow as if inquiring the reason for that passionate expression at that time of the morning. She briefly reported to Larry the conversation with her friend (who he usually referred to as "crazy Lisa" because of her natural talent to get into complicated relationships and to speak about the supernatural) to intentionally distract him. Then she brought Marvin to the kitchen table and turned to the stove to prepare some oatmeal for them. Larry came closer, embraced her from behind, and kissed her neck. She welcomed the peaceful moment and returned the affection.

Marvin took advantage of their distraction and sneaked back to the papers and crayons scattered on the kitchen floor. They smiled, noticing Marvin's opportunism.

"While you finish it, I'll go get the newspapers," Larry said, heading towards the front door.

Anna finished the oatmeal, grabbed some ripe peaches and nectarines, washed them up, and put them all on the table.

"What are you drawing? Umm...it seems very important," she teased, approaching Marvin.

"Just my dreams." He handed the drawing to Anna.

She looked at it curiously. The depiction of his nightmare was not anything scary, though. It was just a house in a river and few trees close by. "Good job!" she said. "Can I suggest something? What if you move the house up a little bit? It seems to be located inside the river."

"The river is dragging the house," Marvin answered, somewhat impatiently.

"You mean it's some sort of a *boathouse*?" she concluded.

"No, the house is being dragged by the flood. A huge flood!" And Marvin made a noise and a movement to represent the scene. "I was inside the house, so you can't see me, but I was there."

Marvin had no way of knowing what a flood meant because he had never seen one. Possibly, he had seen it on TV, and the storm had instigated his imagination, "Who else is in the house with you?" Anna probed.

"I'm alone. I was very scared, but I wanted to save the

lady," he answered, surprising Anna even more.

Larry came back, interrupting the conversation.

"The paper hasn't arrived yet, certainly because of the rain," he said. "A tree fell at the Sullivan's; luckily it didn't hit the house. I'm wondering how many claims we'll have reported today."

"Well, that's what insurance is for, and it wasn't a hurricane," she replied, discouraging him from talking about business at the breakfast table. She carried Marvin back to his chair. "Let's eat with Daddy, Marvin, and then you can finish your drawing."

"It's done," Marvin said.

When Larry left, Anna headed to her diary. She was feeling uncomfortable since their conversation the previous night. She felt pressured. In fact, she was blaming herself. She decided that she needed to write.

Her thoughts wandered for a moment through past events—the day she met Larry at a wedding of a mutual friend, their first date, her own wedding, Marvin's birth—and everything seemed so perfect. Life had no right to change the math, she thought.

Something in her mind made her curious, and she went to the computer to do some research. She thought that clarifying some concepts would be a help. The first thing she found is that mathematics was an *exact science*. Not a surprise, but what did *exact science* mean? Then she read the answer on the screen out loud (to ensure that no other thoughts would take her full attention away): "EXACT SCIENCE: ANY FIELD OF SCIENCE CAPABLE OF ACCURATE QUANTITATIVE EXPRESSIONS, PRECISE PREDICTIONS AND RIGOROUS METHODS OF TESTING HYPOTHESES."

It didn't help. Nothing in her emotions could be "accurately expressed" or "precisely predicted." She couldn't even see hypotheses to consider. Life did not belong to the exact sciences, she concluded.

"Would there be any way to start over from scratch?" she wondered. It was said that nobody fell in love with the same person twice, so there was no way to start over, she concluded disappointedly. Then she typed the word "happiness" and thousands of links came up on the screen. She saw a Snow White picture and thought that movies, books, and soap operas, usually ended with a happily ever after, just like in those fairy tales. A big illusion! *Daily life turned princes into frogs. Would it be a mistake to desire being in love with a partner forever—or at least till death do us part?* She considered that an affirmative answer to this question would be very frustrating. If she accepted this as a solution for the equation, life would be as boring as math. She went back to her diary, wrote her thoughts down, and closed it.

She looked at Marvin playing with a puzzle on the living room rug, and thought that he was the only truth she did not need to decipher. There was no equation hidden in the love she felt for her son, nor in the gratitude that she had for having him.

Chapter 4

At 11:00 a.m., her friend, Lisa, arrived. She was a pretty, shapely, woman, with short, straight ginger hair, in her mid-thirties. She was newly single, recovering from a recent break up with her boyfriend whom she had lived with for two years.

Anna met Lisa by chance, when visiting a mutual friend, and they instantly connected, as if they had known each other their entire lives. Curiously, it wasn't because they had the same likes, but their differences seemed to fill each other's gaps.

Anna came to the door to greet Lisa, and invited her to walk around to see the property.

"So, how's life in this new nest?" Lisa asked when they reached the back yard.

"Well, the house is very comfortable, enough space for Marvin. It couldn't be better."

"Comfortable?! Is that it? You must be kidding me; this house is awesome!" Lisa stated, looking around.

"You just started looking!"

"I don't need to see everything. I can feel the energy. The previous owners might have had a happy life here. What about Larry? Is he excited or does he also think the house is 'comfortable'?"

"He's happy, I guess. He likes the neighborhood. He sought out this property very carefully."

"And have you guys found the missing link?" Lisa probed.

Anna sighed. "Missing link? Do you always have a name for everything?"

"Sorry, I'm just a straightforward person who tries to make

things simpler, remember?"

"How could I forget? You never let me. But I like 'missing link'! Sounds like a title of a book." Anna wondered if her life would ever fit in a book. "Maybe this is what Larry was looking for when he bought this house. People say that things like this usually work, I mean, buying a house, going for a romantic vacation, or even remarrying each other—a wedding party to remind us what we had forgotten." She sighed ironically. "I don't know, I think that when it's supposed to happen it just does so, like when we met each other ten years ago. It just happened, it was our fate. Why do we have to reinvent the wheel now? Doesn't fate have any further plans for life after marriage? Is it a done deal?"

"Sorry to say, but it sounds like you're waiting for a miracle."

"It'd be much easier." Anna sighed again, tired of dealing with her own thoughts.

"And Larry, how's he reacting?"

"He has been patient, he's always there for me, I can't complain. Actually, I can! Why does he have to be so perfect? He's the best husband a woman can have! There are times when I find myself looking for some flaw with him to justify myself, to not feel guilty, but it's just a waste of time. This is my own karma and he has nothing to do with it. Even when he tries to help me, he pushes me away."

"You're not seeing someone, are you?" Lisa gave her a suspicious look.

Anna stayed silent intentionally, because it seemed obvious for anyone to think that there was another man. Eventually, someone would judge her and take it for granted.

"Huh? Are you?" Lisa insisted. "Oh, gosh, I can recognize it from miles."

Lisa had never had undeniable proof that her boyfriend was really cheating on her, but she suspected it. She also rejected reconciliation when he attempted to heal the relationship. Currently, she was struggling with an unresolved feeling.

"No, I'm not." Anna was upset—because at least with her dear friend Lisa she had the right to get upset. "Life is not an exact science, my dear friend. Not always A plus B equals C." Now, she could say that, for it had become clear for her. "And you know what? It might be a good idea!" She quipped. "If I meet someone interesting, I may fall in love again."

"Are you saying that you don't love Larry anymore?" Lisa was surprised with Anna's Freudian slip.

"I'm just kidding," Anna said, her tone turning impatient. "I do love him. Maybe I just don't remember how it works. Maybe we're just getting old, and it's time to change our perspective on marriage. I don't know. How am I supposed to know? Maybe the problem is me. I just hope that all this is only a phase that will eventually pass. I can even hear God's voice roaring from above: 'See Anna, life is so simple, and you are so dramatic!'."

Lisa looked at her friend with compassion. But she felt unable to help, her own situation being no better. Instead, she asked Anna about the flowers in the backyard, curious if this was a new ability of Anna's or if the flowers were already there when they moved in.

When Anna invited her to see the inside of the house, Lisa noticed that Marvin hadn't come to jump in her arms yet, as he always did. "How's Marvin? How's the experience with home schooling?" Lisa asked.

"He's doing great, but it's still too soon to tell," Anna said.

"Don't you worry about him feeling apart from the world?"

"I don't see it happening. He has activities with other kids from the home school program. He has made friends. Actually, he is very sociable, more than me, I guess.

"Is Larry still against your decision?"

"He still refuses to invest his time in it, but at least he doesn't bother me anymore. His parents are radically against it, though. But I don't care; it's my job to find the best way to educate my child."

"I think you're crazy. I could never handle this without my partner's support."

"Maybe I am, me and two other million moms in this country."

"Wow. I didn't know there were so many. But, to me, you're still a crazy-adorable-homeschooler mom. Why do you always have to be different?"

"What's the point of not being different?" Anna replied in the same tone.

Although Lisa never wanted to follow Anna's life choices, which included the unfashionable way she often dressed, the healthy eating habits she got from Larry, the homeschooling choice, and her lack of interest in makeup or feminine accessories, which Lisa considered essential, she admired her. Anna had the courage to stick up for what she believed. She enjoyed Anna's company, her way of seeing the world. Anna's spontaneity was what attracted Lisa most. Anna was adventurous and had no perfect measurements for consequences, at least in Lisa's eyes.

Anna took Lisa for a tour inside the house; afterwards, they settled in the kitchen for a cup of tea.

Marvin was back to his drawing in the living room and came only to get a big kiss from Lisa then rushed back, as if he was busy in the middle of something important.

Lisa showed Anna a new book she was reading about psychology, from a spiritual perspective. The author of the book was a prominent Brazilian medium, who wrote the book through psychograph—the author was a spirit guide. Anna was familiar with Lisa's paranormal interests and, though she never followed the same beliefs, she let Lisa express hers. Besides, she was happy that Lisa was taking steps to get out of her hell.

The pages were filled with yellow highlights, a clear sign of

Lisa's excitement with the reading. "It's about self-forgiveness. You know, I must forgive myself before I forgive Jim. It seems to be the hardest part. Maybe, in the end, I'll find that it was my own fault, I guess."

"How can Jim's betrayal be your fault?" Anna was curious. "Is this book making you feel this way?"

"Not exactly. The book is about how we create resistance to accept our own disturbing behavior; the conclusion is mine. Sometimes I think that I could've done things better; if he sought out another woman, it's because he was unhappy with the one he had."

"I think you're only half right, honey. You never had real proof that he was cheating on you, and even if he was, you never asked for it. If he did it, it was his choice. You should start the reading over. Please, go back to the first page and change your perspective."

Marvin approached them with a new drawing in hand. "Look, Mom. This is me and Dad."

Anna turned her attention to the drawing, which was of a house, a man with a hat, and a child. "I see that you are building a full story," she acknowledged Marvin for the smart way he was expressing his creativity.

"We used to live in this house," Marvin spontaneously added.

"And Mom, where is she?"

"I had no mother. Just my father, my grandma, my aunt, and me. My dad's name was Charlie, and he worked at the hat factory. My name was Marty. I was living with my Grandma, but my dad was living here when the river flooded the town." He pointed to the house on the paper, which has some scribbles representing unidentified details.

Anna stared at the paper speechless. The drawings were becoming a story, a strange story though, for a six-year-old child. She moved her eyes to Lisa, seeking an explanation. Lisa cocked her eyebrows in response, as if asking what is wrong with a child using his imagination to create a story.

Before they could translate their thoughts in words, Marvin returned to his makeshift studio on the living room and grabbed another drawing. This one showed a woman and a man in a canoe, which had the name *Danbury Police* written on the side.

"This is the first flood. This is Mrs. Goodwin," he pointed the woman. "And this man is helping her. He saved Mrs. Goodwin. Her house was half under the water."

Marvin returned quickly to grab another drawing and came back before the two women could exchange a word.

"Here is the city," he showed in the new drawing. "Houses and stores are underwater. All the goods in the basements were lost. It was a huge loss."

The drawing had two parallel lines representing a street with houses on both sides. In the middle of the intersection, there was a very tiny house. Curiously, Marvin had drawn some fish on the street, as if he wanted to show the river running over it.

Anna was astonished at how detailed the picture was and intrigued that Marvin was using words that had never been part of his vocabulary. "How could you imagine all these details, Marvin? You're a true artist! We have an artist in our family!" She declared, disguising her perplexity.

"I didn't imagine it, Mom. I was there when it happened."

Marvin's answer made Anna dizzy.

"Home school is awesome," Lisa mumbled ironically, as Marvin went back to the living room.

Anna gave her a dirty look.

"Maybe it's just an overactive imagination," Lisa said. "Or maybe he is recovering memories from his past life," she added, to apologize for the comment.

"Is this a sort of inspiration from your guardian angel or did you read it in this book too?" Anna said wryly.

"Not in this book, but I've read something about it. If I'm

not wrong, it was in *Oprah Magazine*. Children, at a certain age, remember events from past lives."

"Are you serious? Everything has a spiritual explanation for you?" Anna scoffed. "It's just a childish imagination, don't you see? Awkward, but what else could it be?"

"Maybe Marvin is trying to tell you something. Has he shown any strange behavior lately?" Lisa asked seriously.

"Well, last night he had a rough time, which has become regular during storms, although his reaction had never been as bad. But it doesn't mean—"

"Maybe it doesn't mean anything; maybe it does," Lisa cut her off. "Marvin speaks as if he knows what he is saying. It sounds like some sort of memory. I'm not saying that it is, but it's very peculiar."

"Okay. Tell me what you know about it." Anna surrendered to the seriousness of Lisa's tone.

"I don't know much, but what I read is that it can be caused by some traumatic event from a former life that emerges to be healed."

"You're scaring me," Anna replied. "Marvin never liked storms, and yesterday there was a lot of thunder and lightning. He was frightened," she said trying to find a more reasonable answer.

"Well," Lisa sighed, "if so, you should expect that he would will to forget his nightmares instead of keeping them alive in his drawings. You don't have to take it for granted, but it doesn't hurt to observe. If, in fact, those are memories from a past life, you will know, because he'll tell you things that will surprise you even more."

Anna was thoughtful and turned to watch Marvin distractedly drawing on the living room.

Later in the day, she wrote in her diary:

"Today Lisa called my attention to what she believes are memories emerging from Marvin's past life. It sounds crazy, of course, not a surprise since it's coming from her. I agree that

he's been super creative, making up stories; but should I link his hysterical behavior on rainy days to something so surreal? Maybe Lisa has been reading too much and she has become even more creative than Marvin. But what if she is right? Could it be a clue to find a way to help my child? I don't know. It's not easy for me, as a mom, to accept that my son may have a major problem. Maybe it doesn't cost anything to observe, as Lisa said. Maybe this is something to focus my mind on and forget my own crazy issues: a blessing in disguise."

Chapter 5

Around eleven, a little after Lisa left, one of the Marvin's homeschooled friends arrived with his mother to pick him up. The plan was that Marvin would spend the day with his friend and then sleep over.

As Anna watched the car pull away, she had her fingers crossed and prayed that God would not allow another bad night. More storms were expected that evening.

Once alone, she wrote down a list of errands to run, and got herself ready to get out. She planned a drive to town to grocery shop and ship the birthday present she had bought for her mom.

The driving took her no more than ten minutes in autopilot mode, absorbed in her thoughts and concerns.

She drove to Wooster Square, by Kennedy Park, a small green area located near the Post Office in the center of Danbury.

Kennedy Park was the main spot for day laborers. They arrived early in the morning wearing warm clothes, willing to do a job of any kind offered by contractors that stopped by. From inside her car, Anna watched those young men, Spanish looking, swarming around every truck or van that stopped, and wondered about the types of discomfort they had to deal with to provide for the families, that they left behind in their homelands. How many stories were those tired faces and calloused hands hiding? She had grown up listening to stories from her parents about immigrants; she knew well their struggles and dramas, as well as their hopes.

Danbury had become a city of immigrants from all parts of

the world, mainly from South America, most from Brazil and Ecuador. At the end of the twentieth century, immigrants commercially populated Main Street, in the area where most of the historical events of the city had taken place, beginning in 1776, when the commissioners of the new American Army chose Danbury for a place to deposit for military stores.

After the Danbury Fair Mall was built in 1986, many Main Street merchants had closed their doors due to emptying of the city center. This was the time when, coincidentally, immigrants began to arrive in waves. The closed stores re-opened with products to serve immigrant communities that included, as well as the South Americans, Italians, Asians, Arabs, Indians, and Portuguese. Some of them were now well established in town.

The Post office was an old building that replaced the old train station in the beginning of the past century. Anna was disappointed that the line was very long for that time of day, but one of the two postmen on duty was friendly and funny, making costumers laugh, and distracting them from the length of the line. There was Frank Sinatra songs playing on a CD player on the shelf behind the counter, and sometimes one of the postmen ventured to sing along. Anna acknowledged that those men knew how to create a nice environment at work; they could be there simply following their routine, but they chose to make their work hours as pleasant as possible. Small things, coming from unknown special people, made life more enjoyable, she thought. It lifted her mood.

After shipping the package, Anna desired a cup of coffee to warm up a bit. Fall was playing with the weather, changing between cold, warm, windy and rainy days, occasionally dropping the temperature abruptly during the day, just like what was happening that late morning.

She entered a small convenience store where the coffee was self-service, in carafes in the front right corner of the store. She chose a black decaf and refrained from adding cream.

When she was deciding whether or not to sweeten her coffee, she noticed a set of large, framed black and white photographs hanging on the wall right in front of her. They were pictures of a flooded town from decades earlier. They showed the damage to the streets and a temporary shelter where people had sought out help. If the convenience store were an alternative coffee shop, the pictures would have been cool, but what were they doing here? Anna wondered. Maybe the owner had taken the pictures himself and wanted to show off his skills, scooping the media, doing history. She asked the attendant about the origin of the photos, and he said that it was Danbury in the time of the Great Flood of 1955.

It seemed like a coincidence that she encountered these pictures on the same day that Marvin was telling stories and drawing about a flood. She strived to dismiss the connection, but she could not ignore it. She had never entered the convenience store before, and she had just gone in there because there was no other option for coffee nearby.

She paid for the coffee and headed back to the street.

It was only a short walk to the public library. She was curious about the tragedy in the photos and any connection with Marvin's dreams and drawings. When she entered the library, she saw an announcement for a children's music program the library was hosting and she regretted not having known about it beforehand because Marvin would have enjoyed it.

At the front desk, she asked the clerk for some material about the Great Flood of 1955.

The girl brought her to the historical room, a small room in the corner of the library. Then, she took a yellow thick folder from a file cabinet and handled it to Anna. "Here is the best collection of material we have," she said.

As Anna opened her mouth to thank her, a man entered the room, demanding some information, speaking Portuguese. When the girl responded, Anna recognized that she was Brazilian, though she had no accent when she spoke to her in English. She had desires to speak to them; however, she only glanced at the pair and said nothing. She had other priorities and was excited to open that Pandora's box. The clerk left the room followed by the man, and closed the glass door behind her.

Anna pulled a chair out from the conference table, the only table in the small room. Its walls were covered with shelves packed with old books. As she sat down, she noticed a man at the opposite end of the table, absorbed in some research. She couldn't help noticing that he was handsome and wondered why she had not noticed his presence before.

She first pulled out a thin booklet with a yellow and red cover titled "Danbury Flood Pictures." It was a pictorial review of the disaster of Oct. 15-16, 1955, as she read on the bottom of the cover. She flipped the pages of the booklet with some anxiety, and after finishing it, she noticed a thick white envelope, which was full of newspaper clippings. She slid them out on the table.

She learned that in 1955 two hurricanes, *Connie* and *Diane*, swept through Connecticut, and unleashed a devastating flood, the worst natural disaster in state records. Many deaths were reported after a trace of devastating damages. The first hurricane hit in August, and the city was still recovering when an even bigger storm hit on October 15. Stores and houses on Main Street and surrounding areas were greatly affected, and because the waters of the Still River took long to recede, losses were very high. The city center, after that, underwent profound transformation and new stores replaced houses on Main Street. The city made efforts to prevent further spillovers including channeling the Still River. For that, many buildings on the course of the river had to be demolished.

A picture caught Anna's attention. It was a shot of the flooded corner of Main Street and White Street with a little cabin with a traffic light on top in the middle of the intersection. Marvin had drawn a similar little house at the intersection of his imaginary city.

Another photo, though, took her breath away. It was of an elderly woman, with white hair and a long dress, being helped by two men to board a canoe. "Danbury Police" was written on the side of the canoe.

Anna covered her mouth with her hand as if trying to prevent her voice from coming out. "Oh... my... God! How can it be possible?" she couldn't help saying.

The man at the other end of the table looked up. "It was a big tragedy, wasn't it?"

"I beg your pardon?" she said surprised.

"I said it was a big tragedy, wasn't it?" he repeated in a low voice as if to remind her that this was a library.

"Did I say it out loud?" she whispered.

"Yes," he also whispered. Before she could say another word, he stood up and pulled his chair closer.

"I'm Ralph."

"I'm Anna," she replied, feeling a little confused with the stranger's unexpected approach.

"I could not help noticing, you looked anxious. Are you doing some research?" he asked, trying to keep his voice quiet.

"Kind of."

"Do you come here often?" He had a charismatic look that made Anna feel odd.

She looked at the man, apparently in his early forties, casually dressed, and found him interesting. She wondered if he was flirting with her in the library and if so, she wasn't sure how she felt about that. *Hasn't he noticed that I have something shiny on my ring finger?*

"This is my first time here. You?" she said in neutral tone.

"I brought my son to the children's program," he said. "I like this cultural environment. My ex-wife always asked me to bring him, and I ended up getting used to it. It seems that he has a lot of fun here."

Anna nodded, hardly handling his gaze. He had managed to tell her that he was divorced—and that he was free.

The next question had clear second intentions. "Did you bring your kids too?"

"No. I didn't know about the program. Actually, I just came here because I saw some pictures of this flood," she showed him the booklet.

"A calamity. My grandfather told me many stories about it. He had a friend, Burt Taylor, who ran a car repair service by the river in Georgetown. They think that the Norwalk River washed his body into the ocean. They never found him."

"I bet there were many losses."

"Are you a writer? Journalist?"

Anna thought for a moment before answering, weighing whether to tell him the truth. "My six-year-old son made some drawings of this flood," she said. "I was intrigued by his cleverness. My husband and I are accustomed to his intelligence, but this time he surprised us." She had managed to tell him that she was married. "None of us knew about this tragedy. We haven't been in town long enough to know much about its history."

"Perhaps he saw something about it at school," he suggested.

"I home school my son."

"Do you?" He seemed surprised and also, glad. "Well, maybe, he saw it on TV."

"I don't think so. I manage what my son watches, and I don't think that *Curious George* would tell him anything about it."

"Well, have you thought about..." he paused, as if deciding whether to say what he had in mind.

Despite the coincidence of the photos, she had hope that he could say something to counter Lisa's suggestion about past life memories. His pause made her a little anxious. Maybe he was only guessing to keep the conversation running and had nothing else to say. But he said exactly what she did not want to hear.

"Maybe he has the gift of remembering past lives."

Now, that it was said, she didn't know what to do with it. Her heart beat rapidly. First Lisa and now this guy. Was it only a coincidence or was it a natural event that everyone on earth was aware of, but her? "What do you know about it?" She lowered her voice. "My friend said the same thing, and I feel like I'm lost in the woods."

"This is not as unnatural as people think," he said. "In some cases children can even remember names of their relatives, places where they lived, events they experienced..." He paused, looking at her intently as if to gauge her reaction. "I'm a therapist," he said, pulling out a business card from his pocket and placing it on the table in front of her.

She read it briefly—Dr. Ralph Stevenson, Licensed Psychotherapist and Counselor—and looked up at him. "So it seems that you have something to tell me about it?"

"I can refer you to some books," he said, disappointing her.

She had hoped that he would have a simple answer, a magic formula to deal with the situation and how to help her son. "I appreciate that," she said. "I thought it was part of your job, though."

"In fact it is. I do Past Life Regression."

She caught her breath.

"Usually, memories arise to help heal some issue that a child carries to this life, usually the effect of a traumatic event in his former life."

"My son has been behaving hysterically on rainy days for a long time now," she said. "But only recently he started telling these strange stories."

The therapist nodded. Anna felt disarmed, and started to consider him not only a source of information, but also of help. After all, he seemed to be a good person; he was serious about her affliction—and he was a *therapist*, and a *therapist* would not be in a library flirting with a married woman, she concluded.

"There are simple things you can do to check out whether those are past life memories," he said. "Pay close attention to his stories, but treat whatever comes up as naturally as possible. You can ask questions but be careful not to put pressure on him."

She liked the way he talked, though he hadn't said anything new. Lisa had said kind of the same, but what was next?

"If that doesn't produce answers," he continued, "you can try a regression."

"Regression?" Do you mean hypnosis or something like that? Is it safe for children?"

He opened his mouth to answer, but a young girl, with a very gentle smile, entered the room bringing his son over. The child resembled his father and looked like in Marvin's age.

"This is my son, Jonathan," Ralph said to Anna. "Say 'hi' to Anna, son."

"Hi," Jonathan said, giving his father a dirty look, like a jealous son watching over his divorced father.

Anna responded with a friendly smile. She sympathized with Jonathan at first sight and wished that Marvin could be there to meet him.

Ralph stood up and announced that he needed to leave. He told Anna to think about what he said, and if she wanted to schedule an appointment to know more about Regression, she should feel free to contact him. It would be more than a pleasure to help her son.

Later, driving back home, she gazed at Ralph's business card once more. It represented an open door. His appearance was providential, and the help for her child was a reasonable justification for a new contact. He had left a strange impression on her though. She couldn't tell whether he had a second intention; he was too clever.

She tried to ward off thoughts, threw the card inside her purse, and turned the radio on.

Chapter 6

When Anna got home, she took a relaxing shower then wrapped herself in a warm and comfortable bathrobe, letting her hair air dry. She went to the kitchen for a cup of tea and to write in her diary.

Marvin's drawings were still on the kitchen table. Anna stared for a while at the drawings, her mind distant, wondering about what was going through her child's mind. Now that she had seen the pictures and read about the *Great Flood of 1955*, the drawings looked more impressive.

Her gaze shifted to the window, and she thought of Ralph. Not even for a moment had she forgotten him. Nor had the strange sensation left her. She felt as if something good—or exciting?—had finally happened in her emotionally linear life. She tried to rationalize it; after all, her worries about Marvin were playing a big role in her emotions, and Ralph represented potential help that had appeared as if sent by God.

She sat at the kitchen table and wrote in her diary:

What a strange feeling at a time already so confusing.

However, how can I deny that I felt very comfortable with him? Something strange like... She thought for a moment, trying to find the right word. *Affinity! Exactly, as if I could trust my fears and my innermost feelings to a man I just met.*

And his eyes! They seemed to look inside of me.

I admit he is attractive, but I know my limits and I do not want to come anywhere near them.

Better not to take a risk.

I just want to help my son. My son is my life. That's all I care about at this moment.

She read what she had written and was surprised by her own audacity.

Outside, Larry's car arrived in the driveway, and she put the diary away. Larry came in and kissed her as usual, asking for Marvin. When Anna said Marvin was sleeping over at his friend's, Larry picked up. "We don't have wine at home, but I can go out to get some," he suggested with melted, hopeful eyes.

Anna pulled her bathrobe more tightly around her. "I need to tell you something."

"What is it?"

"It's about Marvin." Anna led Larry to Marvin's drawings on the kitchen table.

"He's still drawing his dream," Larry observed.

"I went to the public library today," she said. "Have you heard about a flood that hit Danbury in 1955?"

"I've read about it once," Larry examined the drawings.

"I saw pictures of the flood today that were just like these drawings. Lisa says there are children who remember past lives."

"Crazy idea, don't you think? What else can you expect from Lisa?"

"I thought it was at first, too. But you should see the similarity of these drawings with the pictures. You'd be shocked."

He shifted his gaze to her, puzzled. "C'mon Anna, you're not being influenced by Marvin's nightmares, are you? Children has good imaginations. Marvin had a nightmare and drew what he remembered. Isn't what he does when you tell him stories and ask him to draw what most caught his attention?"

"It's not only the drawings. He refers to this flood as if he had experienced that tragedy. He speaks of details—"

"These are only drawings, Anna," he cut her off, impatiently. "Look: river, houses, fishes; things children draw."

His skepticism rattled Anna. Of course, he was right, she told herself. The pictures were all a coincidence.

Transcendental things, spiritual subjects in general, were not Larry's favorite subjects. Neither was he the kind of man given to deep discussion about intimate feelings or anything that touched on the imagination. He had firm ideas about practical matters— the way a business was run and family matters—and didn't see the need to change them. For Larry, the math of life was simple and it was difficult for him to understand why some people needed to complicate simple things.

"I'll take a shower; then we can order something for dinner." Looking irritated, Larry headed upstairs.

Left alone in the kitchen, Anna felt like an ingenuous believer. Larry's skepticism had shaken her, but her mother's instinct was telling her not to give up. She wandered into the den, and then went to the office in the basement, and sat at the computer. Typing into the search field, she pulled up dozens of links about the *Great Flood of 1955*. She clicked on several of them and read about towns affected by the tragedy.

On one site, she stumbled across the same photo she had seen in the library—the elderly woman in the canoe being helped by two men. She went back to kitchen, grabbed Marvin's drawing, and brought it back to the office to compare. Marvin's drawing was childish and crude of course, but all the essential elements were there. The words "Danbury Police" written on the side of the canoe was the most impressive coincidence.

It was too much to ignore. She called Lisa. At least Lisa would take her seriously. But Lisa did not answer the phone, and Anna hung up without leaving a message.

She was growing anxious. Clearly, there was some connection between Marvin's pictures and the long ago storm. What Marvin had told her was something real, not merely a fantasy. And if he was talking about past life experiences, why were they coming up now? Where were they leading? She wished that Marvin was there with her; at least she would know that he was safe by her side.

Driven by this thought, she headed to the bedroom to get dressed. She was determined to bring Marvin back home; she didn't want him away from her that night.

When Larry came out from the bathroom in his pajamas, he found Anna in the kitchen with her purse in hand, searching for her car keys.

"Going out?"

"I'll go to pick up Marvin," she answered without interrupting her search.

"You said he'd sleep over. Did something happen, did someone call?"

"No. I just don't want Marvin away from me tonight."

Larry stood in front of her, staring at her. His silence made her nervous.

"What?" She yelled impatiently, annoyed with his judgmental attitude. "Check out the weather; there is a storm coming. I just—"

"Anna, listen," he interrupted her reasonably.

She cut off him sharply: "No, you listen. If you don't want to know because you have all the answers, that's fine. At least let me do what I think is best for my son."

She finally found the keys on the kitchen counter, where she had left them when she got home with the groceries. Ignoring Larry, she headed out.

Larry looked both astonished and hurt. For him, it was evident that the new house hadn't brought the desired effect to their lives; on the contrary, Anna's behavior worsened, he concluded. He also considered that Anna, instead, was the one who had problems and needed help, not Marvin.

Chapter 7

The trip to the nearby town of Redding was about twenty minutes. She used the time to organize her ideas and cool down her emotions. Half way, raindrops began to fall on the windshield, and, within seconds, it poured, limiting her visibility. Undiscouraged, she thanked God that she'd had the intuition to pick up Marvin. If she had heeded Larry and opted to stay at home, panic would be floating through her.

The car felt like it was floating on the road, and she slowed down. When she felt safer, she tried to call the house to let Karen know her plans, but her cell phone was out of service.

When Anna finally arrived, Karen came to meet her at the front door. Anna immediately saw the worry in her expression. She had a cordless phone in hands; she had been trying to call Anna.

She brought Anna to the bedroom where Marvin was hiding between the bed and the wall. He was hysterical, and nobody could either stop him from crying or remove him from there. Only Anna was able to comfort the frightened and trembling child in her arms.

Karen left them alone in the room, closing the door behind her. She needed to take care of her own son who had witnessed Marvin's panic and how he ran through the house as if in search of a safe place to survive the end of the world.

Anna lay in the bed with her distraught son and cuddled with him. She could think of nothing to do but whisper comforting words, be present with him, and wait for nature to perform its work.

A flash of lightening at the window shifted her attention to the objects in the room. She grabbed an action figure from the top of the dresser and faked a conversation with it.

"What do you feel when it starts raining?" she whispered, and it seemed to grab Marvin's attention instantly.

"I feel fear," Anna said gruffly to indicate the soldier was talking.

"But the rain is a good thing." Anna said in her own voice. "It helps the plants grow, fertilizes the soil, and cleans the air."

The distraction worked. Marvin's trembling body calmed, and he wiped his wet cheek.

"I'm afraid it won't stop and it'll flood the house," he said.

Anna was speechless for a moment. "You're safe here." She kissed his forehead and squeezed him against her chest.

They cuddled for few minutes, and when the rain receded, Marvin seemed to regain his strength. "Mom, can you bring me to Grandma's house?"

"Yes, sweetie; your father has a meeting in Philadelphia, and we'll be joining him on the trip. I wish it could be on your grandma's birthday, we could surprise her, but—"

"I'm not talking about your mom." Marvin cut her off. "I want to go to see Grandma Lucy." She lives near the train tracks."

Anna had no idea to whom Marvin was referring. "Who is this Grandma Lucy?"

"She's Dad's mom. Dad and I used to visit her every Sunday and spend time at her house."

Larry mother's name wasn't Lucy. Anna had no idea what to say.

Just then, Karen came in to check on them, and Anna was glad that she was saved from responding.

On the way home, Anna chatted about different subjects with Marvin to make him comfortable during the trip. She saw not far away ahead a deer crossing the road. "Can you see that deer?" she pointed.

Marvin, in his booster seat, stretched his neck to the middle of the car. Limited by the seat belt he could only see that the deer was disappearing on the dark roadside.

"When we see a deer crossing the roads we have to be careful," she explained as she slowed. "After one deer, its whole family may follow."

As soon as she said it, a deer crossed the road right in front of the car, closer than she could expect, and she had to zigzag not to hit him. It was a scare, and luckily, the car did not slide on the wet pavement and they were able to get home safe.

Larry came to meet them at the garage door, holding some computer printouts. "I've been selfish, not listening to what you've been tried to tell me," he said, handing the papers to her. The printouts were some past life articles from blogs and websites and excerpts from books. Anna felt as if someone removed a stone from her heart, and she relaxed into a smile. She didn't actually need to read all those papers to understand what Larry was proposing to her.

"It seems that the cavalry arrived," she said with a friendly gaze.

"I tried to find evidence that you and your crazy friend are wrong, and I finally had to admit that it's possible." He lowered his gaze to the papers and back to Anna twice, words stuck in his throat.

"I want you to know that I'm trying, but I can't see things like you do," he finally said. "All my research led me to consider that it's a possibility rather than a fact, but I'll give you my support to find the answer."

Anna sighed. At least he was willing to try.

She told him briefly what happened at Karen's house, and proposed that they talk in the morning. She was both physically and emotionally tired after all she experienced during the day.

But in the morning, they had only a brief conversation before Larry headed to work. She had not told Larry about

"Grandma Lucy." For her, it was a sign that she still wasn't comfortable with Larry's interest.

Marvin seemed to be in a good place that morning, far from all that happened the night before. He was distracted in the living room, dividing his attention between the puzzle on the floor and Curious George on TV. As a homeschooler, she knew how important it was to respect his pace and sometimes just let him be.

She spent the morning organizing the house. The physical activities left her mind free to wander. Now, she was curious to know more about "Grandma Lucy," but decided to curb her anxiety and let nature work.

The rest of the week passed in silence about the flood and dreams, and Anna concluded that Marvin's memories were triggered only by the proximity of rainy days. On Sunday afternoon, though, she learned otherwise.

It was a beautiful bright day. Larry went out to buy a blower to clean up the yard which was covered with yellow leaves.

Anna was on the couch reading one of the books she had found at the library about children who had past life memories. Absorbed by the reading, she didn't notice when Marvin approached her.

"I'm ready," he said.

She interrupted her reading and looked at his serious expression. He was dressed up and had put on his shoes with socks, something he had never done before without Anna's help, his hair neatly combed, styled with gel he probably found in the bath cabinet.

"Wow, what is this?" Anna smiled, thinking he was joking, possibly copying some cartoon character. "Ready for what?" she asked.

"You said we were going to visit Grandma Lucy. Today is the day she always expects us to come." His voice, matching his looks, sounded different, somewhat older.

She put the book aside. Nature was back at work, and it seemed that the day had arrived.

"But I don't know where she lives," Anna said, disguising her surprise.

"Near the train tracks, I told you already," he was impatient.

"Well, the train tracks can be a little long for us to knock on every door close by."

"It's near the hat factory," he stated.

"Well, that narrows the options, but... does this factory have a name?"

"Mallory."

At this point, she could not contain herself. She brought Marvin to the computer and entered "Mallory hat factory-Danbury" in a search engine. Articles and pictures popped up on the screen and she found that the Mallory Hat Company had been a big factory located in Danbury, which stopped its operations in the middle 60's, when men's hats were no longer a mandatory accessory.

What she found wasn't exactly a picture but a painting of the factory and she could not recognize its location in town. As far as she knew, there was no such place in Danbury. The street in front of the factory crossed under the railroad track, as well as the entrance of the factory.

She showed the picture to Marvin and he put his thumbs up. She searched for the address and the map showed the corner of Rose Street that, in fact, ran under a train track.

"Umm"... she was intrigued. "I guess today is a good day for time travel," she said to herself.

Anna parked the car right after she passed under the train tracks on Rose Street, in front of a steel framed fence, with a gate protecting an abandoned, empty lot. She followed the train tracks with her gaze. This had been the exact location of the factory. For some reason, though, the whole factory had been demolished, and all that was left was some cement flooring beneath the growing weeds. She saw that across the street a remaining building that belonged to the factory was still there.

She was astonished! It was a six-floor building, with a windowed facade, which still bore the name "Mallory Hat Co, 1923" above the fourth floor. The solid building was in good shape. Fairfield Processing Company was running the place.

She noticed Marvin standing still in front of the gate staring at the empty lot as if he were associating it with something. She approached and crouched down beside him. "Does it look familiar?"

He didn't say a word, but she could sense how deeply the devastated place hit him. Anna wondered what could be passing through Marvin's mind. He had been expecting something else. Maybe he was wandering in the past, seeing the movement of factory's routine, the trucks coming and going, the employees walking through the patio, the tall chimney blowing the smoke out. Maybe he was only disappointed.

Anna gave him a little time before she asked: "Well, we found the factory...or at least where it used to be. Why don't we go to see Grandma Lucy now?"

He turned to her and smiled with mysterious eyes.

"Can you tell me where she lives? Do you recognize this area?"

Marvin took her hand and started to walk up the hill, which became steep after the factory. He was looking carefully at the houses. Suddenly, he stopped at the corner of Grandview Street and pointed across the street to an old two-story house, with brownish wood siding, a white bay window in the center, and a small porch at the entrance on the right, probably built in the nineteenth century.

"There! The first house on the corner," he said confidently.

A strange sensation squeezed Anna's heart. She felt as if

some sort of "mysterious power" were guiding Marvin, bringing both of them into a surreal tunnel where anything would be possible—like Alice in Wonderland—and she feared that from this point, the adventure had no U-turn.

She managed not to show Marvin her anxiety, took a deep breath, and said, mostly to herself: "Well, we made it until here...let's finish this."

Chapter 8

They stood for a moment in front of the house, which was only ten feet away from the sidewalk. Decorative garden statues in the small grassy front yard and the recently painted trim of the windows and the front door diverted attention from the general maintenance the aged house urgently needed. Anna wanted to see some signs of life, but the curtains in the bay window were blocking her view. In other circumstances, she'd consider snooping in someone else's house as disrespectful, but she was trying to gain time, hoping for some clue about what to do.

Marvin released his hand from hers and walked to the porch in front of the house. There he made himself comfortable in an old rocking chair, which seemed to be an old acquaintance.

Anna crouched by his side. "Son, listen," she said. "Even if you find your grandma or anyone else you can remember..." Anna trailed off and raised her eyebrows, taking a deep breath, thinking of the eccentricity of her own words, before continuing. "...they won't know who you are. We need to take it easy until we can explain—"

The front door opened. A woman, apparently in her sixties, had noticed the intruders on her porch and came out to check on them.

Anna was instantly on her feet, but words refused to come out of her mouth. It was bad enough to be caught on some else's property but the only explanation she had to give was embarrassing. "Sorry to bother you," she finally said. "I'm looking for a woman named Lucy..." She trailed, realizing that she did not know Grandma Lucy's last name.

"Lucy Baker," Marvin said rocking hard in the chair.

The woman gave Anna a strange look. "Lucy Baker is the name of my mother. But she died a long time ago. What is it?"

How obvious! Anna thought. *A woman who was a grandmother in 1955 could not be still alive in 2002.*

Marvin lost interest in the chair. He stood up and came to snuggle at her waist. Anna stroked his hair.

"Sorry, I'm Anna Dawson," Anna said offering to shake hands.

"Ellen," the woman accepted Anna's hand hesitantly.

"Are you Ellie?" Marvin asked suspiciously. "You can't be. Ellie is a young girl."

Marvin's comment caused the woman to frown.

"If you have a minute, I can explain," Anna said, hurriedly.

"Nobody has called me by my nickname for a long time." Ellen's expression was one of astonishment. After a moment of hesitation, Ellen finally motioned Anna to enter. "Would you like to come in?" she said.

The front door led straight to a living room that was crowded with memorabilia and antique furnishings. Every corner was filled with care. The richness of detail caught Anna's attention. Small wooden birds sat on the windowsill. A weeping fern hung in a sunny spot. Small lamps made of stamped fabric were well distributed throughout the room. And a foot size teddy bear with a bead necklace sat on a crafted wooden chair with a brown leather seat. What most impressed Anna though, were the framed photographs hanging on the wall and over the china cabinet. Many of them were also grouped on the top of an old piano. Most of them were black and white. Everything in that room felt like time travel and she felt a strange sensation.

Ellen invited Anna to sit on a couch covered in mustard yellow fabric.

Marvin looked over the pictures and the decorations as if he recognized them and they induced fond memories. He approached a picture hanging on the wall of a woman with a calm countenance and gray hair. "This is Grandma," he said, pointing the photo.

Anna replied with a faint smile and a compassionate gaze. She gave Ellen an apologetic look.

Ellen's eyes grew round as Marvin identified other members of her family providing names and kinship. Finally, he came to a photo of a boy, about fifteen-years-old, next to a man in his thirties. "This is my Dad, and this is me," he pointed.

Driven by curiosity, Anna approached the photo over the piano. The resemblance of the boy in the picture to Marvin was remarkable. The expression in his eyes and the shape of his forehead were simply identical to Marvin. Then, she turned back to Ellen.

"This is my son, Marvin," she started. "I know it sounds strange..." she trailed, looking for words. "My son gets hysterical in rainstorms, and recently, he began to tell me stories about a flood that he said he remembered. He made drawings and named people, who he said were family. I decided to see where his stories would lead me."

"And they brought you to my house," Ellen said.

Anna gave her a pleading look. "He told me his name was Marty, and he lived with his grandma next to the hat factory. He brought me here, because he recognized the house."

"That's impossible," Ellen said with confidence, looking at Marvin playing with the teddy bear, as if he had found another old friend. "As far as I know Marty is still alive."

Anna became confused. If Marty was still alive, her theories were all wrong. "I don't understand," Anna said. "How could he recognize your entire family in these pictures? At first, I didn't want to believe either, but it is unlikely that a six-year-old child can imagine all that stuff."

"Your son has an interesting gift," Ellen said in a friendly tone. "I've heard about children who say they belonged to another family in a previous life, but he cannot be our Marty."

Ellen sounded calm, but Anna could sense that she was barely holding her emotions in check.

"Why don't you ask him about his mother?" Ellen fixed her hair showing a slight tremble in her hands, then turned her gaze to Marvin. "If he can only tell us what my family always wanted to know, I'll give him credit."

Anna pulled her son around to look at him in the eyes. "Marvin, do you remember your mother? What was her name?"

"My mother is you; I have no other mother," he answered with certainty.

Anna looked at Ellen, while Marvin returned to the teddy bear.

"Marty, in fact, was abandoned by his mother when he still was a baby," Ellen reported. "But Georgia reappeared after fifteen years in the fall of 1955. She took Marty with her without his father's permission. When my mother was told about it, she fell ill and never recovered. My brother Charlie, Marty's dad, also never overcame the loss. He tried by all means to get some information about his boy. He first thought that something could have happened to them because of the terrible flood, but no bodies were found. He gave up only after years of an unsuccessful search. After the hat factory closed its doors, he started his own business, then, his business became his partner in life." Ellen paused, collecting her thoughts. "I was twenty-one when Georgia came back, and Marty was almost sixteen. My nephew and I were very close in our childhood. After my mom passed away, ten years after this incident, my brother Charlie wanted to sell the house. I was about to get married and I asked him to let me stay living here. If one day Marty returned to town, it was here that he would come first. I never lost hope."

Anna sensed the sorrow underlying Ellen's sigh. Marvin's memories were revealing a sad history of this family, although it showed an intriguing gap in his story. Why could he not remember his mother who virtually kidnapped him from his family? "I don't know, all this is new for me," Anna said. "But, what if something happened to your nephew and he never had a chance to come back?"

Ellen was silent for a moment, and Anna hoped that she was taking her words into a consideration. But when Ellen spoke, she seemed lost in the past. "Georgia went back to California when Marty was four months old and told Charlie she wasn't able to pursue her dream of become an actress if she had a child to raise." Ellen paused, and Anna sensed her effort in sharing those bitter memories. "Fifteen years passed in silence," Ellen continued, "and one day she reappeared in town, claiming to be sorry for having abandoned her child and that she had never forgotten Charlie. She must have been a good actress, because Charlie almost trusted her. The day she left, he was busy with the flood and the damages caused to the factory, but he could see when Marty got into Georgia's car. It was the last time he saw his son, and he never heard from him or from Georgia again."

Anna felt her heart tighten in her chest. Her child's problem became smaller before the drama that lay beneath this family. "And Charlie, is he still…"

"Yes, he's alive. He lives by himself in a cottage by Candlewood Lake. My brother is seventy-eight now, and only a shadow of what he used to be."

Anna looked at Marvin still distracted with the teddy bear. "I think that Marvin would love to meet Charlie," Anna said.

"I don't think that is a good idea," Ellen was emphatic. "Your son is an adorable boy, but there's no evidence that my nephew died and now is back as your child. I don't know what makes you think that's possible, but I don't want to see my brother going again through all his misfortune. In fact, he never overcame his loss, he just buried all the sorrow in his heart, and he's at an age now that'd be a risk to stir it up."

"Maybe Marvin can bring him some hope; children often do," Anna insisted.

Ellen said nothing. Her gaze expressed a pain that Anna decided to respect. She thanked Ellen for her hospitality. She reached after a pen and a piece of paper in her purse and wrote down her phone number. She handed it to Ellen in case she changed her mind about Charlie.

When Ellen held the piece of paper, her gaze became distant as if she was wresting with an idea. "Wait a minute," she said before leaving the room.

Anna could hear her laboring up the stairs to the second floor. She snuggled Marvin, wondering how this visit would affect him. Her intuition was telling her that this visit hadn't been in vain and it wasn't by chance that their lives were crossing.

Ellen returned, holding an old notebook. "This is Georgia's diary," she said, handing it to Anna. "Charlie kept it among her belongs in the attic. I guess he doesn't even remember anymore. Something is telling me that you should read it. Maybe it will make sense to you and help you understand my brother's pain. You don't need to return it; my desire was always to burn everything that brings back memories of that woman, but something prevented me from doing it."

Anna stared at the notebook speechless, surprised by the offer. Then she thanked Ellen and gave her a warm hug. Marvin also offered his love in a hug, which Ellen, fighting her own resistance, wasn't able to fully accept.

When they got back home, Anna let Marvin choose what to do and he decided to go play in his tent in the attic. Wearing headphones, Larry was busy in the backyard with the leaf blower.

Anna held Georgia's old and yellowed notebook as if it were a sacred document. The person who wrote the diary, despite how crazy it sounded, was possibly her son's mother in a former life. It could represent a source of help for her son, she thought, or maybe only confessions of a solitary woman who made a bad choice in life. Anna sat down at the kitchen table, took a deep breath, and carefully opened the diary to its first page.

Chapter 9

August 26, 1950.

I'm looking at this man lying in my bed, and after five years, sometimes I still feel like he is a stranger. I owe Jerry though, I've learned more from him about acting and plays than from the acting classes I attended. He is charming, protective, and my best friend no doubt, but, maybe it was a mistake becoming more than friends. I also owe this man all tears he wiped from my face, from my life. I truly love this man, but every time he touches me, I feel like it is my dear one who is touching me. My body does not recognize his, and my dear one is all that comes every time he runs his fingers through my hair.

This is the life that I chose and, after all, it's how it's supposed to be, not exactly as I dreamed though. Everyone around me, in this acting business, has his or her own drama. Pete, the director of the play, was widowed last year and still wears black. I think he is always angry, yelling at everyone's mistakes, because he blames his job for preventing him from being with his wife when she needed him. Frank, the producer, loves Sara, who loves Jim, the guy from the play Sara worked on before she came to be part of our crew. Jim isn't interested in Sara or in any other girl. I wonder if she ever noticed that or if she just can't accept his sexual preferences. I have caught her crying for him many times while Frank strives to help her to feel better.

In the spotlight, everyone looks happy and successful, but backstage, when the characters leave us, our lives are full of unfinished business. People come to this place in pursuit of dreams, but this is not a place for dreamers. We are not real people here. Off stage, most of the time, we see only characters, masquerading their sadness, loneliness, fears and sorrows, often sinking their emptiness in drinks and tobacco.

To be honest, the most real person here is Jennifer, the girl I met a week ago at the bar. She made a choice in life that I never would have, but she seemed to have the perfect sense of how far she is from her way to heaven. She seemed to know exactly what she was doing. She agreed to the price she had to pay to travel on the road she chose. I don't see many people who agree to pay the price. Some don't even want to take a look at the bill. They complain about the charges, forgetting that it was their own choice. Everything in life has a price. My price is to be away from my son, from my dear one, and from my peace.

Georgia closed her diary; it was 9:00 p.m. Time flew when she started to release her emotions on its pages. From the desk, near to the window of the sixth floor, she could see the lights of the city that never slept and enjoy the fresh breeze that traveled above the traffic.

Jerry was passed out in bed, and she couldn't remember the last time he went to bed that early. Their job had turned them both into night owls, mostly working, often socializing at parties and with friends and sometimes gambling just for fun. Jerry always advised that "building strong and lasting relationships is the key to success in all kinds of business." *Stage versus screen* was a subject of inflamed discussion. Jerry constantly encouraged Georgia to consider the tempting offers she got along the way to switch her perspectives, but she wasn't interested in screen. Although she grew up inspired by the Garlands and Hayworths of the screen, she fell in love with the stage on day one. The first time she entered a big theater, she stood in the center of the stage and closed her eyes. She could hear the voices in the silent empty chamber; she could feel the warmth from the audience on her skin. The smell was familiar and pleasant. The place felt like home. She had the opportunity to perform in front of a camera once for a TV commercial. She later described it as "performing in a cold cage with a lifeless, threatening monster watching you behind a square, dark lens."

She was a talented, fast learner, and well disciplined. Those qualities and, of course, her beauty brought her performances special attention from directors, producers and artists. She received invitations for all sorts of events and parties. For Jerry, the socializing was the best side of the business, but it had soon become a heavy burden for Georgia. She missed the warm coziness of a home with a regular family. Being an actress was not like a regular job, nor was she living in a normal world where people went to work in the morning and came back home at the end of the day to enjoy family.

Jerry had come home earlier this evening. He had been taciturn; he looked sad and smelled of alcohol, both unusual. She was worried. He had been putting off seeing a doctor since his last visit to Doctor Kaminski, when he had gotten a prescription and lots of advice about things to avoid, from sugar to alcohol, red meat, and tobacco. He had also been told to add fruits and vegetables to his diet. "You're only forty-five, too young to feel so dumpy, and smart enough not to become a slave to some drug," Dr. Kaminski warned.

The symptoms had started as increased fatigue. Doctor Kaminski then ran a blood test and found anemia. Something of a maverick, Dr. Kaminski believed that a healthy diet and a change in life style could be the most effective healing process in a long run.

"It's your choice," added Doctor Kaminski, looking up earnestly over his glasses. "Disease calls for change. You may change your habits or face the drug's side effects, which are often quite uncomfortable. You still have plenty of time, but don't take this matter lightly."

Jerry laughed broadly looking at the list. "You want to make me a vegetarian! Golly! Where am I going to eat? I don't have a housewife. You are taking this too seriously, doctor; all I'm asking is—"

"A quick fix, I know," the doctor interrupted him; he was familiar with this type of behavior. "Some serious diseases are silent," he said, "I need to keep an eye on you. Nothing can be more deadly dangerous than a stubborn sick man that refuses to surrender to his doctor's advice."

Jerry did not follow the doctor's advice. When he started to lose weight, he realized that something was wrong. He kept it secret from Georgia, as well as a persistent abdominal pain. She'd send him back to the doctor, and this he wanted to avoid; he did not want to find out what he already suspected.

Georgia put the diary in the desktop drawer and turned to Jerry in bed. She could stay up writing or combing her hair, or even reading in bed by his side; nothing seemed to disturb Jerry's sleep. She could go to the living room to watch The Goldbergs, her favorite show, or something else on TV or put the new Ella Fitzgerald record on the Victrola and enjoy a glass of wine, but she rather lay down by his side.

Jerry seemed in a state of deep oblivion. His chest barely moved with a peaceful breathing. She ran her fingers lightly through his soft, black hair, and her chest tightened. She wished she could stretch out this rare moment of solitude. She was glad that she had finally spotted the ghost that had been haunting her for so long. In the afternoon, while walking in the city, she had come to a serious conclusion: she had reached her limits.

She was twenty-eight now, but she looked older. The nightlife wasn't the only thief taking away her youth. There was also the unfinished business that had tormented her every single day for the last ten years, since the moment she had given up love, family, and a possible normal happy life. The young girl had made a bad decision and the adult was facing the aftermath. At eighteen, she hadn't been able to fight back the sweeping dream that possessed her, a dream that started when she was only thirteen and became overpowering as she grew older.

She had fallen for Charlie in high school. He was smarter than the other kids, and had caught her attention at first sight, but it still took two years before they started dating. He loved her since the first moment, but he was clever and had good timing. He was always around when she needed him, but was confident enough to eventually stay away and let her breathe, like the tide, hydrating the sand as it advances, and receding slowly to let it enjoy the sun. That captivated her more than all the schemes and maneuvers the other boys at school performed to catch her attention. They became friends, and it satisfied them until the last year of school, when their first kiss sparked their hearts and transformed their warming friendship into an ardent romance. They became inseparable, until fate changed their lives.

Georgia's father was a simple man, who had emigrated from South America at the end of the nineteenth century and settled down in Atlanta, Georgia, where he learned how to build a house, from the foundation to the roof. Through a decade of hard work, he became an experienced contractor. He was a man with a restless spirit, though. He decided to travel around the country in search of investors and ended up in Connecticut, where he met the love of his life. The marriage lasted only eleven years. His wife died when Georgia, their only daughter, was ten. He never felt comfortable with the cold in the Northeast, and without hesitation, he accepted an offer from a friend to work for a company in Los Angeles, building scenery for show business.

Georgia was seventeen when she moved with her father to Los Angeles. She promised she'd come back to Charlie and wrote him many letters, sharing all she had seen in her dreamland. In only few weeks, with the help of her father, she was already attending acting classes, meeting influential people from show business and making friends.

On the same day when she visited Million Dollar Theater —before it became the Mecca of the Spanish language entertainment—and stepped for the first time on a big stage, she found that she was pregnant. She was so excited and so involved with her new life that she had ignored the signs in her body until this day. It was almost twelve weeks now. The baby was silently growing inside her womb, a reminder of the love she had left behind. Her world collapsed, she was confused and lost. She stopped writing Charlie. If he knew, he would ask her to come back, and it would be the end of her dreams.

It was the toughest time she ever went through. Advice to consider an abortion came from everywhere, but she fought against the world to let the baby come to life, and it was a lonely battle, since she never told Charlie. Time went on, and when the pregnancy was in an advanced stage, she almost gave up on her dreams. When she heard the baby's first cries, her heart broke into pieces. She managed to accommodate the baby into her new life, but only thinking of Charlie was devastating. It was unjust to the father of her child, the man she still loved like no other.

One day she saw Charlie in a dream. He was cold and distant, and when she came closer, she became paralyzed by the hatred in his gaze. She woke up frightened, feeling guilty and selfish for hiding the baby from him. She decided to go back to Connecticut.

The baby became the party of Charlie's house for those three months she stayed with Charlie and his family. The day she had left Charlie and the baby, her heart stayed behind. Since then, she lived with a hole in her chest, an empty space that she strived to ignore for the first few years. In those years, she succeeded, more or less, when all was new and attractive.

Years had passed at a fast pace since then. She never thought it would be so long before she went back. She had lost her father after only five years of living in LA. She felt alone in the world and was considering the renunciation of her dreams when Jerry came to her life in 1945. It was as if heaven had sent her an angel. He occupied all empty spaces in her life, taught her how to be a good actress and a better person. He fertilized the seeds of her dreams and made them blossom. He protected her from troubles and vultures; he loved her. She was grateful for him, and they had a good time together, but soon she learned that being loved wasn't enough. She needed to be able to love too, but how to love without a heart?

Jerry made a small movement in bed that brought Georgia back, but just for a few seconds. *He is almost ten now. Does he know about me? Did Charlie tell him my name?* She wondered, looking vaguely to the ceiling. *Did Charlie get married? Of course, he did! He is not a man that the girls in town would let be alone. Does Marty call her 'Mom'?* Those answers she could easily have had, if she had sent the letters she wrote, but she hadn't. She was afraid to know. She had always assumed that when the moment arrived, she'd just go back, but life washed all her plans away. She had never even sent her son a picture. He had never seen her face. Would he forgive her?

Georgia turned to her side and gazed at Jerry again. This time she didn't touch him, just looked at his face, wondering. She knew she couldn't stop the voice of life within, urging her to fix the past. She needed to go back. Nevertheless, this wonderful man at her side deserved better than that. She should not be so inconsequent this time. She had learned many lessons; she had grown up. The woman needed now to take charge of the girl.

She considered talking to Jerry in the morning, opening her heart broadly to figure the best way—or the least painful one—to break the news to him. Listening to opinions, before making decisions—turning the periscope to different perspectives—was something that he had always advocated. He was mature, emotionally balanced, and an intelligent man. He knew about her unfinished business. He'd possibly understand her decision, although it would be heartbreak.

After all, there was a chance that it would not be a goodbye. She might go back to Connecticut only to find that she had become an unwelcome ghost that nobody wanted to see.

In the morning, Jerry was the first to awake. He checked the clock on the bedside table, only to find how late it was. He sat on the edge of the bed with a heavy feeling in his head. Georgia made a movement and he twisted to gaze at her. She was still asleep. Then he carefully got up and headed to the kitchen to brew some coffee.

A few minutes later, Georgia stretched her arms, searching for Jerry in bed. The smell of fresh coffee invited her to get up, though she wanted to stay a little longer.

She met Jerry in the kitchen. He was leaning against the sink, enjoying his cup of coffee. She kissed him good morning, and poured some coffee in a mug. "There's something that I want to talk to you about," she said earnestly, stirring her coffee. The sooner she'd let him know her thoughts, the better she'd manage her anxiety. "I know it's a heavy conversation for this time of the day…"

"I know," he nodded with a hazy gaze.

"You know?" she was surprised.

"I know; I owe you a word. I've been hiding this to save you from unnecessary worries." He took a sip of coffee. "I went to see Doctor Kaminski last week."

She frowned. The doctor's name gave her a bad feeling.

"I've been feeling extremely tired, as you know. I also have this persistent pain in my abdomen that I never told you about. He ordered a few tests, and yesterday I went back to get the results."

He paused and lowered his gaze to the mug between his trembling hands. "I'm sorry. I guess I thought that I was invincible." He smiled faintly. "This is not going to be easy; Doctor Kaminski said that the later it is detected, the harder it is to treat... but it's not too late, though."

Georgia knew what he meant. Cancer! The word that nobody wanted to say. The word itself sounded gruesome, like death!

"Why wouldn't you tell me?" she thought, but didn't ask. Instead, she came closer and rested his head on her chest, tenderly. "Oh, Jerry, Jerry!" she finally said, sinking into his pain. "How much time?"

"Months, maybe a year... he couldn't tell." He straightened up and gently pushed her back to gaze in her eyes, with his optimistic smile. "He said I can fight back, and I will."

Georgia felt devastated, for both of them. She could see the deep fear in his eyes. "We will," she said, taken by compassion. "We will..." she repeated. While a warm tear rolled down her face, the image of Charlie and her baby faded in the distance.

Chapter 10

Larry took a break from his work in the backyard for a glass of water. "Hey, I didn't know you were back!" He said to Anna still at the kitchen table.

"We just got home," she answered softly, closing Georgia's diary and trying to bring herself back from far away. "You're working hard out there, aren't you?" She forced her attention on him.

"I know. In one week the grass will be covered in yellow again. This is endless!"

"You wanted a house, you got it. We should hire a landscaper."

"And miss all the fun?"

Larry reached for a glass in the cabinet and placed it in the fridge door water dispenser. "Where'd you go?" he asked.

"Would you like the short or the long version?"

He finished filling the glass, pulled out a chair, and sat in front of her. He knew, when she says that, she has something important to share. He took a sip and gave her his full attention.

"I found that you're not the only father of Marvin," she decided to start with a bit of suspense, which caused Larry to spit the water out, almost choking. "Sorry," she rushed to cool him down, holding back her laughter. "I didn't mean to scare you. It's about Marvin's past life."

Larry wiped his mouth, frowning, as though he wasn't prepared yet to come back to the subject.

"He brought me to a house where he claimed his grandma lived. And in fact, it was 'the house.' Her daughter still lives there. He showed me a picture of a boy—"

"You're kidding, right? Did you go to somebody's house with this story?" Larry cut her off. His reaction was a bucket of cold water on Anna's excitement.

"Yes, you know that I will do whatever it takes to help Marvin," she replied, holding her ground.

Larry was visibly upset, but Anna sensed his effort to be polite. "I told you; I want to help," he said, "but you can't just go bother people you don't know with a problem that is ours!"

She lowered her gaze to the diary as if she found an ally there, and it seemed to bring her serenity. She flipped through the pages of the worn notebook, coming to a dried rose, brown with age. "Can you believe that this rose died decades ago and is still a part of someone's story?"

Larry ran his hand through his black sweaty hair, and took a long, impatient breath. "Look, sweetie, I really want to help you, but you're acting as if my help is the last thing you want. I know you like to be self-sufficient, taking charge over Marvin's problems, making your own decisions, but you can't do crazy things like this. What did you tell them?" His voice rose. "That our son was part of their family in the past and now that he remembers, he deserves a reunion? And for what? To talk about old times, to be invited to Thanksgiving dinner, to have his Christmas stocking hanging on their fire-place?"

Anna kept her expression steady, but her voice was firm. "I don't know, Larry. I'm still seeking answers. Do you think I knew what to say when I saw that strange woman in front of me or when Marvin began to name her relatives in those pictures? Why don't you try to stop being so judgmental and try to understand your son instead? "

"I feel like I already saw this movie," he said with annoyance. "We went through the same turbulence at the time of the home school decision. You asked my opinion, but you had already decided. The 'in depth' chat we had, was a one-way conversation, for you to convince me that it was the best thing to do, and for that, you became calm like you're doing now! Then you became angry, when I refused to yield to your arguments." He got up, barely holding his temper, and threw the rest of the water in the sink. "I'm getting used to the steps you take to make your opinion prevail, Anna, and the more aware of it I become the less patience I have."

After years of being the perfect husband that never complained, never claimed his rights, and never attempted to make his opinion prevail, Larry was finally getting his point across. Anna was surprised, and somewhat touched. She disguised her joy though, she wanted see how far he'd go.

"And it seems that we're not done with that conversation yet," she said, with the same calm voice.

Larry was prevented from responding as Marvin came to the kitchen. "Are you mad at me, Dad?" He stood in the kitchen door with a sad gaze and a frightened expression.

Larry again ran his hand through his hair as he felt he was losing control over his own family. Then approached Marvin, crouching in front of him. "No, son, Daddy is not mad at you. Your mom and I are only having a conversation."

"Don't be mad at Mom, Daddy," Marvin said with a pleading tone. "It was my idea to go see Grandma Lucy, but she wasn't there. She is dead. Ellie said she died because of me. She didn't know that I died, nobody knows because I had no way to tell them."

Larry was speechless. He could read Anna's eyes saying: "See now? It's not about me or you; this is about him." He looked back to the child and the innocent expression behind those little chestnut eyes disarmed Larry. He felt like his family was traveling on a parallel path, which was inaccessible to him. "We need to talk," he finally said to Anna.

"Talk to your son. What are you afraid of?"

Larry squinted. "Now you're treating me like a child," he said quite offended, and went back to his work in the backyard.

For the rest of the day, they barely talked to each other. Larry made himself busy, organizing personal stuff that had not been unpacked since they moved in.

Believing he needed time alone, Anna spent the evening entertaining Marvin until he fell asleep later this night. Then she went to the kitchen, planning to dive again into Georgia's diary. But she couldn't focus. She was feeling unexpected attracted to Larry after the discussion in the afternoon, as if his new attitude had been the missing ingredient to spice their marriage again. *He could have that confidence more often, and show that he knows the woman he has*, she thought. It didn't matter if he pointed out her flaws or if what he said was not always a compliment. She didn't want to be perfect. She just wanted to be herself before the man she chose, knowing that he really could see her.

She went to the bedroom. Asleep, Larry lay quietly in their bed in the dim light. She stood still for a moment in front of the bed, sensing that he was just pretending he was already sleeping. She turned the bedside table lamp off, silently undressed, and smoothly assaulted Larry under the covers. He pretended not to be interested as long as he could—no more than few seconds—before surrendering unconditionally. The energy was intense as if they wanted to merge into just one body, one soul. It was a rare moment of silent perfection for a couple that was almost never able even to find perfection in the realm of words.

Afterwards, Larry easily fell asleep, this time for good. But Anna's mind started to wander through the events of the day. After lying awake for while, she decided to get up and return to Georgia's diary.

She made a quick stop at Marvin's bedroom to check on him, and headed to the kitchen to make a warm cup of tea, just right to relax. When the tea had brewed, she set at the kitchen table with the notebook in her hands, wondering about what else was to come. When she opened it, she saw that Georgia had skipped through time as she wrote.

Chapter 11

September 7, 1950

Last night I spent time with Jennifer. We are getting along well. I don't mind her job; it's her choice. She is smart and an easy talker; normal as any regular person, even a better person than many.

She told me her life story, how she became what she is now. Jen's father was a Mexican immigrant and her mom an American white woman. They got divorced when she was only five-years-old, and two years later, her father brought her with him to Mexico. She never saw her mother again until the time she turned eighteen and was able to make her way back to the U.S. against her father's will. In Ohio, she discovered that her dad had actually kidnapped her. After learning about her dramatic story and her father's cruelty, she never went back to Mexico. But she never felt that living with her mom was home either. Her mom was a hoarder and had problems dealing with people. Jennifer entered into the world of prostitution to support her mom financially. When her mom died, she met a man who brought her to California.

After listening to Jen's story, I wondered what leads a father to do such crazy thing to his own daughter. If the answer is "he missed her so much that he could not help it," I know what he meant. Oh Golly, I really know it! I put myself in his shoes and fantasized about doing the same—not that I would do it, of course or even think that it's right... But curiously, for the first time I had the sensation of having my son close to me, like in a dream. I didn't see it; I actually felt it, like something real.

Maybe there is something that I still can do to stop this pain, although, looking at Jen, and what her life turned into, I feel so selfish. How could I possibly imagine that I could have found peace leaving behind my son and the man that I loved like no other? I spoke to Jerry and he said that these are emotions I have stifled. He's right. For all these years, I've denied myself the right to think about it. Yet, after hearing Jen's story, the sensation of having my son close to me is an unexpected call that I can't get rid of.

Reading Georgia's diary, Anna fell into a different reality. Georgia touched her heart. As time went by, Georgia became more and more drawn to the idea of going back to see her son with the hope of regaining Charlie's affection. For page after page, day after day, month after month, she made plans, just waiting for the right time, when she would have courage enough to face all the damage she had left behind to follow her dreams.

Anna was curious why she just didn't do it; Georgia seemed to be stuck to Jerry for a reason that was not clearly explained in the diary, as if she was waiting for something to happen to him. She did not mention the progression of Jerry's disease.

The next morning, Anna woke at 9:00 a.m. She was tired and groggy. An extended time in bed on that chilly morning would be totally justified, but she needed to check on Marvin. He was still sleeping, and she let him stay in bed a little longer. Larry had gone to work and left her a note on the kitchen table, a reminder about the three-day conference in Philadelphia this week and the plans they had made to turn it into a family trip. She rubbed her sleepy eyes as she realized that she'd forgotten it.

Anna wasn't hungry enough for breakfast. She had a glass of water instead, and dialed Lisa's number.

The phone rang a few times before Lisa grabbed it. "I hope you have a good reason to call me at this time." Lisa sounded like she just woke—and in a bad mood.

"I don't like Mondays either, but it's nine o'clock. Don't you work today?" Anna said.

"I'll work later today. You know, my schedule is crazy."

"Did you work last night?"

"No, I just hung out with friends and had some wine…"

A short moment of silence and Anna concluded: "Okay, I'll call you later."

"Really?" Lisa protested. "You just woke me up, and now you'll hang up on me? Why don't you tell me what is going on?"

"I have a lot to tell you, actually. Remember that conversation we had about Marvin's dreams and drawings? You suggested that they were past life memories?"

"Yes I do, and now you're calling to tell me I'm crazy? Tell me something new."

"Not exactly," Anna smiled. "Marvin took me on a tour through his past life, including his former family and the house where his grandma used to live…" She heard a disturbing noise on the other side of the line. "Lisa? You're still there?"

"Sorry, I'm still here. Just dropped my phone," Lisa finally answered breathing hard. "Did I hear well? Where did Marvin bring you?"

"Yes, you heard just right," Anna assured her. "Why don't you get your butt out of bed and come over for breakfast?"

"Just give me a few minutes because I need to get ready to go to work after." Lisa said promptly, hanging up.

It could be a long wait before Lisa arrived. Anna knew about her sacred ritual, which included endlessly trying on outfits, applying makeup, matching bracelets, earrings, and necklaces, styling her hair, and double-checking every detail. Only then would Lisa leave her nest.

Although the house was chilly inside, the warm rays of the sun shining in through the glass door were inviting. Anna opened the sliding door widely, taking a deep breath, enjoying the smell of autumn, the morning breeze, and the sun's warmth bathing her face. She was inspired to set up breakfast on the deck table while waiting for Lisa. She prepared some toast, jelly, some organic peaches and grapes, and hot water for tea or herbal coffee, her favorite since she had kicked her caffeine addition. She brought everything outside and sat down on a deck chair to enjoy the sun.

When Lisa arrived, Anna realized that almost an hour had passed since they talked over the phone.

"I feel like I was hit by a truck," Lisa complained at the breakfast table.

"Have some coffee," Anna suggested.

"But it has no caffeine," Lisa mumbled.

"I have black tea?"

Lisa nodded, and Anna brought a box of tea bags for her. After few sips, Lisa perked up and seemed ready for the news.

"So, Marvin came up with the name of his grandma," Anna started.

"A name?" Lisa's eyes widened. "Wow, this is getting warm!"

"He told me her name was Lucy and showed me where she used to live. So, there was only one way to know if it was a fantasy of his 'creative mind'," Anna continued.

"And you went there to check. Is she still living there?" Lisa stopped in the midst of spreading jelly on her toast.

"I asked myself the same stupid question before we got there, only to realize that a grandma from the fifties couldn't still be alive."

"Duh," Lisa agreed.

"I had no idea what I was going to say when a woman came to the door. She confirmed that this Grandma Lucy had lived there, and guess what? She was her daughter!"

Lisa's jaw dropped and kept on dropping as Anna told each detail of the conversation with Ellen she could remember. At the end of her story, she went into the house to get Georgia's diary.

Lisa held the notebook with the same astonished expression Anna had when she first touched it. She opened it carefully, running her gaze through the pages.

"I read almost half of it already. I don't understand how Marvin can't remember her," Anna mused. "Ellen's story doesn't match his exactly. I understand that she can't believe on a strange boy, who fell from the sky, claiming to be her nephew reincarnated—unless we're living in India. For one thing, she'd have to accept that her nephew died, and it seems that she's not ready for that yet."

"And Ellen's version is that Georgia kidnapped her own son?" Lisa probed.

Anna nodded. "To me, it doesn't sound like Georgia was a person who could do something so stupid to her son and the man she loved." She cocked her eyebrow: "As you can see, it seems that Marvin's memories are only the tip of the iceberg. This family has been struggling with this terrible drama for so long..."

"Maybe Marvin is only a messenger. Maybe he's not the same boy who was kidnapped by this woman," Lisa suggested. "If he is the same boy, the existence of his mother could be a repressed memory, what Freud defines as a 'traumatic experiences pushed out of consciousness.' People block out frightening episodes of abuse, for instance."

Anna sighed and her gaze became vague, as she pondered the possibilities. Besides being funny and witty, Lisa could be smart and thoughtful. She had a bachelor's degree in psychology, and her passion for children brought her back to school to prepare herself for a career as a child life specialist to help children and their families navigate the emotionally and physically demanding process of coping with hospitalization.

Marvin had fallen in love with her fun and skilled way with kids.

"I had the same thought," Anna finally said. "After I read this diary, I felt even more bound to understand what my son is going through." She paused to organize her thoughts. "There's one more thing..." she trailed off.

"What is that?"

"I felt a sort of connection with this woman," Anna smiled softly, recalling pleasant memories. "Her thoughts, her feelings, her story... I feel like I can fully grasp her, and I see many similarities in our lives." Anna grabbed the notebook and shuffled something through the pages. "Listen to this." She cleared her throat. *"Jerry is a wonderful man. Any woman would raise hands to heaven for having him. He always tries to guess my desires and fulfill my needs. He's smiling, intelligent, fun, always loving, and above of all, he is my best friend. Yet, I often feel like I can't be present with him, as if my body is here but my soul is somewhere else, sometimes living in the past, sometimes wandering through the future I dream of."*

Anna put the notebook down. "When I read this diary, I have hope that, hidden somewhere in these pages, there is something that can help me find answers to my questions. I don't know yet why it came into my hands, but I feel like this is not only about Marvin." And, because Lisa stayed staring at her silently, she pleaded. "You think I'm crazy?"

"You need help, girl," Lisa said earnestly.

Anna gave her a wry look. "You don't mean it."

"I'm serious. You should look for professional help. You're getting too involved; you may easily get lost. You won't be able to see the whole picture without outside help."

Anna thought of Ralph, which unsettled her.

"Did you tell Larry about all this?" Lisa asked.

"I did." Anna sighed in annoyance.

"What did he say?"

"He got mad at me. He thinks it was crazy, going to bother somebody else with a problem that is ours. You know, he is still trying to get into the whole idea, but I don't see many improvements."

"Maybe he's feeling threatened, and he is just scared."

"Threatened by what?"

"Well, maybe this is one more thing taking your attention from him."

"What am I supposed to do? I didn't invent this," Anna cried. "Besides, this is not about us; this is about what Marvin has been dealing with for a while. This is not a reason for him to be jealous or act like a needy child."

They had to stop the conversation as Marvin had wakened and came outside, looking cute in his pajamas and slippers, with his friend, an old Amish cloth dog, in his arms. He snuggled against Anna.

"Good morning, sweetie." Anna kissed his forehead. "Say 'hi' to Lisa."

"Hi, Lisa," Marvin said rubbing his sleepy eyes.

"Hi, Marvin," Lisa answered. "Come here for a big kiss."

Marvin sprang into Lisa's arms.

"Why don't you join us for breakfast?" Lisa said, while trying to smooth his disheveled hair.

"Can I have a peach?" he asked.

Anna gave him the fruit. Marvin grabbed it and slipped away to sit on the deck steps, watching a squirrel playing with an acorn on the grass.

Chapter 12

During the rest of the morning, Anna set Marvin busy with some educational activities. She considered Lisa's suggestion, but she couldn't tell if that strange man with a winsome smile represented help or trouble. She fought back her fears. *This is not about me!* She tried to convince herself. He had come to her, as fate would have, and she should not refuse the answers life was offering for her prayers. She got Ralph's business card from her purse, but she still paced in the house for few minutes holding the card, until she finally decided to free her mind of all judgment and dial Ralph's number. Whatever he had to offer in the field of psychology or Past Life Regression seemed the only possible or practical next step that she could take to deepen her investigation.

The phone rang twice and a male voice answered. "Good morning, Dr. Stevenson speaking."

"Hi, this is Anna. Maybe you don't remember me... We met at the Library."

"Hi Anna, of course I do. How's your son doing?"

It was comforting that he actually remembered. "He's doing great, thank you for asking. I have made some progress in my son's dreams but I'm still lost. To be honest, I feel more lost than ever."

"It happens often, in the beginning, when you're still crawling on an unknown land."

"I think it's time to accept your suggestion and schedule an appointment. We need help, I guess," she smiled. "I want to know more about regression therapy."

"That'll be great, but I...don't...have...any time for today," he said haltingly, as if running through his agenda. "I'm booked. Actually, it's a short day for me, I have to take care of my son, I'm sorry."

"I wasn't expecting anything that soon anyway; anytime during the next week will work for me."

"I have Wednesday at 3:00 pm. Does that work for you?"

"We'll be away for a couple of days. We're going to see my parents in Philadelphia."

"In that case, if you have time this afternoon, I'll be at Meckauer Park with my son. You and your son can come to join us. We can talk, and I can take a close look at your son."

Anna was surprised at the invitation. It seemed too casual for her, not a doctor's visit. He sounded nice, but what was his real intention? "We don't want to bother you in your spare time," she said.

"Not a problem at all. I think your son will be a better buddy for my son than me at the park."

Anna hesitated before saying "yes" and they agreed on 4 o'clock.

When Anna parked the car at Meckauer Park, she spotted Ralph in the distance in the playground area, sitting at a picnic table, watching the kids play. Some children were around, as the weather was just right for outdoor activity, but she couldn't see his son among the others. When they approached though, she saw the boy running toward his father.

Anna and Ralph greeted each other. Disguising the joy she felt at the reencounter, Anna rushed to introduce Marvin.

"Do you play soccer?" Jonathan asked Marvin.

"I'd like to," Marvin answered.

Anna was surprised. "Really? You never told me that."

Jonathan invited Marvin to follow him, an experienced user of that playground.

Ralph and Anna smiled at each other. "You can enroll your son in a soccer academy, unless you are able to teach it to him, too," Ralph joked. "It's good if he learns it as a child. It will be easier when he grows up."

"You mean... to become a professional player? Is there a school for that? I always thought of it more like a gift. In Brazil, the boys are born knowing how to play soccer. It's in their blood."

"So, are you from Brazil?"

"My parents are."

"Huh, so they are happy that Brazil won the World Cup this year in Japan."

"Oh yeah, my dad almost had a heart attack. He went crazy!"

Ralph invited her to sit on the bench.

"So, what is a grown up man doing in a park at this time of the day?" she teased.

"I came to bring my son, as you know," he replied in the vein.

She glanced around and only saw young moms with their kids. "Yeah, it's very common here," she said ironically.

"My ex-wife has an odd schedule."

"What does she do?"

"She's a doctor at Danbury Hospital. My schedule is more flexible, since I'm my own boss."

"Aw, it's very nice of you," she smiled. "Do you mind if I ask why a woman can get divorced from a man who prioritizes his son over his job?"

"Absolutely, but probably you don't have time for the answer. I'd need the ten years we lived together to tell you all the reasons," he smiled. "Briefly, I'd say we lost our connection. It tends to happen when one stops respecting differences."

"I'm sorry. Of course there's not only 'one reason' when a couple break up after living together for so long."

"I'm glad you understand that," he amended.

"And you never found someone again?"

"It was only two years ago. I made a couple of attempts, but they didn't work out. It takes a while to get rid of the previous relationship's patterns and be ready for the next. I decided to take a break to get myself together and wait for Mrs. Right," he smiled again.

Anna thought that they should change the subject and talk about Marvin instead. After all, this wasn't a date. She shouldn't be nosing into his life.

Jonathan called for help on the swing. Ralph stood up and left Anna alone with her thoughts. She saw that Marvin copied Jonathan, but Ralph offered to help him, too.

When he came back, he tried to resume the conversation at the same point where they stopped.

"What about you?" he asked. "How's your marriage going? Did you find 'Mr. Right'? I guess so."

She regretted that she had brought the subject up. She didn't want to keep this personal assessment going on. "Marvelous," she said in an impulsive way. There was no point in complaining about the perfect life she had. "Larry is the best husband a woman could wish for." She completed her speech with a smile, as if she really meant it.

"I'd say, from my professional experience, it is quite rare to hear that." He praised her while looking at her sharply as if he didn't quite believe what she has said.

She was still deciding if she would consider Ralph's cleverness as insolence, when he said. "I don't want to sound disrespectful, but I want you to know that I had an interest in you since the first time I saw you in the Library, and I'm glad that we met again."

Anna's heartbeat sped up and she felt unsettled on the bench. Now that he'd said that, everything that had been in the realm of fantasy dropped into the real world, and she didn't know what to do with his unexpected confession. She thought that he was very clever—the cleverest man she had ever met—and easy to play with. But, now he'd pushed the wrong button, and the game had to end. It upset her. She decided to face what she was afraid to hear; since the game was definitely about to end, she at least would know it for sure. "Interest, uh... what kind?" she asked, diverting her gaze from his, playing with the tip of her ponytail.

"I would have told you that day in the library if I had time," he said. "My son Jonathan began to tell me his memories about his past life in Italy when he was four."

Anna was surprised. *Why didn't he tell me before? Everything would have been easier*, she thought, easing her breathing.

"At that time," he continued, "I was a doctor following the 'masters of psychology', and it cost me a huge effort to overcome my disbeliefs, and a lot of research to understand my son. When I finally discovered the amazing reality that he was revealing to me, I fell in love with the subject and dove into Past Life Regression research. Then I added what I learned, little by little into my practice, to help others deal with something that had made me feel so helpless when it first arose on my son's life."

Anna felt a mix of relief and disappointment. Everything that she had been feeling and guessing about this interesting man was now floating in a spiral. "So, you thought that my son and I were potential patients," she concluded wryly.

He smiled. "I know I shouldn't meet potential patients in a park, but I kind of like to break the rules. I like to see my patients in a natural environment, where they look more real and I can read them better."

Anna stared at him for a moment and felt that the more she knew about him the more she was dazzled. "So, what a coincidence! I went to the Library looking for answers, and you just fell from the sky!"

"Well, everything happens for a reason, don't you think?" he said.

"Do you believe in fate?" she asked back.

He thought for a moment. "I don't know what you call 'fate'. I rather believe that we're not alone. I believe we live many lives and make some friends who eventually come to help us."

"You mean we're surrounded by ghosts or guardian angels?" She made a spooky face.

"You can name it freely, but what I mean is," he settled on the bench. "There is a powerful intelligence that created this whole mechanism called the 'universe', and every piece of this wonderful puzzle we call 'life' falls into place with perfect timing. I can see this clearly through my patients' eyes. How one life interacts with another is just an amazing example of the perfect universal laws settled by this supreme intelligence."

She liked the wise way he spoke and felt even more compelled to deepen the conversation. "I've been struggling to understand life lately," she said. "What I recently found is that life is not an 'exact science' as you're saying. Sometimes, I'm even surprised how 'wrong' and 'right' trade places and turn life into a no-right-answer question."

"I see where you are going: the unknown!"

"The unknown?" she sounded disappointed. "Is that it? Just like my mom: 'this is God's mystery, Anna'. She says that about everything she can't explain."

"Exactly!" he said. "A child looks at a simple addition problem as a mystery, and an adult looks at life with the same innocent expression in his face. The answer is always there, but the unknown is a mystery until the moment we become aware of it."

"It sounds like life is a riddle one has to solve," she amended, feeling a bit despondent.

"Or to have faith that the 'right answer' will come to us eventually, when we are ready and open for it."

"'Seek and you shall find'?"

"Yep!"

"It sounds so religious, doesn't it?" she smiled.

"And you don't like it? I mean religion," he concluded.

"I'm not judgmental. I just don't buy it. People abdicate their own gut to follow someone who is paid to tell them what to believe in."

"Maybe we're talking about different subjects. One thing is the truth. The other thing is the human organization around it."

"Truth..." she laughs wryly. " Who knows it?"

"You're right. Nobody knows everything," he said. "I think truth unfolds itself as we grow older. The way to find it is a journey that makes life more interesting."

Anna was thoughtful and glanced around. The boys were now playing on the monkey bar and on the slide. Anna waved her hand and smiled to reassure Marvin that she was watching him. "So, what did you learn from your son's memories? Do you mind sharing?" Anna asked.

"Not at all," Ralph said. "Jonathan was five. It was a bad moment in our marriage, and we decided to take a little vacation. We rented a cottage on a lake in New York. First day, I took Jonathan to spend time in a boat. He was excited; this was all new to him. As soon as we boarded, he told me his 'gondola' was more comfortable than that boat. It was strange to me that he knew what a gondola was, but I thought he was fantasizing about his first time in a boat. Then he told me stories about his life as a 'merchant in Venice' for the entire boat ride."

"That sounds familiar," Anna joked, thinking of the Shakespeare play.

"To make a long story short," he continued, "he told me he was this Venetian merchant who had the habit of navigating his gondola through the city once a week to watch what people were wearing."

"Did he have any problems? I mean, you said that children remember past lives to heal from traumas."

"Well, he told me how he died. It was pretty traumatic, but he never showed signs that it was an issue in this present life." Ralph shook his head slowly. "The purpose of the memories isn't always clear. At the time, I had no clue what was happening. I decided to investigate. I wanted to understand this peculiar phenomenon, although my wife was against it. She thought I was wasting my time around fantasies, and it made everything harder."

"Why?"

He thought for a moment. "Here's the thing: my son's memories, as far as I can tell, were to heal her."

"To heal your wife?"

"She had terrible migraines, and Jonathan kept talking about this woman who put a bullet in her own head."

"A suicide!"

"According to him, she didn't die. At that time, the doctors could not remove the bullet without causing serious damage to her brain. She lived the rest of her life with that bullet inside her head. One day though, during the therapy with my son, I had a clear glimpse that this woman was my ex-wife. I tried to convince her that she could find healing by having contact with her past life, but she refused. She was a newly graduated doctor and had a career to pursue. As a doctor, I went in the opposite direction, and our connection fell away."

"And your marriage came to an end." Anna concluded for him.

He nodded. There was a shadow of sadness in his eyes. "Being divorced is not fun, especially if you have an adorable child who deserves two parents at home."

Anna pictured herself on the foggy road on which she needed light and guidance to travel.

She caught a glimpse of what he said about coincidences and pieces falling into place. This interesting and emotionally rich man hadn't crossed her way by chance. She gave him a gentle smile. It was time to dispense with formalities and open her heart.

She told him the evolution of Marvin's memories since the day he first spoke about his grandma to their visit to her house. She mentioned Georgia's diary as well and how she felt bound to her life story.

Ralph listened silently until she finished. "It seems clear that your son came back to life to bring peace to this family, and it's up to them to accept it or not," he said. "From what you tell me, he has many points of connection with this family." And with a smile, he concluded. "The evidence is strong enough to ensure a successful procedure."

"English, please," she begged.

"Sorry. What I mean is if we find out what is blocking the connection between the woman, they're calling his mother, and your son, maybe we'll find a lot hidden behind it."

"So you're saying we should submit Marvin to a regression session?"

"Don't be scared. I'll do it at a pace to respect your son's limits. Actually, he'll be the easiest part."

"And what is the hardest?"

"You." He had a hint of compassion in his gaze.

"Me?" She was astonished. "I'm all about it. I thought you were going to say that they are the hardest part. Ellen doesn't believe and won't let us even meet Charlie, the father, who may be just as skeptical. She's holding on to the hope that the boy is still alive."

"I'm sure you'll find a way to make them believe when the right moment arises. For now, there is not much we can do about them. You have to focus on what is in your hand."

"My hand? I tried to understand what is going on with my child, and it led me to this family's drama," she cried. "I don't even think I can count on my husband. Larry has no patience and he is so…limited!"

"It seems that we have to remove some obstacles from the path before we start our journey." Ralph said thoughtfully. "I suggest that we start with two steps: First we have a regression with Marvin at your home. I guess it is easier than convincing your husband to come to my office. Then I can proceed with your regression in my office."

"My regression?"

"I like to follow my gut, and it's telling me that you need to dig a bit in your past."

Anna found herself liking the idea.

"I have this Wednesday at 3:00 p.m., and my nights are open for a home visit, as I guess your husband works during the day."

"That'd be great, but I told you about the trip we have this week."

He stared at her with disappointment. She sensed that, and didn't take long to decide.

"You know what? My husband is going for a conference in Philadelphia, and the only reason I'm going is to see my parents, but I guess, they can wait..." Anna made up her mind. "I'll take the Wednesday, and I'll talk to Larry about your visit."

Ralph let a grin sparkle his face.

The late afternoon was becoming chilly, and most of the moms were leaving the park. Anna and Ralph agreed that it was time to go.

As Anna buckled Marvin into his car seat, a shadow fell over his face. "Mom, can Jonathan be my friend?"

"Why not?"

"I don't know. He's like his father."

"Well, if he's like his father, you definitely should be his friend," Anna said, surprised with his strange question. She smoothed Marvin's hair before closing his door and going around to the driver's side.

Chapter 13

Larry centered the red rose bouquet on the kitchen table. One thing he had learned from his father was that flowers elicited forgiveness and were the best way to show that you cared. Additionally, they were beautiful and smelled nice. To Larry, they were better than words. The flowers were insurance that Anna would not slip away again.

He still had the sensation of her skin against his the night before. The image of her in the midst of their ecstasy hadn't left his mind and he hadn't been able to focus on his work that day.

He had cut work short and was disappointed to find that Anna wasn't at home. He called her cell phone and left a message; he called again five minutes later and again had no response. He could either fall into self-pity or give wings to an imaginative jealousy, but he chose to be patient and wait. He spent some time deciding whether to leave the flowers resting on the table or to place them in a vase. The final decision was that the nice and well-done wrapping should be maintained to save the beauty of the arrangement. Then he settled himself into his big chair in the living room and turned on the news.

When Anna and Marvin arrived, Marvin was the one who jumped into his arms.

"Where've you been? I called you, left a message..." He stood between Anna and the roses on the table.

Anna reached her cell phone from her purse and confirmed that she had two missed calls from him. "I'm so sorry." She finally kissed him hello. "I brought Marvin to the park and left my purse inside the car."

Marvin had wriggled free and vanished into his bedroom upstairs.

"By the way, this is for you." Larry stepped aside so Anna could see the bouquet.

Murmuring her surprise and appreciation, she bent over to smell one of the blooms. Larry put his arms around her waist. Anna tried to guess his intentions. "Umm... it seems that the witch deserves a chance," she said archly, leaning back against him.

"You know that whatever I said doesn't change what I feel," he replied, filling her cheek with gentle kisses.

She closed her eyes to receive them. On the ride back home, she had tried to figure out how to tell Larry about Ralph and the conversation they had had. What if Larry opposed her plans?

She slipped out of his arms to grab a vase from the kitchen cabinet. As she grabbed the bouquet, she saw a card: *"To my beloved wife, to reassure you that in the good and the not so good moments, I will always love you."*

Anna gave him a compassionate look. She felt guilty for not wanting to melt in his arms—and for the conversation she was planning to have.

She approached him and snuggled into his arms anyway. "How was your day?" she whispered, leaning her head on his chest.

"Slow. I think I was anxious to go home. Yours?"

"Good! Lisa came for breakfast, then Marvin and I had our usual activities. I also found more information about..." She hesitated. Why did this subject make her so uncomfortable?

"His past life memories," Larry concluded for her. "Don't worry. I'm not going to throw stones on you because of this. I just don't like when you do..."

"Crazy things." Now she finished for him.

She left his arms again and went back to the roses while Larry changed the subject. "Aren't you excited to see your parents? How long has it been since you've seen them, three months, four?"

"Since July, which was only two months ago."

"Right! It seems so long ago…"

She took the scissors from the kitchen cabinet drawer and cut the bottoms of the stems at an angle, before putting each bloom in the vase. "I found a therapist to help Marvin," she arranged the bouquet in the vase.

"A therapist?"

"His name is Dr. Ralph Stevenson; have you heard about him? He seems to be competent, very accessible, friendly, and most importantly, he had the same experience with his son. Isn't it amazing? He knows exactly what we're looking for, which, for me, is a plus." She gazed at Larry, letting him know that she was prepared to fight for it.

He stared at her, thwarted. It was one more thing that she'd decided without asking his opinion beforehand. However, he was committed to not getting into a fight. He took a deep breath. "It sounds like you got a good referral. I suppose you went over more than one to compare?"

"To be honest, I wasn't looking for that." She finished with the flowers and showed him the nice arrangement. She leaned to smell them before placing them back on the kitchen table. She gently hugged him. "I know I should've asked your opinion first but… this is a long story. Do you mind if I take care of Marvin first? He needs a shower."

He cocked his eyebrow and nodded.

After Marvin had been tucked into bed, they sat at the kitchen table over cups of tea. "I'm all ears," Larry said, running his thumbnail along the teacup's edge. "How did you find this Dr. Stevenson? At the park?"

"I met him by chance at the library. I think I called attention to myself because I was so astonished after finding those pictures. He told me that his son had memories about a past life in Italy, which led him into specialization in Regression Therapy." She decided to omit their encounter at the park for peace's sake.

"It sounds too overwhelming for a little child," Larry protested, uncomfortable with the stranger that Anna, all of a sudden, was welcoming into their lives.

"Ralph said it's totally safe; he'll respect Marvin's limits."

"I'm surprised that you call this doctor by his first name! Wouldn't 'Dr. Stevenson' be more appropriate?"

"Well, maybe." Anna was embarrassed. "Anyway, he said he can come over for a home visit—maybe tomorrow night—and you can meet him. He wants to perform the first session here to make you comfortable with someone taking your child on this unusual trip."

"I admit that it's very unusual for a therapist to offer home visits," Larry was sarcastic. "But, anyway, we're taking off on Wednesday morning; we need time tomorrow night to pack."

Anna took a moment. "The thing is," she finally said, "do you mind if we don't go with you? I want to see my parents, but I'm so focused on Marvin at this moment... I don't want to take a vacation when things are just starting to pick up. I feel like I shouldn't take a break now. I'd be anxious to come back home." After a pause, she concluded with a faint smile, "As you see, I wouldn't be good company on this trip. I'm sorry."

Larry was speechless for a moment. Once again, Anna surpassed his expectations, taking one step ahead and leaving him behind. She was unavoidably sliding through his fingers.

"I can agree that you're doing your best to help Marvin, but it sounds like you're already losing your mind." He was grouchy, his patience quickly fading, and he was just about to retract the white flag.

"I know we made plans for this trip, but it's not a real vacation. You'll be at the conference all day long, and I'll be stuck at my parent's. We can plan another trip, a weekend together, a real vacation," she argued. "I can also pack your stuff tomorrow during the day, so you'll have tomorrow evening free for the session."

Larry ran his hand through his hair nervously, a habit of his, and tried to follow her. "What you're saying is that you want to change our plans? You decided to get a therapist for Marvin, and also want to bring this man to our house to take care of my own son? Outstanding! What else did you decide?"

Anna felt the tension in his voice. For her, the matter shouldn't degenerate into a war. The goal, after all, was to help their mutual son. What happened to the perfect man she married? He had become a stubborn naysayer, she thought. "That's not fair, Larry. This is exclusively about our son."

"You already made up your mind, like always. You never ask my opinion. He's 'our' son only when you need my agreement. Beyond that, you have the right to make decisions on your own."

"But I'm here, right now, sharing this decision with you," she cried.

"The decision you made with another man," he raised his voice, impatiently.

"Are you... jealous?" she gave him a surprising look.

"Is there any reason to be?" His eyes narrowed.

"You're scared," she recalled Lisa's comment.

"Well, it can happen when you love."

She felt disarmed. "Isn't love supposed to bring you confidence and a giving attitude?" She said in a more peaceful tone.

"What about reciprocity?" He frowned.

"It's not about us."

"You keep repeating this over and over. You wanted to home school Marvin, and I agreed. I bought this house to give us a fresh start, and I'm doing everything to help you with your endless confusion. What I see is that you're using Marvin's discomfort on rainy days to run away from your own problems. Yes, this is about us!"

Anna felt offended. He was distorting her intentions.

"You prefer to listen to your crazy friend or to a stranger that you met by chance, instead of focusing on finding a solution to our lives," Larry continued.

"Very easy for you to judge me," she said dryly. "What if things are not supposed to be as you expect? You want peace over wreckage. You don't want to know what's going on around you, with your wife or your son. In your life, it's all predictable, simple math, like 'buy a house and start fresh.' I'm sorry, Larry, if I and Marvin have problems. We didn't mean to have them." Anna pushed her chair back and stood up.

This night, she wrote in her diary.

I want to know what love is, I mean, love between a man and woman. It may be an old question, but I have never had a convincing answer.

Chapter 14

"Why did you sleep in my bed last night, mom?" Marvin asked, at the breakfast table.

"I just wanted to be with you for a minute and fell asleep, sweetie."

Marvin looked suspicious at Anna, took another spoonful of his cereal, and kept talking. Both Anna and Larry were very quiet this morning. "Are we still going to see Grandpa and Grandma tomorrow?"

Larry glanced at Anna, challenging her to respond.

"Do you want to go?" Anna asked Marvin back.

"Of course, I do" he answered. "I miss Grandpa and Grandma."

"Then we'll go to see Grandpa and Grandma," Anna said, watching Larry's reaction as Marvin became cheerful.

The night had taken its toll and Anna came up with a proposal. "I have a deal," she said to Larry in a low voice. "Would you like to hear it?"

He gave her a wry, wordless look as if saying that he wanted out of the game.

"We'll go with you," she said, ignoring his indifference. "In exchange, I want to schedule the regression session for tonight."

Larry was silent for a moment. "You should not promise something to him before you listen to my answer," Larry finally said. "Your strategy is a bad joke. What if I say 'no'?"

"It's your choice." Anna shrugged.

Larry finished his breakfast silently, kissed his son, and left.

Anna called Larry's cell phone many times during the morning, but he never answered. She thought of leaving a message, yelling at him, provoking him, even pleading for reconsideration, but she restrained herself. He couldn't use a child to play such a dirty game. It was hard for her to accept that he had been very smart. He delivered a perfect checkmate and there was no legal move to escape the threat. It wasn't fair!

Finally, she grabbed the phone once more, this time to call Ralph and cancel the Wednesday appointment, but an inexplicable feeling kept her from pressing the 'call' button. Maybe a miracle could still happen.

She called Lisa, instead, and invited her friend over. She needed to vent.

Lisa arrived in a cheerful mood. She showed Anna a necklace she had just gotten as a present.

"It's beautiful, isn't it?" she showed the necklace, which was made with red and yellow beads. She explained, "The reds are açaí berries, and the yellows, coconut skin, a present from a Brazilian friend."

"Umm, I'm jealous now," Anna played. "I haven't seen one of these. It's very pretty! Is he a friend or something else?"

"I think he is interested. He's shy, though, I can't tell."

"This is unique, and he was very sensitive to choose it." Anna took a very close look at the necklace. "I'd say ninety percent chance," she stated earnestly.

"Chance of what, that it's real?"

"That he is interested. Besides, you're pretty and funny. Hard to resist."

"Thank you! You made my day."

Lisa laughed, as Anna whispered, "I wish someone could make mine."

"What's going on now? You look a little bit down."

"I'm mad and angry and cranky! My marriage has become a battle field, and there's this stupid trip that I don't want to make."

The house phone rang. Anna turned her head slightly and saw an unrecognized number on the Caller ID. Someone was leaving a message and it caught her attention: "Hi, Anna. This is Ellen. May you, please…" Anna jumped over the phone and grabbed it, panting.

"Hi, Ellen, this is Anna." She made signs at Lisa to explain that this was "the" Ellen.

"Oh, hi Anna! I was about to leave a message."

"Sorry, I was a little busy here. I'm glad you called." Anna couldn't contain her excitement at hearing Ellen's voice.

"I'm calling to ask you, if you have a spare moment today, would you please come to my house and bring your son with you? I'd like to take a closer look at this boy."

Anna was stunned. "I can come now if you don't mind."

As Ellen agreed, they hung up the phone.

"Do you believe in miracles?" Anna said to Lisa. Rushing to get Marvin appropriately dressed, she invited Lisa to come along.

"I kind of hoped you'd invite me," Lisa grinned. "I don't want to miss it."

As Ellen opened the front door, Anna greeted her and rushed to introduce Lisa to make sure that Ellen would be comfortable with her presence. Marvin hugged Ellen, and this time she looked more comfortable with his affection.

Looking around at the old-fashioned furnishings, Lisa felt uncomfortable with the energy she immediately sensed in the room. Many mixed memories were present, not quite pleasant though, and she could feel it in her stomach (she had this gift and sometimes she wished she hadn't, especially in moments like this).

Ellen motioned them to sit on the couch. "After your last visit, I couldn't stop thinking about all that you told me," she said. "It still sounds too strange to me, but..." She was twisting her clenched hands. "The reason I invited you is because there's someone who wants to meet your son."

Anna's curiosity turned into astonishment when a man of medium height, apparently in his seventies, appeared in the door to the kitchen. He had resigned green eyes, as though he hadn't much to hope for at his age. A deep sensation of familiarity followed by a déjà-vu made Anna dizzy. She exchanged a look with Lisa who sensed Anna's reaction and gave her back a supporting look.

"I want to introduce you to my brother Charlie," Ellen said.

Anna shook the man's hand, making an effort to pull herself together then introduced Lisa and Marvin. "You don't look like my dad Charlie. He has dark hair and is younger," Marvin said earnestly.

No one knew what to say and the silence was uncomfortable.

"I don't think this is going to work," Charlie said, giving Ellen a dirty look.

"I know you," Lisa said, trying to wipe out the embarrassing vibration, "from the Danbury Hospital! If I'm not wrong, you went there when you got a bad cut on your hand while working in your backyard."

"I remember the accident, but unfortunately I don't remember you, young lady," said Charlie politely.

"Small world," Anna mumbled.

Since they'd stood up for the introductions, Ellen invited everyone back to the couch. In spite of Marvin's reaction to Charlie, Ellen didn't give up. She grabbed the picture of his family and asked Marvin to point his father in it. Marvin, without hesitating, pointed to Charlie, and then gave a suspicious look to that man in front of him. He switched his gaze alternately from the picture to Charlie, as though trying to find similarities between them.

"Don't you think that it's him?" Anna tried to help him.

"This picture was taken a long time ago. People age as time goes by. How do you think he looks like now?"

Marvin gazed at Ellen in the picture and compared it to her present appearance. He did the same again to Charlie, and finally seemed to recognize him, because he smiled and approached Charlie. "This is you, and there is me," he pointed at the picture. "And this is your friend Frank," he added naturally.

Charlie looked straight at Marvin, and it seemed that he had finally found words to say, when Marvin interrupted him. "Where is Mr. Bogart?" Marvin asked.

Charlie was stunned. He looked at Ellen who returned the gaze as if saying "I told you!" He took a moment to catch his breath, managing to answer in an even low voice. "Mr. Bogart was old and had to make his way to wherever dogs go after they die."

Marvin nodded, as he knew this was the truth.

"Mr. Bogart was our dog. I named him after the Casablanca actor Humphrey Bogart," Charlie explained, without moving his gaze away from Marvin. "He was a Great Dane, a clumsy big dog. He was part of our small family. He loved to take car rides and go places. By coincidence, he died the same year Humphrey passed away in 1957, two years after Marty was gone."

Anna had imagined Charlie as a senile, old man. He looked great though for his age. Considering Lisa's comment about his accident, it seemed obvious that he drew his strength from being active.

Anna observed him with a sort of admiration. His hair was like cotton that he capriciously combed from left to right, and his green eyes, even surrounded by the wrinkled skin, were clear like a peaceful lake. Anna felt like she could just sit there and look at him. She remembered Ralph's words about "perfect timing," "universal laws," and about nobody being alone. She felt that they weren't alone; invisible hands were performing wise and silent work. "I know, this is a lot to process," Anna finally said. "Since Marvin began to tell me about his past life, my intention was only to find the truth, to help my son with his unusual behavior on rainy days. I thought that, by exposing him to what he believes to be real, I could bring some light to a situation that I had no clue how to deal with."

"It is a lot to process," Charlie agreed emphatically, "We need more evidence than names. Your son may be a very special child—I don't want be disrespectful in any way—but he can't be my son, who I still hope is alive."

"When was the last time you heard from your son, Mr. Baker?" Lisa intervened. "I mean, after all these years without a word, if I had even a hint, I would follow it until the end of the world."

Charlie looked uncomfortable. "The fact that I never had a word about what happened to my son doesn't mean that I have to believe in whatever anybody tells me." He paused, and his gaze became vague, as if he were sorting out old memories. "The first years were the worst of my life, worse even than the first time Georgia left. She was my first love; she was just someone...unforgettable." Charlie's eyes shone. "And you never expect anything bad from someone you love, but she unfortunately did the worst." Charlie came back to the present. "If your boy could tell me what happened after that day, or where she is—something real—maybe I could accept that my son is dead, if he is dead." His voice sounded bitter, but not angry. His eyes were wet.

Ellen cleared her throat. "The reason that I called you today," she said to Anna "is because I trust in your intentions. We don't want to embarrass your son or be disrespectful. We want to make it easier for you..."

"And what is it?" Anna felt like it was a bad omen.

Ellen looked at Charlie as if passing the burden of explanation to him.

"When Ellen told me about your son," Charlie said, "I thought it was a bad joke, but I couldn't get it out of my mind. Ellen said that you were not one of those people who come to snoop into somebody else's life. She told me about your concerns and that your son is having some troubles. Then I thought of a way we could make this easier for all of us."

"Okay," said Anna, somewhat suspiciously.

"The reason that I wanted to see your son," Charlie continued, "was to check something on him."

"And what is it?" She was quite uncomfortable.

"I did research on the subject, past life memories. It is said that when a person comes back to life, he can carry on his body the same birthmark he had in the previous life. My son, Marty, had a birthmark on the back of his neck, a well shaped little red heart."

Marvin had never had any birthmark and Anna was more disappointed than she could have expected. Even so, she pulled Marvin closer for a double check on the back of his neck and at the base of his skull only to find what she already knew. "Is it that simple?" She wondered aloud. "Could a birthmark be better evidence than all he remembers about people who he never met in this life?"

Lisa kindly touched her arm.

Charlie reached a folded old piece of paper from the pocket of his button-down denim shirt, and unfolded it carefully under Anna's curious eyes. The paper was an old reward sign offering twenty thousand dollars to whoever could bring any reliable information about the missing fifteen-year-old boy. It had a non-expiration note at the bottom. Marty's picture was stamped in the center.

"With all my respects," Charlie handed the paper over to Anna. "I had many people coming to me in the past with false information. It was big money, and I guess it still is. You could buy a house with it at that time. I made available all that I had to get any clue about my son. Unfortunately, the offer attracted many swindlers. Many years later, I still had people knocking upon my door, trying to deceive me with stories they invented in an attempt to redeem the prize. The last one was a woman who brought me a picture of a thirty-year-old man. His resemblance to my son was impressive. She gave me a phone number and I called the man. He wasn't able to answer the simplest personal questions I asked." And after a pause, Charlie sighed and concluded. "After all this years, I'm still offering this prize and still hope that someone out there can bring me some news about my son, a question that I hope not to carry to the grave unanswered."

"This is disappointing for me as well," Ellen said with a friendly voice. "Your child has impressed us greatly. But reincarnation is a subjective matter. We'd be very thankful for anything anyone could tell us about our Marty, but we cannot rely on something without evidence."

Anna felt too discouraged to argue.

"At least, if your son could tell us about his mother…" Ellen insisted, "If he could say something that leads us to any clue about what happened…"

"I had no mother, I already told you," Marvin said with his childish simplicity.

"We'd be glad to help you with your son's problem, but I believe there's nothing we can do," Charlie added.

"Don't worry, I'm already looking for professional help," Anna said, fighting back a tear. "I guess we should go now." She stood up. "Thank you for your kindness, and sorry if we caused any discomfort."

She took Marvin's hand, gave a long and meaningful look at Charlie, and walked toward the front door followed by Lisa.

"Take good care of him tonight," Ellen said.

"Humiliation!" Anna finally said in the midst of a silent car ride. A tear slid down her face. "They think that it's money that I want?"

"Of course not," Lisa tried to be comforting. "They just wanted to tell you that they had reasons not to believe your story, at least without 'evidence'."

"I know, but he didn't even have a good conversation with Marvin. He could've asked more questions, anything..."

"It's okay, Mom, they don't know me because I have a different body now," Marvin said.

"You're right, sweet heart. I'm sorry that they didn't."

"Don't be sorry; they will."

When they arrived home, as soon as Anna had a private moment with Lisa, she collapsed in tears.

"What am I going to do now? I'm not asking for anything for myself, for God's sake."

Lisa took a tissue from her purse and handed it to Anna. "I can imagine how you feel, but you have to be patient."

"How can I be patient? I'm in a war with Larry because of this. Ellen and Charlie don't want to believe in something that is screaming in their faces. I feel like I'm in a protest march that everybody left, and I'm standing there alone holding the flag."

"I know, but it's my role to remind you that past life memory isn't the most popular subject," Lisa said. "You said you're already looking for professional help, are you?"

"Yes." She wiped her tears, trying to get her strength back. "But that has been another battle; Larry doesn't get it."

"Get what?"

"Past Life Regression, a kind of hypnosis. There's a doctor in Bethel, I met him the other day."

"Umm. It sounds interesting! Did you schedule an appointment?"

"I did, but I'll have to postpone it. We're going to Philadelphia tomorrow. Larry has a conference there."

"And why do you have to go?"

"I don't have to; but I don't want..." Anna's expression went blank as if she had just thought of something. "Why did Ellen tell me to take good care of Marvin tonight? What did she mean?"

"Maybe she was thinking of the rain," Lisa guessed.

"Seriously!? The sky is clear."

"Check the forecast. Chance of precipitation is one hundred percent," Lisa informed her. "And I think it's time for me to hit the road. I'd like to stay a little more with you, my friend, but I've got to work."

When Anna was alone with her thoughts, she tried to find comfort in Ralph's words. Was she supposed to have faith that the truth would unfold in its own pace? Faith! The only thing left for a person that never really had it, she thought in herself. Maybe that's what faith was: to believe, even when nothing seemed to be working out.

Chapter 15

Anna spent part of the afternoon packing. Her suitcase, she filled in just few minutes with casual garments, jeans, light sweaters, cotton t-shirts, and her favorite comfy pajamas. She had neither plans nor motivation to do anything but stay at her parents' home enjoying the good food her mother always made and her father's stories that he told so proudly. On Larry's suitcase, she spent more time. (She had grown up watching her mom packing for her father, as it was part of her Brazilian culture, and Larry loved that Anna had learned this from her mom.) She packed dress pants and shirts, as well as socks, underwear, and ties. All were carefully folded. When she was finished, she examined her handiwork. *Too perfect!* she thought. She slightly tousled the navy blue button-down shirt on the top of the pile—his favorite—as if taking revenge of his perfection.

She also took a moment to call Ralph and cancel her appointment. She was glad when the call went to the answering machine. She didn't want to explain herself. At the park, she had been so decided and glowing. Now she was feeling drained and lifeless. She wasn't giving up; a few days away from her problems now sounded providential. She'd recover her strength in the loving arms of her family.

She left a prolix message, and got cut off before it was over and felt irritated with herself.

When Larry got home, a little after 5:00 p.m., he found all curtains closed. A couple of windows in the living room had only the rods, installed by the previous homeowner (one of the things they still had to fix in the house) and Anna had hung bed sheets over them to cover the outside view. It had started to rain in the late afternoon.

"Are we expecting a hurricane?" Larry asked ironically, shedding his suitcase on the couch.

"We don't need a hurricane; you know what a regular rainstorm does," Anna answered dryly. She was still angry at him.

"Isn't this a little drastic?"

"You don't wait until you're thirsty to dig a well," she responded, with the same tone. "Thanks for not answering my calls, by the way."

"Sorry, it was a busy day," he said, with a sly smile that he tried to hide turning his head.

Anna caught him from the corner of her eyes, but decided to avoid a fight.

Marvin was playing in his bedroom, bringing life to his toys long before it started raining. As soon as the rain picked up though, Marvin began to tremble, as if his sixth sense was capturing the vibration of the falling rain outside. The double-paned glass window and the blinds were preventing him from seeing or hearing it. Anna came to check on him and watched him grab a couple of his stuffed dinosaurs and sneak to a makeshift hideout underneath the bed. She was worried. She went to her knees and lifted the bed skirt to find Marvin. He was fine, although quiet and gloomy. Later, she read some bedtime stories to keep his mind busy and decided to stay in bed with him until he fell asleep. Larry was doing some work in preparation for the conference.

Before she left Marvin's room, the rain turned into a storm, and, at this point, the seal of the windows proved insufficient to prevent them from hearing it. The roar of the wind shaking the tree foliage, and the thick raindrops hitting the window panes were clearly amplified in Marvin's head. Anna could tell by the expression of terror on his face when he suddenly woke up. She watched as his gaze became distant and his body tensed into rigidity. Whispering words of encouragement and support, Anna cuddled with him in bed.

At the next thunderclap, he burst into tears, and Anna held him even tighter.

But Marvin cried incessantly, and none of her efforts were effective to prevent his tears from cascading, his hysteria from worsening, or to distract his frightened soul. *Oh, God!* She pleaded, and squeezed him against her chest, helpless, as if she wanted to take Marvin's pain into herself.

Inside, Anna's anger was growing. She thought of Charlie and Ellie, and even Larry. All those who could help her child were now enjoying the comfort of their indifference, their selfishness.

Her inconsolable child was pushing Anna's strength to its limit. She felt as though she was close to losing hope and faith and patience and even civility. She was about to scream at God. Instead, she silently released her tears, along with her child.

Only a few minutes has passed. The growing anguish turned Anna's expression into a coldness. She brought Marvin down to the basement where Larry was working at his desk. Seeing Marvin in Anna's arms, Larry sprang to his feet, his face showing his concern. Anna stood before him and flicked a scathing gaze in his direction. This is what I've been trying to tell you—her eyes on fire seemed to say. When Larry reached out a hand to soothe Marvin, Anna passed the child to him. Marvin fought not to leave the safety of his mother's arms, but Anna was determined. She kissed Marvin's forehead and mouthed to Larry "good luck" before leaving them alone.

She went back to the living room and cuddled into a ball on the couch, covering her ears with pillows not to hear Marvin's cry. Larry definitely needed that, she was decided. Her heart was tightened; it was an extraordinary effort, being away from his child at this moment, but deep inside, she knew that it wouldn't last long.

Less than five minutes passed when Larry came after her, Marvin inconsolably in his arms. "This is not fair; this is not the time for this. Can you please help?" he said in a pleading, low voice.

Anna got up and took Marvin back into her arms. His crying suddenly receded, and he seemed to feel more comfortable. But it was only for few seconds. Marvin cried throughout the night, alternating moments of more or less distress. They took turns in the attempt to give him some relief, seldom successfully.

Larry brought over some covers and pillows, and they settled on the basement couch, where the sounds of the night were less frightening. At about 3:00 a.m. Larry, whose eyes were reddish and whose expression was drawn, reached his limits and drifted off. Anna told him to go to bed. "You have a busy day tomorrow."

They needed to leave the house no later than 5:30. He needed to rest for the long drive. "You're right," he said, staggering to his feet, "I need to get some sleep. You'd better stay home tomorrow and do whatever you think will help him. I'll explain to your parents what happened."

Anna nodded. She was speechless. A miracle in course.

"Thank God!" she mouthed, eyes closed, once Larry had left.

A few minutes later, the rain slowed to a drizzle. Marvin became quiet, but still didn't want to leave Anna's lap. Every attempt to put him to bed led to a new crisis. In order to keep him in a calm and comfortable mood, she held him in her arms, bouncing on the rocking chair and whispering lullabies.

At 5:00 a.m., Larry woke up and got ready to leave. He found Anna sleeping on the chair in the living room, with Marvin asleep in her lap. His approach was enough to wake her up. He came closer to kiss her goodbye and was glad to see Marvin sleeping like a little angel.

"Is it time?" she whispered groggily.

He nodded. "Look, you take care of this boy, okay?"

She sighed, and turned her gaze to heaven.

"About the therapy..." he said, "you know what you're doing, don't you?"

She nodded silently in expectation as he continued.

"So, do what you think is best, and when you're done, come back to me, okay? I may not know about psychology, past life, all that stuff, but one thing I know: I love you. I don't want to lose you or my son. My family is the most precious thing I have in life."

He gave her a still kiss, as though he was only making a physical bridge for his feelings to pass. She closed her eyes to receive it.

He kissed Marvin's forehead, grabbed his suitcase, and walked toward the front door.

"Hey," Anna whispered.

He turned around. Her eyes were tired, but tender. "I like when we fight on the same side. Thank you!" She said with a hint of a smile.

Holding Marvin in her arms, she opened the curtain slightly to watch him pass by outside the window. The rain had ceased, and she suddenly saw some stars in a clear spot in the cloudy sky. She sent a prayer out into the opening in the heavens.

Chapter 16

Her hands were sweaty—as always when she was nervous. She looked around, taking account of details. The waiting room walls were light brown to match the carpet and the furniture. There were three comfortable, large armchairs by the longest wall and, above them, three paintings of delicate flowers resting on a narrow wooden hanging shelf. Soft music filled the air, bringing an almost sacred sensation.

She sat on a chair on the opposite side of the receptionist's desk, near an open cabinet filled with all sorts of reading material and a well cared for bonsai. She thought that if a waiting room told something about the officeholder within, this one was a spoiler. But the absence of a receptionist was strange as was the fact that the front door of the building was locked downstairs. Thanks to a man in the driveway, she had found the back door unlocked and was able to sneak inside the building. A "do not disturb" sign hanging on the knob of a closed door indicated that Ralph was busy with a client in his office.

She sorted through the magazines and chose one about health. She tried to focus on reading it but the letters became blurred as her mind wandered away.

She was about to have her first Past Life Regression session and had no clue what to expect. She was excited, though skeptical, not because she didn't trust him—he was probably the only one she'd trusted on this matter—but because she did not think she could enter into the required deep state of relaxation.

She felt like the clock, hanging on the wall in front of her, slowed down to the point that it seemed to be still. "Maybe the battery needs to be replaced," she thought. Then she checked on her cell phone and realized that the clock was precise: ten minutes before 3:00 p.m. Nobody had called for an appointment after she cancelled hers. First thing in the morning, she had grabbed the phone and, fingers crossed, called Ralph. Then she called Lisa and pleaded with her to watch Marvin.

When she saw the name "Doctor Stevenson" on the front door, it had seemed quite strange. For the first time she thought of him as a doctor, and of herself as a patient. She realized she should not be dressed the way she had in skinny white jeans and high heels, not-too-high, but high enough to enhance her sensual Brazilian body type. She had also put on discreet make up and let her black wavy hair loose. It cascaded over a maroon leather jacket.

Now she was uncomfortable. She thought she was calling too much attention to herself, when the occasion did not call for it. Then she pulled a band out of her purse and tied her hair in a ponytail.

Ten minutes after 3:00, a pretty young woman came out of Ralph's office. She was dressed in an attractive way, if not sensual. Anna tugged the band out of her hair before Ralph came to greet her.

"I'm glad you made it," he said with a friendly smile.

"Yeah!" she agreed. "It seems that the universe is conspiring in my favor."

"I can see that. Why don't you come to my office?"

She entered Ralph's office with the same curiosity that she had when scanning the waiting room. The first thing she noticed was a picture of Ralph's son on the bookcase located behind a small wooden desk. Next, she saw an inviting chaise lounge, with an olive slipcover and a tufted back pillow. Behind it, two rectangular windows, with half-closed olive curtains cutting the bright light coming from outside. She complimented Ralph on the appearance of the room while walking toward his desk and touching a small statue of an ancient man with a wise face.

"Is she another potential client that you met by chance at the library?" she taunted him, as she ran her eyes across the room.

"You mean Beth? She is my niece, my oldest brother's daughter."

"Oh." She blushed. But she still couldn't help being jealous. The feeling had been growing within her since she saw the girl and she was mad that she could not take control over it.

Ralph offered her a chair and sat right in front of her. She met his gaze unexpectedly and could not resist it. Silently, they stared at each other. For few seconds the world stopped around them. She realized that every time she saw him, she felt more and more taken by his charm, as if taking one more step toward a deep and mysterious valley. She couldn't let the door open to this feeling, though, even slightly. She wished she could know what was passing through his mind.

"I guess you don't know much about what is going to happen," Ralph broke the silence.

"Not really." She glanced around uncomfortably. "I'm feeling guilty that Marvin is the one who should be here, especially after what happened last night."

"And what did happen last night?"

She told him briefly about the hard time they had at home.

"I understand your concerns," he said after. "However, it will be better if you have a broader understanding in advance about hypnosis. You'll be more able to help him yourself." He asked some formal questions and wrote down some notes in a small notebook. When he started with a preliminary explanation, she finally began to relax.

"Hypnosis is not something to be afraid of. It's only a deep state of relaxation that causes the memory to sharpen. Sometimes you fall into this state without realizing it, when driving a car or watching a movie. These are moments when your thought goes away and you seem to be somewhere else. I will guide you through an initial relaxation, and then I'll give you commands to go back on your timeline. You will be conscious the whole time, and I want you to know that you'll always be safe. You can open your eyes at any time if you feel stressed out or uncomfortable. But you can do other things as well. If a scene or emotion feels uncomfortable, you can just float over it and be detached as if you're watching a movie. Just know that you're safe."

She glanced at the chaise lounge and wondered how she could feel comfortable with that charming man freely watching her lie with her eyes closed. "Will I remember when it's done?"

"Yes. Not only remember. You'll be able to understand the connection between the memories that emerge and your present life."

"This is interesting. I accept reincarnation, but I never figured how it works. Knowing that I can face myself in another life kind of freaks me out," she said. "I just hope that I don't fall asleep before we start; I had a pretty bad night."

"Don't worry. That's not going to happen. Is there anything else you'd like to ask before we start?"

She shook her head and he motioned her to make herself comfortable, suggesting that she take off her jacket and hang it on the chair. She accepted the suggestion, but when she lay down on the chaise lounge, she felt exposed, a tension that began to dissipate only when his soft voice started to lead her to focus on her breath.

Using visualization and imagery, he guided her to a stress free place. Anna felt her breathing slow. She released her hands that were clasped over her chest to relax on either side of her body.

When her breathing became calm and deep, he went to the next step. "I'll start counting from ten to one, and you will deepen into a beautiful state of relaxation. Let your mind be free. Don't try to analyze or judge any image that emerges. You'll be only the observer, so watch them. Observe the feelings attached to all images and don't try to understand or to criticize what you see. You'll be able to do that later."

Anna felt her body melting on the chaise lounge, and her head spinning. She felt safe though, and enjoyed the sensetion.

"Ten...nine...eight... You feel at peace, more and more relaxed. Seven...six...five... You go deeper and deeper in this state of calmness and relaxation. Four, three, two...one." He let her be for a moment. "Now I want you to go to back in time to the most significant event in your childhood. Let your mind bring the memories of this time. Focus on the little girl or baby that you once were."

He let a minute pass silently. Then he guided her to look around, observe her hands, her feet, and the clothes she wore. Tension grew on her face and hands.

"I'm a girl, a little girl. I'm wearing a gray dress and shoes," she said.

"What's your age?"

"Ten. My father is by my side and he's crying. We're both sitting on the bed in his bedroom where my mom lies. She's pale and her eyes are half-open and still. She's wearing a beige nightgown. She's dead. He's crying because my mom died. I'm sad, but I'm not crying." Anna's expression looked like a scared little girl.

"What year is it?" he asked.

"It's 1932. My mother was sick, very sick. I feel guilty. My father is trying to console me. He said that it wasn't my fault. I'm scared. He says he'll protect me. He always did all that I wanted. He was my father before."

"Had he been your father?" Ralph caught the link.

"Yes. This isn't the first time he's my father."

"And why do you feel guilt?"

"My father had to spend his time taking care of me, but he

should've been taking care of her instead; she'd been ill for so long."

She became silent. When she said nothing more, Ralph intervened. "Now, I want you to go to the previous time with your father."

Anna grew more and more tense. Her palms were sweating. "My father hates me."

"Why does he hate you?"

"My mother died giving birth to me. He blames me."

"What year is it?"

"It's 1770."

"What's your age?"

"I just turned sixteen. My name is Lucia. I live in a town called Olinda in a very poor house. It's hot, and the house smells like smoke from a wood burning stove. My father is handicapped; he uses me to make money."

"In what country is this town located?"

"It's in Brazil."

She became silent; the memories disturbed her deeply. The image of the man was threatening.

"How does your father use you?"

"He makes me lie with men. He hits me with a wooden stick if I refuse. The men are dirty and smell of tobacco. They ride horses. They call me *a filha do aleijado.*"

"What does it mean?"

"*The daughter of the lame man.* Most of them respect me; some bring me presents expecting special treatment in exchange. There's one of them that I like. I like when he comes, but he doesn't come often. He's the only one who talks to me and asks me questions. He makes me feel loved. I feel like I have known him for a long time. But he's married and seems unhappy. I dream of running away with him...but my father needs me. He can't work on the plantation. My mother was the one who provided for the family before I was born. I have a sister older than me, but she is mentally ill."

She became silent and Ralph intervened with a soft low voice.

"I want you to look with love at this girl you once were. I want you to know that it wasn't your fault that your mom died. We can't control life. No one knows when it's time for us to leave this life for another. It's God's will. It wasn't your fault. Free this girl you once were from guilt. Tell her that what happened belongs to the past."

Anna relaxed again as the memories of this time faded. Ralph let her rest for a couple of minutes and jotted in his notebook. "I want you to keep going in time. Feel safe to explore the next most important moments of your lives."

Another silent minute passed. "I'm a young French woman in the 19th century. There are many people in the room; they are talking to the souls. The souls make the table shake and spin. My sister and her husband are sitting at the table as I'm, too. My sister hates me... she's Lisa."

Anna had revealed a name, and Ralph wrote it down. Anna had grown tense. Her sweaty hands were wetting the fabric of her shirt.

"Why does she hate you?"

"I live with my sister and her husband. Our parents are deceased and she's the only family I have. I'm pregnant. It's her husband's baby. She can't have a baby, and she thinks that I did it because I love him. But I'd never do anything to hurt my sister. He seduced me; he forced me. I tried to resist, but she doesn't believe me. She thinks that I seduced him."

Anna moaned, experiencing extreme pain. She writhed on the chair, her hands pressing her tummy, reviving the birth of a beautiful baby. The midwife pulled out the baby and her sister took the newborn in her arms. Then, she relaxed as the pain had gone away.

"It's a boy," Anna smiled. She became silent for a moment enjoying the image of the baby in her sister's arms. Then the tension came back to her voice. "My sister wants to keep the baby, and asked me to leave their lives. She says this is the only way she can forgive me."

Anna cried.

"Did you give her the baby," Ralph probed.

"I had no choice. I don't want her to hate me."

"Did you leave the house?"

"Yes, I did. I had no choice."

"Did you ever see the baby again in this life?"

"No. I never went back. I wandered through Paris for a year, until I was rescued by a good man who brought me to his house. I was very sick and I died, regardless of his care."

Anna became quiet, as these memories faded. A few minutes passed before something new emerged.

"What do you see now?" asked Ralph, his voice barely above a whisper.

"I see a man lying in bed. He's sick. He's not my husband, but—I don't understand—he is my husband. We never got married."

"Maybe he's just your partner," Ralph suggested.

"We live together..." Anna confirmed. This time the memories were not so clear. She was in a bedroom with a dim light. The man was lying on a walnut wood bed with a paneled headboard and footboard. An untouched bowl of soup was resting on a tray on the bedside table. She forced herself to see the man's face. He was terminally ill, skin over bones. "He's the same husband I have now. He's dying, but he smiles. I'm so sad; he's a good man. I had many losses, people that I love..."

"How old are you?"

"Thirty-two, maybe thirty-three... Someone is waiting for me but I can't see his face."

"Is this person a man or a child?"

"A man."

"Can you go closer to see who he is?"

"He's not in the same place as me. I just know he's waiting

for me."

"Why don't you go to meet him?"

"I can't. I have to stay with my husband. He has cancer; he doesn't have much time. Only after he dies, I'll be free to go."

Anna started to sob silently. It lasted several minutes during which she didn't say a word until she calmed down. She stayed silent, in a relaxed state for few more minutes. Ralph checked the clock. It was time to bring her back. He waited one more minute only to make sure that she had nothing else to say then started to guide her to the countdown back to consciousness.

The regression was over. She opened her eyes and saw Ralph by her side with a friendly smile. "Welcome back. How do you feel?"

She thought for a moment, assessing her feelings. She felt good, so relaxed that she couldn't talk. The memories were so vivid, as if she just had woken up from a dream.

"I'm cold," she said, rubbing her arms.

Ralph grabbed her jacket and handed it to her. She put it on and stayed leaning on the chaise lounge, now feeling completely comfortable under his attentive eyes.

"Is there something you want to ask...or share?" he offered.

"I do have many questions," she said emphatically. "Is this couch a sort of time travel machine?"

He smiled, and just cocked his eyebrow as a confirmation.

"Is it that easy for anyone to go back in time like this?" she asked.

"For some people it takes a few sessions until they can see even a slight image. Others are like you. It depends how near to the surface the memories are."

"But I was never good at relaxation."

"Remember when I said that we're never alone?"

Anna nodded, not sure what he meant. "It was an amazing experience! I felt so present with those people. I had this feeling that I had complete knowledge of everything about them."

She was talking in a slow pace, as if the memories were still floating above her head and she didn't want to let them go. "Are these memories real or could I possibly be making them up?"

"That, you can tell better than me. Only you can tell if all that you saw and felt made sense to your life. You revealed names, ages, situations, and precise information. You also experienced feelings that only you know how they impact your present life."

She nodded. "The little girl feeling so guilty..." she recalled her first memory. "I can see clearly myself in her skin. This is a feeling that I have always had but I never suspected that it was guilt. I always felt like everything that happened around me, in some way, was my fault. But the little girl just took it away from me. Is it always that easy?"

"You weren't guilty; it wasn't your fault that your mother died when you were born. Nevertheless, if that wasn't the case, if instead, you had done something bad in the past, the healing could be harder, though still possible through regression. When you bring a past event to consciousness you can see that you are no longer the person you once were, the person who didn't have the knowledge or the strength that now you have to overcome fear and make better choices in life, so you're able to forgive yourself."

Anna thought for a moment. "This is so amazing!" she finally said. "Is this how life works? We bring our baggage from one life to another as unfinished business that we still have to work out. It reminds me of what you said about '*things falling into place in perfect timing....*'"

"And I remember you saying that '*life is not an exact science.*'"

She was surprised, and glad that he also remembered things they said to each other. It proved that he cared about her. Since their very first encounter, he had revealed himself as a man with a sharp vision, and it was what most attracted her. *This is the moment when someone connects to your soul,* she said to herself, *the moment when a person actually sees you. It is the key he used to open the door that, more and more I'm feeling unable to close.* She gazed at him, once again admiring his cleverness and his experience to deal with the human mind. "And I suppose that now you can explain it better to me," she teased.

"You're entirely able to understand it for yourself," he said earnestly.

"Not even a hint?" she pleaded.

"A hint. Okay." He thought for a moment. "I suggest you to pay close attention to the patterns that this experience revealed to you. Maybe, at first you cannot see them clearly, but as time goes by, things will make more sense."

"Patterns?" She was surprised with his enigmatic answer.

He bit his upper lip slightly, figuring out how to break it in simple words.

"Galileo Galilei said that the *'universe is written in mathematical language and that until we learn the language and become familiar with the characters in which it's written, we'll be wandering about in a dark labyrinth'*. And, guess what? One of the principles of mathematics is that *'mathematic seeks out patterns and use them to formulate new conjectures.'*"

He paused for a moment to let her digest his words. "We live many lives, as today you had the opportunity to experience by yourself. In each life, we have many experiences. We make choices, we suffer, we love, and we create bad and good connections with people. Very often, we fall into patterns because of unresolved feelings caused by traumatic events in our journey. Now, connect this to what Galileo said: until we learn the language, we'll be wandering about in a dark labyrinth."

Anna gave him her full attention, noticing his words building connections within her head.

"I'm glad that the first thing you brought to your conscience was guilt," he continued.

"I don't understand," she said.

"The ultimate goal of our souls is perfection, and this is a long journey. You, Anna, in your present life, are the sum of all experiences you had. Many patterns were created as the result of good and bad things that happened to you, as well as the good and bad choices you made in life. This is a process of learning and don't fool yourself that you can reach perfection as a beginner. Once you remove guilt from your path, you'll understand that you're a spiritual being in progress, dealing with all the inheritance from your past. To live in this world without any information about spiritual life is to live in a dark place. That's why we need to learn the language of the universe. Life, like everything else, becomes more manageable when we know how it works."

"Otherwise we'll be wandering about in a dark labyrinth," Anna repeated after him, thinking of her own life. "It makes a lot of sense."

He nodded with satisfaction.

"Larry was my husband before." She recalled the last images she saw. "The way he died explains why he is so obsessed with his health now. This is a pattern, isn't it?"

He nodded once again.

Bringing memories of Larry to consciousness, she noticed a change in her feelings about him. She couldn't define it. They had been together before and had a story that transcended their present life. He'd always been a good man, always there for her, although in the past life she had had a shadow hanging over her feelings. She remembered the shadow of the other man waiting for her. Maybe being confused about their relationship was a pattern that she needed to break, she thought. She should love him. But was love a matter of choice? She couldn't agree with that. Real love screams out itself, you don't need to rationalize it..."

"We create patterns with the way we love as well," Ralph said, bringing her back from her thoughts.

She gave him a surrendering look. He read her mind! *Was it only a professional skill?* She thought. *What a scary connection!*

"I guess you have a lot to digest," Ralph brought her back again. "Would you want to see me again? This week, next week?..."

"Of course I do!" she reacted instantly. "But...this wasn't supposed to be about me. My son..."

"He is the easiest part."

"I see; I'm the hardest," she acknowledged, catching the pattern. "No guilt," she corrected herself with a smile. "But still..."

"Can you do me a favor?" he interrupted her. She nodded, helpless. "Tonight, make him lie in your arms, very comfortable, and ask him to close his eyes and tell what he sees in the moment that his phobia emerged. Children at his age have memories very near to the surface. Don't be afraid. Just use love. You're ready to help your own child. And remember, we're not alone."

Anna wondered if she was up to it. She'd love to have her son in the skilled hands of this wise man instead, but because he said so, she would try.

She slid her legs off the chaise lounge and reached for her shoes. She put them on and stood up at the same time that he did. Without intention, they wound up too close to each other, so close that she could feel his energy. She was paralyzed before him. For a moment, the whole world disappeared for her, and he was the only thing left. She never felt him that close before, never felt so incapable of holding onto her reality. How she wanted to surrender to her grateful heart and kiss him, deeply and lingeringly.

"I'll see you tomorrow at 6:00 p.m.," he said gently,

dragging her back to reality, saving her from doing something that she would regret later.

"Tomorrow, at 6:00," she repeated automatically. It was strange that he took patients in the evening.

"One more thing," he said. "Control your impulse to reveal to people what you've learned. Nobody has the right to interfere in someone's path, except with supportive words and selfless love."

Anna nodded, though not getting exactly what he meant.

Chapter 17

When Anna arrived at home in the early evening, Marvin was passed out on the couch in front of the television and Lisa was seated on the carpet floor by the coffee table, painting her toenails with a dark red nail polish.

"I'm so sorry, Lisa. You don't deserve it, I'm a bad friend," Anna pleaded, shedding her purse and the car keys on the side table.

"It's okay." Lisa gave Anna an inquisitive look. "But I was worried about you."

"How's everything? Did he give you a hard time?" Anna asked.

"We had a lot of fun as always, but this time I defeated him. You can relax tonight; I put him out of combat for you."

Anna grabbed the remote on the coffee table and turned the TV off as she always did when Marvin fell asleep watching his cartoons in the evening.

"By the way, you have few messages," Lisa pointed the answer machine.

Anna crouched down by Marvin's side and kissed his forehead, a long, fond kiss. She felt her heart full of love for her son as she kissed him, a love a thousand times deeper than she had ever felt before. Maybe she was just still high from the altered state of conscience she had experienced. Colors had deepened and every little thing seemed more meaningful to her after this afternoon. She had a peaceful feeling of lightness inside her chest, as though her heart was radiating a glorious light.

Anna kissed Marvin again, thinking that life would be

easier if we could always choose to be with the ones we loved. She was thinking about Ralph. She had fallen for him. A tiny teardrop rolled down her face. She gently pulled the blanket up to warm up the kid as the night outside had become chilly.

"Are you okay?" Lisa was worried.

Anna nodded, wiping her face.

"C'mon, what's wrong?" Lisa insisted.

"Nothing. Everything is wonderful," Anna smiled.

Lisa gave her a suspicious look. "You go to a doctor visit, dressed to kill, and come back with this smile on your face. You better tell me what happened out there, girl. I hope you're not in trouble."

Anna stood up. "Do you mind if I take a minute to check out the messages. I also need to call Larry; I'll be short, I promise."

Lisa turned her eyes back to her nails and nodded showing that she was okay with that. She wanted to finish painting her nails in order to give Anna her full attention when she came back. Lisa was curious; eager to hear from her, but nothing in the world had enough power or a justified meaning to get Lisa's attention when she painted her nails. Anna knew that, and felt comfortable to leave her friend for while.

In the kitchen, Anna reviewed the messages. The only important ones were one from Larry and another from her mother. She picked up the cordless phone to call her husband.

The conversation was smooth and loving. Larry's voice from his Philadelphia hotel room was singularly soft and she enjoyed listening to him, as she gazed at a picture of them with Marvin on the refrigerator door. She told him about Marvin, that he was well. He told her he missed her, and she said the same. She could sense Larry smiling on the other end of the line. That was all he wanted to hear. And she meant it. It was like she could, for the first time, separate what she felt for Larry and for Ralph. Larry was reality, security, daily life, friendship, complacency, and family. Ralph was... maybe just a dream. So palpable though, and too fulfilling to just let it go. He fulfilled a hole in her heart, a place that had been unoccupied for her entire life. Wasn't it a place for a husband to occupy? This place demanded sensations stronger than the sweet complacency of a regular marriage. Like when we fall in love—what an addictive sensation! Larry had his place in her heart, but his place was never here. This place was for Ralph or for someone else or for... nobody.

It was an unidentified, unconscious demand and she couldn't remember when it started. As far as she could tell, she was born with this gap. She recognized it, she could catch it in the moments when it surfaced, like a whale that shows only the tip of its tail, intentionally hiding its massive body as to not to scare the sailors. This flash never lasted long, though. It was impossible to hold onto long enough to see it thoroughly. When she projected this feeling onto Ralph, however, then she could get a good look at it. He was the materialization of her famine, and she could keep him alive as long as she wanted, but only in this realm. She knew that if she tried to bring him to reality all the magic would instantly be gone.

Larry had made plans with Anna's parents for dinner, and he was late. He needed to rush to the shower. Anna didn't say a word about the session. It would be better in person. She asked him to tell her mom she'd call her in the morning.

After hanging up, her mind wandered back to her memories of Larry in her past life. He was there, she recalled. He didn't come to her life by chance. They were not young kids hastily deciding to get married, as she had often thought. Their destinies were connected; they were supposed to be together. But why didn't she love him with all her heart? Had something happened in their past that was now preventing her from loving him? She ran the tip of her index finger over the family photo on the fridge. *What a riddle!*

"Can anything be better than a beautiful family like that?" Lisa stood in the opening between the kitchen and the living room, airing her nails. She walked to the kitchen table and made herself comfortable on a chair as if telling Anna that she was ready to listen.

"Can I ask you something?" Anna said.

"Yep. I'm all yours."

Anna took a seat at the table. "You're always so available when I ask you to help me with Marvin. I mean... this is your day off, and you're my friend, not my babysitter. I really appreciate it, but why don't you ever say 'no' to me?"

"What a strange question, girl! You're my friend, a sister that I never had." Lisa said frowning. "And you know that I love this boy as if he was my own son."

Anna stared at Lisa with a smile on her face. She could easily see the connection between them from this life to the past when they were sisters. She instantly recalled Ralph's words: "we need to learn the language of the universe. Life, like everything else, becomes more manageable when we know how it works..."

"You're the sister I never had as well—at least in this life." Lisa looked at her curiously and Anna continued, "Don't take me wrong, but...have you ever considered having your own child? You're young, have a great job, and are very good with children. You'd be a great mom."

Lisa's gaze became distant. "Bob and I tried once, but for some reason it didn't happen. Maybe it's just as well. I'd be attached forever to that betrayer. You know, I'm not lucky with the male species. I think I have a kind of magnet that attracts bad stuff to my life."

Lisa always sounded stronger than she was. But now, Anna could see through her. "Remember that book you showed me other day? If I'm not wrong, it said something about *how we create resistance to accept our own disturbing behavior.*"

"I'm surprised that you remember."

"I didn't get it at first," Anna continued, "but now I see what you meant when you said you need to forgive yourself in the first place. I can see a pattern in the way you blame yourself for something that maybe you don't even know when it started."

"You call it a pattern; I call it being a magnet. In one way or another, I'm still single and alone. And human biology being what it is, we still need a man to have a baby—unfortunately."

"Well, you can have a foster child," Anna insisted. "There are so many children out there who'd be more than happy having a mom like you."

"Umm...I don't know. I love kids, but I already have so many little ones under my supervision at the hospital. They're enough for me. I guess this is my role in this life."

"You do a great job there, but they're not yours. I just wondered if you feel that you don't deserve having your own."

Lisa came up short with nothing more to say.

Anna was stunned. The issues experienced by Anna's sister in the nineteenth century seemed to perfectly match Lisa's present unconscious conflicts. But a voice inside prevented her from revealing it to Lisa. *"Nobody has the right to interfere in someone's path, except with supportive words and a selfless love,"* she finally realized what Ralph had said. The experience Anna had was for herself, the inner voice said. She would heed the voice, but she wished it could turn into help for others. She had never felt like she had any ability to help anyone.

Anyway, what could she tell Lisa? That 200 years ago, she had had a baby with Lisa's husband? That she had betrayed her sister, even against her own will? That Lisa had stolen the baby and shooed Anna out of the house? Amazingly, Anna forgave her. Lisa was a dear friend, and it was frustrating to see her lost in a maze of patterns that originated in a distant past.

"I think you're trying to distract me from asking you about your doctor's appointment," Lisa finally said.

"Maybe another day, I don't want to hold you here any longer," Anna tried to get out of it.

"I have nobody waiting for me at home, I don't have to wake up early tomorrow, and I'm not leaving, until you tell me about that smile in your face, those tears in your eyes, and the reason for all this." Lisa stood her ground.

Anna swallowed hard. She had to make up something to say, something that sounded convincing. Maybe she could tell Lisa everything, except the part that concerned her. "Okay, I can try, but I'm not sure I can. There's so much to digest," Anna said in a surrendered voice. "I just need to catch my breath after all I went through. I feel like my head is a big balloon, full of information that I still can't fully access."

"And where'd you go, who's this doctor?" Lisa was dying of curiosity.

"His name is Dr. Ralph Stevenson." Anna felt that it sounded weird saying his name in such a formal way. "I met him by chance at the library other day."

"Dr. Ralph Stevenson..." Lisa repeated slowly. "It sounds familiar. Where's he from?"

"He's local, very competent... Oh, my gosh!" Anna moved a hand to her forehead. "I forgot to pay him. What an airhead I am!" Anna realized that money had never been a part of their conversation. "Anyway, I'm going to see him again tomorrow."

"So, you're going to give me the opportunity to say 'no' to you. I'll have a full schedule tomorrow, honey; I can't help you," Lisa teased.

"C'mon, Lisa..."

"Okay, but you gotta tell me how it was. Did you go through past lives?"

"Yeees..." Anna was reluctant.

"Did you see anything?"

"Umm... it is hard to explain. I saw things, but there were so many feelings attached. I can tell you the images, but it's all about feelings, sensations. I mean, it's like we see through feelings. The sensation is somewhat scary. You just know, beyond an unquestionable certainty, that you've lived before."

Anna intended to make Lisa understand that she couldn't tell her everything, for it was a very personal experience, but Lisa caught her. "Can you stop beating around the bush and tell me what you saw?"

"I saw a man who was Larry in a previous life; he was a sick man. He died quite young after a prolonged illness," Anna said, as her mind went back to the memories. "It was so sad. He looked so haggard in bed."

"When was it?" Lisa probed.

"I don't know. It seemed not long ago; This memory was different from the others I accessed, though. I don't know where or when it happened," Anna was intrigued.

"Was he your husband again?"

"Kind of, we lived together, in a nice apartment, though at this time it was gloomy, with sorrow casting shadows on our lives. I felt like I didn't want to be there, but I had to be. He needed me. My life was on hold, as if I was just waiting for him die, to open my cage and fly away."

The remembrance of the unrevealed figure of a man came to her mind.

"You think this has something to do with Marvin's memories?" Lisa said.

"I don't know," Anna replied on autopilot. Her mind had gone into a sort of trance. "What's wrong with Marvin?" She asked all of a sudden.

Lisa looked at her friend as if trying to figure out where she was.

A scream of despair came from the living room. Lisa was on her feet instantly, and rushed to check on Marvin. Anna took a moment to wake up from the trance and realize what was happening before she followed Lisa.

She found Lisa sitting on the couch, holding Marvin in her lap, his head resting on her chest. He was sweaty and breathing heavily, unconscious it seemed. The dim lamp light showed the tension on his face. For an instant, Anna saw Lisa as her older sister, replacing her in the care of her son.

"Why did you leave me, Mom?" Marvin asked all of a sudden.

"She didn't leave you; she was just a little late," Lisa tried to comfort him.

"Daddy is so sad, Mom," he said.

"He's okay. Your mom called him…"

"Sh-sh-sh…" Anna shushed Lisa with a gesture. Marvin wasn't awake, and he wasn't talking about the present. Anna came closer and sat down on the edge of the couch, remembering Ralph's recommendation.

"Mommy is here," Anna said in a whisper, "and I want to ask you a few questions. Do you mind?"

"Okay, Mom," he agreed.

Lisa sensed the moment and became quiet and attentive as she stroked Marvin's head.

"Would you like to tell me something?" Anna asked not sure what to say.

"I already told you," he answered bluntly. "Daddy is so sad because you left him."

"Who's your dad, what's his name?"

"His name is Charlie."

Anna exchanged an astonished gaze with Lisa. "Is he the same man you met at Ellen's house?"

"Yes, but he's younger. He's tough, a hard worker, but he's been so sad lately. He doesn't want to tell me, but I know that it's because of you."

Marvin sounded very confident. Anna's heart pounded and she sat back, trying to put two and two together. If she had been his mother, the sick man in her memories was Jerry,

Georgia's partner. Charlie was the shadowy man. Jerry's sickness was what was holding Georgia back from going back to Connecticut.

"Have you ever seen me? How do I look?" Anna asked, realizing how close she was to finding the answer Charlie and Ellie were longing for.

"I don't think I have. My father doesn't like to talk about you."

"But you left him too, didn't you?" Anna probed.

"I left him the day I died," Marvin said straight and naturally.

Anna gazed at Lisa, striving to hold her emotions. "How old were you?" she continued.

"I was fifteen."

"Do you mind telling me what happened on the day you died?"

Tension grew on Marvin's face and his body stiffened. After a moment, he began to speak, his voice sounded like a 15-year-old boy's. "There's an old lady in the water. She's wearing a nightgown... she is clinging to the branches of a tree, fighting against the water that's coming up fast. I need to help her."

Marvin made small movements with his head and his body. Lisa struggled to hold him, feeling the tension growing in his muscles, and she looked at Anna as if asking if it was safe to continue. Anna gave her a reassuring look. "What's happening now?"

"I'm inside the house. The water is freezing cold, almost up to my neck. I'm shaking. I'm on the first floor. If I can get upstairs, I can come out through the window and reach her from the roof of the porch."

Marvin became silent, as if he was fighting his way to the second floor of the house.

"The water is getting stronger, moving furniture around, and I've gotten into the second floor with the river growing behind my back. It's very difficult to get around me. The house is shaking. I can't go back. I'm trying to reach the window and save the woman."

Marvin's tension grew even more and he curled up in Lisa's arms. Anna noticed that at this point his body's reaction was very similar to the moments when he had been taken by the storm phobia.

"The house is shaking harder and twisting," he continued.

"Are you alone? Can you shout for help?" Anna inquired.

"I'm alone. I'm striving for survival now. The walls are cracking...it feels like the house is going down in the river."

Marvin was gasping, his voice breaking up. "I'm scared... I don't want to die alone. I'm drowning... I'm swallowing water...I can't breathe..."

Suddenly, Marvin went quiet. His muscles relaxed, and his breath became even.

"What do you see now?" Anna asked in a low voice, intuitively sensing that Marvin still had more to share.

"I'm floating above the river. I'm dead. I can't see the house, only the roof ridge. The house is going down the river along with trees and some debris. I see a bright light... I want to go towards the light. It feels safe."

Marvin became silent and still. Lisa fondly stroked his hair. After a moment, he opened his eyes and gazed at Anna in front of him. She smiled at him with love in her eyes.

"Hi Mom," he said, leaving Lisa's arms to give her a hug. "Sorry that I fell asleep before taking a shower."

Anna was amazed at how naturally he was acting as if nothing out of the ordinary had happened. "It's okay. You can still take it. Go grab your pajamas and wait for me upstairs."

Marvin left her arms and headed upstairs.

"Wow! That was amazing!" Lisa said with startled eyes. "He just told us all we wanted to know. How did you do that?"

Anna leaned back on the couch, defeated by fatigue. The night before had been long and tough, and the day had been emotional.

"Am I wrong, or did he just say that you're the woman who Charlie is blaming for taking his son away?" Lisa asked, still having difficulty catching her breath.

"I guess he did."

"It makes you the woman who wrote that diary…wow!" Lisa connected the dots. "What about the kidnapping thing?"

Anna had the same amazement, but her mind was running slowly now. She was too tired to find the missing link in the story. "If Georgia left with Marty, why did he die alone? Where was she? What did happen that day?"

"It sounds like a thriller," Lisa commented. "It does seem though, that the purpose of Marvin's phobia is to bring this unfinished story to light."

"Isn't it amazing?" Anna smiled, feeling perplexed. She squinted, trying to see farther back in her memories. "During the regression session, I had a vision in which I lived in France, almost a hundred years before Georgia's time. My baby was taken from me. I felt guilty but accepted it, because it would prevent someone from hating me. And I never went back to see my baby because I felt like I made a mistake and didn't deserve to see him again. I was afraid that he would hate me, too." Anna trailed off to connect the dots and see if her words were hitting Lisa in some way, which they didn't seem to. "Now, thinking of Georgia, waiting for so long to go back to see her son…" she continued. "When reading Georgia's diary, I felt so sorry for this frightened woman, as though I could feel her pain. This is why I feel guilty in this life so often!"

"In psychology it's called *'trauma trigger',*" Lisa said. "It's a troubling reminder of a traumatic event, a condition in which a person can't control the recurrence of emotional or physical symptoms. Sometimes, it is very clear, as in Marvin's case or subtle enough to lead the person to react in an unconscious pattern of behavior."

"Exactly! As Georgia, I could clearly feel that I didn't belong to the life I was living. I'd left something behind, and again, guilt prevented me from going back to my loved ones." Anna was surprised as some recent memories emerged in her mind. "I remember being scared when I went into labor with Marvin. I never figured out the reason. After he was born, I felt more and more detached from the life I had before when it was just me and Larry. My connection with Larry faded, and I had the strange desire to run away from my own life, feeling guilty that I wasn't able to fulfill Larry's expectations."

"I'm really jealous!" Lisa said, clearly impressed. "I want to see this doctor. What's his name...?"

"Dr. Ralph Stevenson?"

"Damn it! It sounds familiar, but I can't figure it out."

"I strongly encourage you to see him," Anna said. "I can give you his card. I have his number saved in my phone already."

Anna stood up so quickly that she became lightheaded. She brought her hands to her forehead and threw her body back on the couch to prevent herself from fainting.

"You okay?" Lisa was worried.

"I'm fine. I just realized that I haven't eaten anything since the morning."

"It's late. You should go get something to eat," Lisa said in a motherly tone. "And I've gotta hit the road." Lisa stood up.

Anna nodded as Marvin came back downstairs wearing his pajamas, and claiming that he had taken a shower by himself.

"That was fast," Lisa said suspicious. "Come over here, let me smell you."

Marvin came close and raised his arms, with a mischievous smile on his face. He was familiar with Lisa's inspections and knew that her intention was to tickle his armpits, around his neck, and on his belly, making him burst into laughter.

Later, when Marvin had been put to bed, Anna grabbed Georgia's diary and brought it to the kitchen. She put the kettle on, and reached for a box of chamomile tea bags in the cabinet. Taking her tea into the living room, she curled up on the couch, put the blanket over her feet, and held up the diary, staring at it for a moment. Going through this notebook after all that she learned would be a completely different experience. She wondered if anyone in the whole world ever had the experience of reading a diary written by her own hand in a previous life.

Chapter 18

October 9, 1955

I'm about to cross a bridge. Behind me is the wreckage of my old dreams covering some good memories, and on the other side, a promising land with plenty of hope. But it is unclear like a foggy morning with clouds hanging low in the sky.

I knew that at this point, my mind might be shut and my soul too devastated to make wise decisions, so I had made plans throughout the years. I've always been afraid—just like now—that it would all be too late.

I need to release this dread from my soul. The uncertainty of the future makes me nervous, for it does not depend on me. But I promised myself I'd go back, no matter what, as soon as Jerry's soul rested in peace. The time has arrived and there's no decision left to make. It's done!

I told Jerry my decision when he was still able to articulate meaningful words and I could still see a gleam in his eyes. He wished me luck. He had this enormous heart; he was the biggest soul I ever met. His big smile could make the mostly cloudy day bright. And I'm glad that I could pay him back for all he did for me. I watched over him, seeing his body shrink to skin over bones. But his big smile never left him.

My old acting dream died with him; maybe it had died a long time ago. I don't feel sorry, because the death of my dream sets me free. It charged me a high price. Some dreams are just unaffordable! When we try to live in a dream, we miss the best of life, which is the blessing of living in the present, enjoying what is around us. A dream is only an impulse to achieve goals, not to be lived. Dreams are dreams in all their guises,

not real though, and eventually, we must wake up. The real dream is to be with and enjoy the presence of those we love, and for that, I will do whatever it takes to be with my son..."
Georgia removed the pen from the end of the page, and, before moving to the next, she paused, hesitant with the realization that it could be even harder than expected. She reconsidered her thoughts. *"Or at least to have his forgiveness, if it's still possible. If I still deserve to dream about something, this will be my dream from now on: the three of us together as a family, the family that I never had. Oh, golly! I miss family so much!*

Those were the last words Georgia wrote in her diary. She put it away, on the bed, where she laid all things left to pack in the train case that Jen had promised to give her as a present. She hoped it could fit her make-up, perfume, jewelry, the money she withdrew from the bank, and the letters she never sent to her son, as well as the glass slipper necklace she promised to bring back to Charlie. It was supposed to be proof that she never forgot him, that her love never died. A smile grew upon her face. What a silly teenager's game! It was cute of him though, and she decided to keep her promise.

She was expecting Jen soon and had left many of her clothes and shoes in the closet for her. She had too much for the simplicity of her future life, far from the glamour, the spotlight, and the prying eyes of Los Angeles' high society.

Leaving that place, after all those years, felt unreal. The apartment had become her world, her refuge. The wallpaper in the living room—light blue with white flowers—seemed to reflect her moments with Jerry. Maybe someone with a sensitive soul could feel the vibration in the room, telling about dreams, fellowship, sorrows, and resignation, about how much Jerry had loved her, and how she had taken care of him, silencing her own demands, putting her own plans on hold so he wouldn't be alone, not even for a day, until his last breath. She was grateful for all she learned from Jerry, from life. She would miss the laughter and tears, the great moments that had brought her joy, and the hard ones that made her grow up.

Jennifer knocked on the door at 9:00 a.m. "Only you, Gigi, could make me wake up this early," Jen said, greeting Georgia at the door, her puffed eyes matching her shaggy hair. The previous night had been a busy one.

"I'm sorry, dear. I know it's too early for you, but I gotta split. I checked the map (Georgia had a big map spread over the dinner table). I have 2800 miles between my son and me."

"Aw, I wish you luck, my friend." Jen said. "I'm very jealous…"

"Don't be. You will have your own turning point."

This made Jen uncomfortable. She changed the subject.

"This is the train case I promised you." She handed Georgia a compact case in pink and white. It appeared new, although Jen had been using it for a couple of months. "The good thing about this case is the false bottom where you can hide your valuables." She demonstrated how to access it.

"That's cool! Where'd you buy it? In a magician store?"

"Well, nowadays you need to be careful. Hotel staff are sometimes curious, you know."

"This is awesome! It'll be very useful during the trip."

"Why don't you take a flight? You'd be there at the end of the day, fresh as a daisy."

"I don't mind driving. It'll take only a couple of days, and I can use the time to prepare myself for the battle I will face. I really need this time out."

Jen gave her a compassionate look. "What if…"

"I know," Georgia said. "He can be married, with kids. My son may not forgive me. But I'm prepared. I'm trying to be realistic."

"You don't need to be a pessimist, though." Jen amended.

"What should I do? Fill my head with dreams again? I'm not expecting anything, I don't deserve anything."

"You know that's not true, don't you? Of course, you deserve it, because you're a great woman. I don't need to tell you that. Besides, you wouldn't give up your life, leave behind the great career you have, and travel that far, if you had no dreams in your head."

"I have hope; it's different." Georgia was positive. "C'mon, let's see what you like in my closet," she evaded.

Georgia brought Jen to the bedroom and motioned for her to help herself.

"Oh my gosh!" Jen was impressed. "Is this all for me?"

"Whatever you want; I saved a couple of suitcases that belonged to Jerry, you can use them."

Jen turned to hug Georgia cheerfully, and gazed at all her belongings on the bed. "Wow, that's a lot of money! I thought Jerry's doctors had drained your savings."

"Actually they did. But Jerry had life insurance. I'm not rich, but it'll help."

"It looks like you're all organized."

"Basically! I got stuck at the bank because of the amount."

"I can imagine." Jen turned to examine the clothes in the closet. "Those people work in a bank but they seem to have never seen so much bread."

"I couldn't get the car registration changed out of Jerry's name. But I'll have to transfer the plates to Connecticut, anyway. I don't need to do it twice."

"Good luck with all this time on the road with a car registered in the name of a dead... I'm sorry, I'm talking too much. Let me grab some of those babies and let you go."

Jen sorted out the clothes and chose what suited her, filling all in the suitcases Georgia offered. Meanwhile, Georgia finished packing her valuables in the train case.

"You don't need to rush," she told Jen. "Just do me a favor. When you leave, can you lock the door and drop off the key in mail box 604?"

Jen gave her a hug. "I can't believe you're leaving me,"

Jen's voice was thick with emotion. "I don't have many friends, not like you."

Georgia wiped a tear off her face. "I'll miss you too."

Chapter 19

Anna reached the last page of Georgia's diary before fatigue overcame her, but she did not have the energy to get up and drag herself to bed. The blanket on the couch wasn't enough to protect her from the chilly night. Discomfort triggered awkward dreams with disconnected images. In the morning, Anna was feeling sick.

Her mind was exhausted, her body, heavy and slow. Sitting up on the sofa, she felt like she had lived a thousand years in just one week. But she wanted to take advantage of Larry's absence before he was back with his skepticism. After learning about her previous connection with Larry and the unfinished business she had, preventing her from being fully present with him, the reasons behind Larry's resistance to Marvin's memories had become clearer for her. She knew that it wouldn't change easily.

But what about Ralph? Why had he come into her life so unexpectedly? Did he have any connection to her past life or was he just a doctor trying to compensate for his inability to help his wife by helping others in similar situations? She wondered if everything in life necessarily had a connection to former life experiences. The charming doctor had fallen from the sky with wise words, answers, and guidance that led her to a broader view of life. He dragged her into his energy field. When she was with him, she felt as if she wasn't in the same plane of her life with Larry.

Anna made plans for a quiet morning, hydrating her body with a fresh smoothie. She took time to call her mom and explained Marvin's problems to her in brief.

"Virgem Maria!" her mom expressed in her tongue her catholic faith in the mother of Jesus. "This boy needs to see a priest. Does this town have a church?"

"Of course, Mom. All towns grow around a church. The Saint Peter Church on Main Street has been there at least for 150 years," Anna intentionally tried to distract her mom from the subject.

"An old church doesn't necessary mean the best one," her mom insisted. "Are you going to the services?"

"I will, Mom; don't worry. And don't worry about Marvin either; I'm seeking professional help for him."

As the morning wore on, Anna's unsettled spirit sought new answers. She attempted to bring Marvin back to his revelations through a relaxing conversation, but he slipped away showing little interest in the subject. In the late morning, while Marvin was immersed in a project, she dove into Georgia's diary again.

She was intrigued and disappointed that Georgia had stopped writing before she left L.A. *"I'll do whatever it takes to be with my son..."* Her last words sounded threatening, although... Maybe they hadn't been her last words. For the first time, Anna noticed a torn edge after the last page Georgia had written on. A page had been torn from the notebook! Had she written something on it? If so, what? Anna couldn't help feeling that the missing page had something to do with what was now the biggest question in her mind: What had happened to Georgia? If Marty had drowned in the river as Marvin had recalled, then he did not leave with Georgia. She had not kidnapped her son. What had happened?

Consumed with a new idea, Anna picked up the phone. Lisa unexpectedly answered. "Hi, I was going to leave a message," Anna was surprised. "Have a minute?"

"Yes, I'm on my break," Lisa answered, chewing something from her lunch.

"Good! I need a favor. You said you met Charlie in the hos-

pital, right? Can you access his file and get me his address?"
"What do you have in mind, girl?"
"I don't know yet, maybe a visit."
"I'll be free tomorrow morning. I can go with you."
"No, I need to go by myself for this one."
"Are you sure? That stubborn man upset you."
"I'm sure. Don't worry, I can handle that."
"Okay. Gimme a minute and I'll call you back."
"One more thing, are you available today at 6:00 p.m.? I have another session..."
"You know that I never say 'no'. But you have to drop him off with me. I need to be home tonight."

Anna hung up the phone, and called some friends to babysit for Marvin in the afternoon. Only one was available and only after 4:00 p.m., which made Anna's plan tight. She would have to drop Marvin at the friend's house before going to see Charlie and then drive back to pick him up and drop him at Lisa's apartment, all before getting to Ralph's office by 6:00. But Anna was determined to stick to her plan.

The driving was a challenge; her friend's house was fifteen minutes from Charlie's address, which makes it half hour to commute both ways, and she still had to drive to Lisa. She didn't expected though, that the conversation with Charlie would last long—if she even found him at home.

At 4:20 p.m., she arrived at the address that Lisa had told her. She left the car, and scanned the cozy cottage Charlie lived in. Although fall had begun to sweep vitality from nature, the owner of the cottage had paid meticulous attention to every little detail in the front yard: a few late season flowers, the little statues, the bushes and the grass; the white wooden bench on the porch; the fresh painted rails and steps; the welcome sign on the front door; and the Victorian thermometer hanging outside the window. Everything was well cared for. It was almost as if Charlie was waiting for someone.

Anna rang the bell few times, but when nobody came, she

walked around the back of the house which was quiet and silent on that chilly, gray afternoon. She reached the backyard easily and was impressed with the large garden she found, which held quite a variety of vegetables. She noticed some sort of sprinkle technology around and over the beds, and a few pyramid-shape protections he must had used to keep away small visitors. Even noticing that all were losing color by the fading season, she was impressed with the organization of the garden, and even more with the size of the vegetables.

She went back to the front of the house, and was caught by a neighbor—a middle-aged woman standing on her side of the fence— who was watching Anna's steps inside the property. "If you're looking for Charlie, he is not at home." The woman's face was suspicious.

"Yes, I was looking for Charlie."

The woman eyed Anna up and down. "Are you his friend... relative?"

"A friend." Anna smiled tentatively, uncomfortable with the woman's gaze.

"Charlie goes for a walk at the lake every afternoon."

"So, I presume he won't be back soon."

"Nope."

Anna thanked the woman and left her uncomfortable presence.

The sun was hanging down on the horizon, and the first stars were visible in the sky. Anna drove around by the lake in the faint hope she could still find him. The calmness from the still water invited her to reflect on the beauty of the scene as nature was settling down to welcome the night. Because of the chill, only few people were around, walking, jogging, or just enjoyed the view, so Anna easily spotted Charlie sitting on a bench at the edge of the grass before the sand beach.

She left the car and walked toward him. She stopped a short distance away to watch him for a moment. He was wearing blue jacket with the collar up protecting his neck from the chill. Knowing their connection in the past, she felt a strange feeling growing inside.

Charlie was looking into the distance and didn't notice her presence.

"Hi, Mr. Baker," she said hesitantly, as she approached.

He moved his gaze to her. "Are you stalking me now?" he said, disguising his surprise.

Anna smiled, and shook her head. "I just want to talk, if you don't mind."

Charlie stared at her for a moment. "Be my guest." He motioned for her to sit on the bench.

"This place is beautiful; I haven't been here before," she said.

"I used to come here with Marty to fish, and I always wanted to live nearby. Candlewood Lake was man-made in the 1920's to be the largest in Connecticut. The goal was to store water when the electrical demand was low for power generation when the demand increased. In most places, it's forty feet deep. If you dived around you could see roads, buildings, and even covered bridges that were there before the valley was flooded."

"Wow, I can't imagine that." She was glad that he was talking to her. "Is there a special reason for its name?"

"Have you seen a candlewood tree?"

She shook her head. "I'm a city girl. I don't know much about nature."

"It grows sweetly-scented, bisexual flowers that turn into bright orange, lantern-shaped berries. Hence the name candlewood," he explained with joy on his face. "It originated from South Africa, and it can tolerate drought and extreme low temperatures. The early settlers had used its sapling branches as candles."

"You seem to know a lot about it."

"I wanted to be a botanist when I was young, but I had to

keep a roof over my head. I couldn't afford it."

Anna had witnessed his dreams materialized in the work he did in his yard. "Dreams are good," she said, "they keep us alive."

"Dreams make you irresponsible and inconsequential. Take what life gives you and do your best, if you'll take my advice."

Anna heard bitterness in his voice. "Life can be surprising," she ventured.

"I may sound like an old man, which in fact I am now, but I haven't always been like this."

"I'd love to hear about that."

Charlie gazed at her, earnestly, for the first time, analyzing her intentions and the value of opening his heart to a woman who he did not know and with whom he had reasons to be cautious. "How did you find me here?"

"My friend Lisa works at the hospital; you've met her. And your neighbor seemed to know your schedule."

Charlie gave her a suspicious look. "I already told you that I won't buy your story."

"I don't mind if you don't believe me," she said serenely. "Actually, I'm tired of trying to convince the world of something that nobody is interested in. I've decided to be a little selfish now, and focus on my son and on my own needs."

"Sounds reasonable." Charlie stood up, surprising Anna. "It's getting cold, and soon will be dark. You're welcome to come to my house and finish this conversation if you want?"

Charlie's house inside was warm and charming, and as well organized as its exterior. He offered Anna a cup of tea and filled the teakettle with spring water from a bottle. "Do you know that the more oxygen in the water, the better the tea will taste?" he explained. "Never use tap water or pre heated left over water. Nowadays, people don't pay attention to details and miss the good taste of all things."

"Thanks for sharing. I'm a tea drinker; I should know this." As Anna walked her eyes over the living/dining/kitchen combined space, a photo of Marty on a frame over an old Victrola caught her attention.

She was happy that things had worked out, and she was there, sitting on his couch, watching him prepare tea. Since she had found he was her love from a former life, she had been curious to see if he'd spark some feelings in her. This hadn't happened, but she still liked to watch Charlie as he moved.

Charlie came to join her, and sat on a sofa in front of her. "I'm sorry. I haven't had a guest here for a long time now."

"Don't worry. Your house couldn't be cozier. For a man living by himself, I'm impressed."

"I just think that it's easier to put things right back in place instead of spend time organizing the house every day or weekend."

"I wish my husband could think the same way. He's sloppy, and I'm afraid that he'll pass it on to our son."

Charlie gazed at her earnestly. "You said you came here to talk. I'll warn you, I won't give you information just to add to your story."

"Yes..."she trailed off. "I guess you know I have Georgia's diary."

"I didn't know that." He frowned. "How did you...? That's where you got all the information?"

"No," she cut him off. "Ellen offered it to me. It was a treasure though, for my understanding of Georgia. She seemed so alone, so helpless."

"So you read her plans and her intentions, too."

"Are you talking about the last page? What happened? Did you tear it out?"

"I'm talking about the kidnapping and the threat on the last page, indeed, though that clearly wasn't the last page. Maybe if the page was there, we'd know what she did."

"How did the diary come into your hands?" Anna asked.

"The hotel, where she stayed, was the first place I went to track her down. To my surprise, she never checked out. They brought me to her room, and her belongings were still there. They let me take them as long as I paid the bill."

"Haven't you ever thought that was a sign that something had happened to her?"

"I see what you mean. But she made a silly mistake. She took money and any valuable thing she had with her when she left."

Anna stared at him for a moment with compassion growing in her eyes. "A diary is a place where a woman vents her emotions, Charlie..." she hesitated. "I'm sorry: Mr. Baker."

Charlie cocked his eyebrow, but seemed not to mind, caught by the intimacy of her voice and the picture she was trying to paint of a woman's inner universe.

"Those are only scattered thoughts that crossed her mind at the moment she wrote them down," Anna continued. "It doesn't mean that she was planning something; otherwise she would have kept obsessively going back to the subject, which never happened. Besides, there is so much love on those pages, so much about how she felt her life fragmented by not being with you and your son. If you read it with your heart, you'd see."

"I read it in all possible ways before drawing my conclusions," Charlie was emphatic. "She had everything set up when she arrived in town. She arranged occasional encounters with Marty to gain his trust before she revealed her identity. The car she drove from California wasn't in her name; I called the DMV in Los Angeles. Nobody could track her." Charlie's gaze softened and became distant. "The days she stayed in town were the best of my life. The sound of her voice is still on my mind. She never sounded phony or acted like a scammer. All that we had couldn't be more real, more special. She made me forget fifteen years of longing in only two days with her sincerity, her unique personality, and her humble way of admitting her mistakes. I believed that she was the same girl I met in high school; the free bird that flew away and came back to land in my palm. I could die to defend her integrity, even when her decision was against my own interests." Charlie paused again, and his distant gaze seemed to arrive back from his visions. "But after all, she was an actress. That makes everything she said and did questionable." He turned his wet eyes to Anna. "Do you think that it's easy to judge the only woman I ever loved in this life? It has been a battle inside of me for almost fifty years now. My reason gathered enough information to hate her, but my silly heart refuses to let her go, not before I know for sure... I have condemned and forgiven her every day since then." Charlie wiped his eyes and sighed, getting back his strength. "Now you understand why a single answer would be welcome? Simple evidence that allows me to track her steps is all that I want."

Anna felt deeply sorry for this helpless man. "Yes, I understand," she said, "more than you think. But I also think that you will never get the answer you want. I mean, maybe life is giving you this answer, but not in the way you expect it to come."

Charlie's face crumbled. Maybe nobody had spoken to him with so much affection for decades. Maybe he had never opened his heart to a woman other than Georgia before. "And you think that your story is the answer," he said, still in clear disbelief, but with a more friendly tone.

"My story is your story, Charlie."

"The story you got from that diary and your son's dreams, which—"

"No," she cut him off with serenity in her voice. "What I know about Georgia is not all from that diary or from my child."

"What do you mean?"

Anna opened her mouth to answer, but the piercing kettle whistle went off. "Wait a minute." Charlie went to the stove and poured the water into two teacups.

"Any preference?" he asked about the tea.

"Herbal tea, please, if any. I have a session after this, and I need to be relaxed."

"Sugar?"

"No, thanks; I like it unsweetened."

"Glad you said that. There's no sense in sweetening tea." He handed her a steaming teacup and reclaimed his seat on the sofa. "It seems that you have more to share." Charlie said, staring at her with disbelief in his expression.

Anna took a sip of tea. "As I told you, my first and only interest was to help my son. My first reaction, when he began to tell me about his ancestors, was the same skeptical attitude you have now."

"I know; you can skip that. Just tell me what else you know," he said impatiently.

"I got professional help."

He gave her a questioning look.

"A therapist," she explained.

Charlie cocked his eyebrow in surprise. "I was thinking more of a detective."

"Not a regular therapist," she explained. "I know it sounds outside the norm, but I went through regression therapy, and..." she paused, feeling awkward. "I found that I'm... I'm also involved in this story." She felt like her story was only a fantasy compared to his real life struggle. "Which is..." Anna hesitated, feeling nervous. She placed the teacup on the coffee table to gain time. Her sweating palms would soon make it hard to hold the teacup safely. But as she glanced down at her hands, she was surprised to see that they were dry. She rubbed one hand against the other in disbelief. It seemed to bring clearness to her mind. "In regression, you can access old memories through hypnosis," she said with more confidence.

"I know how it works," Charlie replied to her surprise.

"Well, so you know that it's possible that we can see what we have done in past lives?"

"I didn't say that. I don't believe that anyone can travel in time."

"But it happened to me, Charlie," she shot back. "I know it's crazy, I didn't expect that it could really happen when I went to the session, but I saw myself in past lives as clearly as I see you now."

Charlie was silent as she continued in a calm and confident tone. "I saw myself taking care of an ill man while another man was waiting for me, just like Georgia. My feelings so matched hers! I had felt bound to her since the first page of her diary although it never occurred to me that I could possibly be this woman, whose life is so appealing, so emotionally wealthy. But last night..." Anna trailed off, worried about Charlie's reaction, "my son fell into a sort of spontaneous trance and told me that you are sad because I left you. Then he described in detail his own death, drowning in a river when he was trying to save an elderly woman in the flood."

Charlie frowned and looked unsettled.

"I'm sorry, Charlie, but your son could never come back to you, not the way you expected," she softened her voice, "and I...I have reasons to believe, despite how crazy it sounds, that I was his mother. It's clear to me that life brought us together because of this unfinished business."

Anna stared for a moment at Charlie's wet eyes, and saw him resting his teacup on the coffee table with a strange expression that she could not read until he burst into a nervous laughter.

"So, you think that you and Georgia..." he said between his laughs.

All of a sudden, Charlie stopped laughing, and stared deep into her eyes. "Why are you doing this to me?" he frowned.

"Because...I couldn't imagine another way to tell you this.

I'm not asking you to believe, but I do want your help in figuring out what happened."

Charlie stared at her, silently, and those seconds before he expressed his thoughts again felt like a timeout before a sentence being given. "How can I stop you, Mrs. Dawson?" he said with anger growing in his expression. "I may be an old man, but I'm not senile. I don't believe you; I don't buy your story. I may be the silliest man on earth, but I'm not stupid."

"Yes, you are!" Anna confronted him.

"What? Are you calling me stupid?"

"I didn't mean to, but yes, I guess I am. You don't want to walk through the door that is wide open for you. Why Charlie? Are you afraid to find the truth, so you'd have no reasons to blame anyone else for your disgrace? Why do men have to be such naysayers?"

Charlie grew angrier. "What makes you think that you can come to my house and disrespect me? What do you know about me? What do you think I did my whole life? I looked for answers in all possible ways, but I won't surrender to your fantasies."

Charlie's eyes were bulging with anger. "People think that my garden keeps me alive," he continued, "but this is not the truth. You want to know the truth? The truth is that anger has kept me alive, and has given me strength to live every day of this Goddamn life since October 16, 1955. My garden helps me to forget it for few minutes, maybe hours." His voice was trembling, and he pointed a finger in her face. "You think you are Georgia? So tell me what happened that day. Maybe you can tell me what happened the night before. Where did Georgia and I go to spend the night? How did we make that night so special, even after the water flooded my house?"

Anna was silent and fearful. She had no answers for him, not even a clue about what he was saying. She worried that this level of emotional distress could be bad for him at his age and regretted what she had said.

"I bet you're not able to answer simple questions," Charlie continued, "like what's the color of the car she drove all the way from Los Angeles." Charlie leaped up and went to his old Victrola. He pulled out three old records and placed them on the coffee table in front of her. "Show me the last song we danced to."

Anguish blocked Anna's throat. She should not have come until she had information that is more precise.

"One last thing," he went on. "What did I give to her in 1940 that she should bring to me to prove that she never forgot me, and she never did?"

Charlie's tone was offensive, and Anna felt her eyes fill.

"You're just like the others." Charlie took the teacups on his trembling hands and brought them to the kitchen. "I want you to leave this house and never come back here; otherwise I'll call the police and accuse you of stalking," he said without looking back at her.

Anna was shocked that it had ended up this way and headed for the front door. She stopped though, mid way, and reached for some sheets of paper in her purse, the pages Larry had printed out from his research about past life memories. She put them on the coffee table before she left.

When she got into her car, she rested her head between her hands, taking deep breaths. Then she saw the time. She only had twenty-five minutes to pick up Marvin and drop him at Lisa's, a thirty-minute ride. She had left her cell phone hooked up to the charger in the car and found that she had three missed calls from Lisa. Lisa had left a voice message, but when Anna tried to access her mailbox, the phone was out of service.

The first leg of the trip was fast, without any traffic. As she buckled Marvin into his booster seat, she realized she couldn't make it on time to the session, but she could at least shorten the delay by taking the back roads that zigzagged in a shortcut to Lisa. She stepped hard on the gas pedal and took the phone to play Lisa's message. Lisa was angry, accusing Anna of something that Anna could not hear well, but she clearly heard that Lisa was calling her "liar." Anna sharpened her ears to try and make sense of the message, but Marvin, from the back seat, was calling her attention.

"Mom," Marvin said. "Remember when you told me about the deer?"

"What did you say, sweetie?" Anna said, turning her head slightly to Marvin, while holding her cell phone at her ear.

"You said that a deer walks with its family," he replied, playing with a Spider-Man figurine.

"I said that. Have you seen one?" she asked, pulling up Lisa's number.

Before he answers, Anna looked up and spotted a deer ahead in the middle of the road which took a sharp curve. She dropped the phone and managed to avoid a collision, but when she reached the curve, two more deer were calmly crossing the road. She managed to avoid the first deer, but the second one got scared and moved right in front of the car. Anna jerked the steering wheel violently to the right and again avoided the collision, but as a result, she lost control of the vehicle. The car skidded off the road into the woods, straight towards a tree that Anna managed miraculously to avoid, although the car lost its side mirror. Anna couldn't stop the vehicle, which went down the hill toward to a pond hidden behind the bushes. She hoped that the bushes could stop them, but unfortunately, they didn't. The car hit a bump on the ground, causing Anna's head to hit the windows, at her side, and landed in the water. The nose of the car sank, upending it into a diagonal position.

Slipping in and out of consciousness, Anna heard Marvin crying in the back seat. He sounded faraway. She observed the cold sensation of the water on her feet. Her head was pitched forwards while the seat belt held up her body. She did not seem to be able to move, but had a dim sense that the wet feeling on her face was blood, trickling onto her lips. She could taste it and sensed that she was in serious trouble.

She drifted out of consciousness again. When she came back, she felt strong enough to turn her head towards Marvin, who was now quiet. She tried to call his name, but her voice was barely above a whisper.

She heard a familiar voice clearly saying her name inside the car. She tried to turn her head again but was prevented by a pain that started in her neck and spread to the back of her head. She sensed that someone was sitting in the passenger seat. "Ralph?" she whispered.

"Hi, Anna; I'm glad that you made it."

"No, I didn't. I'm sorry," she replied.

"Yes, you did. Just in time." He held up his hand to check his wristwatch.

"I can't go anywhere. I'm in a car accident, and I'm afraid I'm dead, since I'm talking to someone who can't possibly be here."

"They'll find you soon, don't worry."

"How's Marvin? You see him?"

"He's ok. He's the easiest part, remember?"

Anna tried to gather her power to turn her head towards Ralph, but all her effort only made the pain in her head intensify and she started to drift away again.

"Are you ready?" Ralph insisted.

She opened her eyes slightly and saw the water reaching the edge of her seat.

"Whatever you want, just take us away from here."

"Okay. So, close your eyes and try to relax. You know how it works. This time it will be a little different, and you'll be able to watch your memories in depth." And after a pause, he began to countdown from ten to zero, guiding her in a deep relaxation. Soon, all the pain was gone.

Chapter 20

A persistent knock on the windshield woke Georgia up. She sat up straight, unaware of where she was, her heart racing. She covered her eyes with her hand to protect them from the bright sun crossing the glass directly to her face. Her neck was sore, and her legs numb. Her memory gradually came back, and she realized that she had spent the whole night curled on the front seat of her Chevrolet. She had thought she could get to Connecticut the night before, but fatigue had proved it to be a miscalculation. She had decided to park for a recovering nap at a gas station, which was closed for the day, but she must have slept through the night.

A tall, black middle-aged man, wearing denim overalls over a white t-shirt and a cap, stared at Georgia's movement inside the car with curiosity.

She checked her hair in the mirror and rolled down the window.

"You okay, lady?" the man asked, his eyes scanning the inside of the car.

"I'm sorry," she answered. "It wasn't my intention..." she was embarrassed, afraid he was going to yell at her for being on private property without permission.

"I don't mind if you sleep here; I was just worried that you could be in some trouble. It's not safe for a woman to sleep on the roads. Did you run out of gas?"

She shook her head in response.

"Where are you going, lady?" he said. He seemed to be a good man; she could hear it in the tone of his voice.

"Danbury, Connecticut. I thought I could get there last

night."

He looked down the road, squinting, as if calculating the distance. "Not too far. I'd say two hours, maybe three. We're near to the Pennsylvania border, but you still have a bit of the Empire State to cross." He paused. "You might need to use the restroom. It's in the corner of the store. Nothing fancy though, but it's clean. If you want some fresh coffee, I'll be inside."

He stared at her for a moment, as though trying to read her story in her eyes, and headed to the store.

Georgia glanced around to assess her situation then left the car to attend to nature's calling. Her legs were still not fully responding to her brain. In the rest room, she took time to fix her makeup in the mirror and brushed her hair slightly before enjoying a cup of fresh brewed coffee with the store owner.

He was a lonely man with a pocketful of good memories. He told her, briefly, about his life and his ancestors' striving against slavery. He showed her some pictures, very proud of his lineage. His dreams were behind him in the form of memories and they were as simple as the expression on his face, but still alive in the glare in his eyes.

His name was George Middleton, and she listened to him with great pleasure as if she had missed talking to authentic people, the kind easily found in the countryside—unsophisticated souls, welcoming and heartwarming, smelling of home, like those she knew in her childhood; people who talked as if they'd known her forever. After working for over a decade in show business, she felt like she missed the best part of the human world, and she was happy to be back. She spent more than an hour with him and when she left, he gave her a map of the area, showing the local roads in detail.

It was her fifth day on the road. She couldn't remember when she had had a timeout like that, days with nothing else to do but drive, snoop around places, and let her mind wander.

The last three days she barely spoke, only to check in and out the hotels where she slept over, and to order something to eat along the way. She could breathe the fresh air through the car window, and when she reached into sleepy roads, she slowed down and enjoyed music on the radio. The new hit *Life Could be a Dream*, the Sh-boom song performed by The Crew Cuts or The Chords—it did not matter for her who sang it—was her favorite song. *"If only all my precious plans would come true, if you would let me spend my whole life lovin' you, life could be a dream, sweetheart,"* she sang along cheerfully, thinking of Charlie, the man she left fifteen years ago with a heart full of love for her.

Charlie could be married now, and happy, and if so, she could do nothing but accept it. Marty was her son though, no matter what. He could still be longing for the opportunity to rest his head on his mom's lap. This thought was enough to fill Georgia's heart with hope and joy. But he could also be angry with her and unwilling to meet the woman who had abandoned him to pursue a dream. After fifteen years, without exchanging a single letter with him, she realized how misguided she had been. To shorten the physical distance between her son and herself, she could push the gas pedal to the floor, but to shorten the distance from his heart, she could only stick to hope.

In the middle of the morning, she crossed the border, entering Connecticut. The day had clouded up, matching her feelings. When she saw the first sign indicating Danbury few miles ahead, she felt her palms sweat on the steering wheel and anxiety spread through her. She had to park alongside the road to get herself together. She cried for few minutes.

"C'mon girl," she said to herself, wiping her face, "you can do this."

She fixed her makeup in the mirror. A woman could

completely change her attitude with few changes in her appearance. A couple of minutes later, as rain began to pour, she arrived in town, with her heart pounding heavily and her eyes shining with excitement.

"Oh, my gosh!" she whispered. Her heart melted as she gazed at the houses, buildings, stores, and people on the street. The town seemed more radiant now, more colorful, filled with cars with their swooping decorative fins and sparkling chrome accessories in a wider range of colors, more than the black and brown vehicles that had been there during her time. She drove down Main Street, straight through the heart of the town, noticing all the updates.

She passed the Empress and the Palace theatres, where she many times attended the matinees with Charlie or her girlfriends. And close by, the Masonic Building, where her father used to gather with his friends. In the distance, she glimpsed the centenary Saint Peter Church, where her mother first introduced God to her when she was still a little girl, and although her relationship with the Almighty had never been as close as her mother wished, she enjoyed the church's holy architecture and the memories it held.

She recognized some of the stores, but many were new in business. The old Hotel Green, with 150 rooms and its imposing facade with four giant columns, was just as she remembered it. She had hung out across the street after school, watching the bigwigs arriving in their shiny Fords with their women wearing fancy hats. She had never been inside the Green, since hotels were for out-of-towners, but now she was one of them.

She parked in front of the hotel, and stood for a moment, looking around and enjoying the drizzle on her face, before walking up the stairs toward the front desk to check-in. The rates were not as high as she had once thought, especially compared to those in LA.

"Thank you for choosing the Hotel Green, Miss," the hotel

clerk said after finishing her registration. "I hope you have a great time in the Hat City. Unfortunately, the town is still recovering from the hurricanes. Some areas were flooded; the damage was immense."

"I heard about the hurricanes," she said. "It's a shame."

"Don't worry; hurricanes are a rare event in this area. The fair and most of the attractions in the city are running regularly, and I'll be more than happy to give you details at any time."

Georgia decided not to tell him that she had been born in this town. How the hotel treated visitors was one of the things she had always wanted to know.

The man took over her car and luggage. He gave her the key number 204, and pointed out that the restaurant downstairs was still open. She went up to her room and decided to settled down before making plans for the rest of the day. The man had given her a street view room. She opened the window and breathed in the fresh air. She saw a thermometer attached to the side jamb showing the temperature in the sixties, pleasant. She unpacked some of her clothes and placed them in the wardrobe, but left her valuable things locked inside the false bottom of the train case. Then she kicked her shoes off and threw her body in to bed.

The sensation of being close to her son and Charlie again, of walking on the same land and breathing the same air, made her anxious. She had no idea whatsoever, about the best way to approach them; she didn't even know if they still lived in town. It occurred to her she probably should have checked before she left LA.

She called the front desk and requested a line. Then she dialed 113 for information, and asked for Charlie Baker's phone number. She felt her trembling palms begin to moisten the phone and her breathing became heavy. Her heart sped up in her chest. The seconds that followed felt like an eternity, but the confirmation that he was in town came as a great relief. She wrote down in her diary the number and the address the operator provided, tore out the page, and put it away in her purse.

"Jesus, Georgia! Take it easy, okay?" she said to herself, noticing that she had inadvertently torn out the last page of her diary, rather than a clean page.

A few minutes later, she could no longer resist. She took back the piece of paper from her purse and called the number. While imagining what to say, she heard the tone, ringing endlessly before she hung up. "Of course, a man is not supposed to be at home at this time of the day on a weekday," she thought.

After a refreshing shower, Georgia made her way to the restaurant downstairs and had a light lunch. Then she decided to have a walk in town. She planned to stop by at the centenary Savings Bank, right next door, to open an account. There, she found the first recognizable face, one of the managers, a middle-aged man called Arthur Ramsay. He had a small, thin mustache matching the shape of his mouth, was wearing rounded glasses, and had a prominent forehead. He had been a best friend of her father. She approached his desk and introduced herself.

"Of course, I remember you! You were the apple of your father's eye." The man said cheerful, and invited her to have a seat. "Look at you, so grown up! You're just like your mother at your age."

He was very amiable, with many stories about the time they spent together. For Georgia, recalling her childhood memories was an unexpected pleasure.

"I always thought of your father when the war ended and we had a housing boom in the economy. He could've made more money here in a couple of years than he made his whole life."

"After my mom died, he wasn't the same man," Georgia said. "He gradually lost his ambition to conquer the world."

"I'm so sorry about him, but I can see, by your deposit, that he was also good at passing along his talents."

She didn't want to tell the manager that this money was from Jerry's life insurance; after all, it was a deserved reimbursement.

The next hour she wandered through the town, snooping around, talking to people, delighting her spirit in sweet memories. She saw familiar faces, but not one of her old acquaintances. She couldn't foresee how she would adapt to a small town after living for so long in a big city, but one thing she knew: this was something that she wanted. Time would be the key to this game, and finding her place in town would probably not be as hard as finding her place back in those hearts she had hurt so badly.

In the middle of the afternoon, with the rain still falling steadily, she went back to the hotel to pick up her car for a broader tour. She drove towards the hat factory, where Charlie used to work part-time. Up ahead on the hill, was his mother's house. She parked at distance, and took a moment to revisit the place she last saw Charlie and her baby in his mother's arms. The house was quiet and sad. The green leaves on the tree beside the house were given way to sparse autumn leaves and the surrounding ground was covered in yellow. Her memories were so clear as if no more than a day had passed. In her mind, all was present and vivid, just like the taste of the coffee she had had before leaving the hotel or the bell she just heard from Saint Peter Church a few minutes ago. She could just see Marty coming out of the front door. She just wanted to see the boy he became, and for that, she waited inside the car for three quarters of hour. She had nothing else to do, other than go back to the hotel and wait until Charlie came back home at the end of the day.

Chapter 21

At 6:00 p.m., Georgia decided that it was time. She grabbed the phone and requested a line. She spent a few seconds working up her courage and dialed Charlie's number. The phone rang repeatedly, and she was about to hang up when a male voice responded. "Hello..." Charlie's voice sounded as if in a dream.

Georgia's tongue was paralyzed with emotion. She took a moment as if allowing the voice to penetrate her brain to match the sound of Charlie's voice she had stored in her mind.

"Hello..." he repeated, somewhat impatiently. His voice sounded different than she remembered, but she had never heard Charlie's voice on the phone before.

"It's me," she said hesitantly and, after a moment, added, "It's me, Georgia."

"I know." His voice was low and calm, almost cold. He didn't seem surprised. "So, you're in town."

"I arrived this morning."

They became silent again.

"How long will you stay?"

"I don't know. Forever, I guess."

"How long is your 'forever'?"

She had known it would not be easy, and she was prepared to handle irony, distrust, and even accusations. "How have you been?" she asked.

"Not bad. Yourself?"

"I'm fine. How's Marty, is he okay?"

"He's fine."

Another moment of silence, and Georgia felt her palms

sweaty on the phone. Her heart pounding in her chest was loud. "Are you married? I mean, I don't want to cause you trouble, but there was no other way to reach you."

"That's okay," Charlie mumbled.

"Are you?" she insisted.

"What?"

"Married. I don't want to get you in trouble with your wife."

Charlie stayed silent for a moment.

"I have no wife," Charlie finally said.

Georgia's lips opened in a silent grin. *He's free!* She thought, striving to manage her excitement.

"Why did you come back?"

"It's a long story, hard to tell over the phone. Are you..." she paused hesitant. "I'll understand if you don't want to see me, but there's so much to say."

"Of course there is. Where are you?"

"Hotel Green, room 204."

Charlie became still. For fifteen years, he waited to hear her voice. Fifteen years... every time the phone rang, every day of his life. If not for him, for Marty at least she would certainly call someday, he knew it.

The words hung in the air. Georgia waited.

"Come to my place," he finally said. "You found my phone number, you probably have my address."

"Yes, I do. What time?"

"Well, I'm at home now..."

"Okay."

Hanging up the phone, Georgia managed to even her breath, pressing the phone against her chest. Then she went to check on her makeup. Now, that she heard his voice, fifteen years seemed to have passed in a snap. But looking in the mirror, she saw that time had left its mark. She was thirty-three now, with slight shadows on her lower eyelid. The innocent glow of youth had vanished from her eyes—if only because of grief. She had lotions and powders to disguise her insecurity at that moment though, and one thing that she had learned in show business was how to use them. She fixed small spots here and there, applying some foundation lightly to even out discoloration. Near the inner corners of her under-eye area, where shadows were most prominent she used a brush-on to camouflage dark circles. A rosy hue of rouge applied to the apples of her cheeks and a mauve lipstick finished off the look. Then for the final touch, she put some perfume on—the one Charlie always liked, in case her presence wasn't enough to wake up his memories. She kept on the same yellow dress she wore during the day.

She could walk to Charlie's house, but, because of the unsteady weather, she chose to drive. Less than twenty minutes had passed from the moment she hung up the phone to when she parked on East Franklin Street in front of Charlie's house. The rain had receded, and after one last check in the mirror, she left the car.

Charlie had seen the car arriving through the window and came out of the house. She saw him standing on the porch, and her legs felt wobbly. He was wearing dark gray pants and a blue long-sleeved button-down shirt, which he hadn't tucked in. She wondered how he could still be single in his thirties.

She crossed the street, gazing at him steadily, and stopped at the porch steps. For few seconds, they stood still and silent, gazing at each other.

"Hi," she forced a smile.

Charlie nodded, assessing her physical changes, noticing her hair was slightly shorter, in a modern style. Her face was that of a woman now, and he could see that the light of her youth was still there, bright and majestic.

"It's good to see you," she said.

"It's good to see you, too," he replied, staring at her still in disbelief.

"So..." she said. "This is where you live now."

He finally moved his eyes from her, shaking off his bewilderment. "For seven years now," he said. "The flowers are almost gone for the season, but the Ford..." he pointed to a 1948 green Ford convertible parked on the driveway, shining and well cared for.

She became emotional and speechless, gazing at the car, recalling his dreams about their home, with flowers at the window and a Ford in the garage.

"Is Marty here?"

"No. He lives with my mom and my sister at Rose Hill, same place. He has his room here though. When he becomes tired of listening to women stuff, he comes here to get some relief."

She smiled again, and relaxed slightly. Then she walked up the steps, getting closer to him.

"Nice car," he said, motioning his hand at the 1950 yellow Chevrolet Bel Air Sedan. "Did you drive all the way from California?"

She nodded proudly. "I like this car; I couldn't leave it behind."

"Wow," he said, trying to sound less surprised that he in fact was. "You covered a lot of ground."

For a moment, they got lost in their thoughts, Charlie wondering how unpredictable she was, and Georgia, realizing the weight of what she had done in a man's mind. Driving that far was something impressive indeed.

"You're not going to show me inside?" she humbly asked.

He said nothing, thinking how dangerous it could be to invite her inside. Soon she'd find her way to squeeze into his life again, he thought. Nevertheless, he turned to his left side as if making the way clear for her and motioned slightly. Georgia walked into the house. She stopped right after she crossed the threshold and looked back as if waiting for Charlie's permission to enter in his life. Charlie moved by her to show her the way.

Georgia noticed that he was a neat man, another thing he had learned from his mother. The decor was warm and inviting. The brown fabric sofa set matched the curtains. The walls were green and a large gray rug covered the living room floor. A charming fireplace and some pictures hanging on the wall made it hard to believe that he was a man living by himself. The wooden buffet with china on the shelves, separating the dining from the living room, seemed unusual.

She examined every detail, until she came to a picture of him with his relatives in a small frame over a wooden Victrola cabinet. She came closer and picked it up. Tears began to well on her eyes as she identified the young boy in the picture with his grandma and aunt Ellie. She turned to say something, but Charlie anticipated her thoughts. "He was twelve at that time," he said.

Georgia turned his gaze to the photo and back again to Charlie.

"Does he know about me?" she said, wiping her face.

Charlie lowered his gaze for a moment. "On Marty's first birthday, I had a conversation with my mom. We agreed that, since you faded out and never came back, Marty would have to hear about you from your mouth. We'd never be in your way, but it'd be your choice. If you never came back, there was no point in keeping you alive in his memory."

She lowered her gaze to the picture in her hands, hit by the truth of his words. "I wanted so much to know about him, about you," she said. "I wrote so many letters..."

"Letters?" he said in disbelief. "I never got any letter from you."

"I never had courage to mail them," she gave him a helpless look.

"And... may I ask why?"

"It wasn't easy for me to leave here," she said, collecting her thoughts. "I became sad and empty. It took me months to recover, and I thought that if I kept coming here or even writing... if I knew about you and Marty, I couldn't stay there and help my father, and pursue my dream."

"Out of sight, out of mind," he concluded in disappointment.

"I always had hope that I could come back at any time...I know you'll never understand," she replied. "I don't expect that anybody understands."

At least she knew that she could not expect anyone's compassion. But, why on earth did she have to come back now? Charlie thought. "Why did you change your mind now?"

"Nothing changed," she replied with surrendered eyes. "That's the reason, I guess. I just realized that nothing ever changed since I left," she paused. "I found what I was looking for, Charlie. I realized my dream, but I was never happy. I was a fool thinking that I could be. I realized that I could only make it if you and our son were there with me." She paused, and changed direction. "But you never came to find me either. Many times, I looked for you in the middle of the audience, hoping you'd just come and take me away with you, even against my will. Why did you never come?"

Charlie stared deep into her eyes for a moment sensing the accusative tone of her voice, but didn't respond. "Can you give me a minute?" he said instead.

He left toward his bedroom upstairs. Georgia took the opportunity to relieve the tension in her legs and sat on the couch.

Charlie came back with a hardcover book in his hand. He reached for a picture inside, which he used as a bookmark, and handed it to her. It was a photo of Marty, who looked a little younger than in the other picture.

She smile, puzzled by the meaning of it. "What's this?" she said.

"Take a look."

"It's Marty, nine- or ten-years-old, I guess. He's so cute."

"Take a better look."

Georgia moved her gaze from Marty to the photo's background and recognized the street and the town where he was standing. "God! When was this?"

"About five years ago. Marty began to ask about his mother; he claimed he had the right to meet you. I wrote you a letter, but it came back undeliverable. Then we went to LA, only to find that you and your father had moved years before. We stayed in town for a couple of days looking for you, until Marty gave up and asked me to go home. Since then, he hasn't mentioned you again."

Georgia was speechless, staring at Charlie.

"I still wonder about how it would've ended if we had found you," he continued. "I still don't know if it was what I wanted. You probably were busy, maybe married to someone with a similar dream. I just wanted him to stop asking, and it was a relief when he did."

Georgia lowered her gaze to the photo again, now striving to prevent tears from falling. "After a few months there, I realized that I'd made a mistake," she said. "My dream was coming true; many doors were open to me, but something wasn't right. I began to consider a change in my plans and come back, but my father was ill, and we had no money to hire a nurse. I had to organize my schedule around his needs. In 1945, he passed away, and I decided that nothing else could hold me there."

Charlie sat on the sofa in front of her. "I'm sorry about your father," he said, thinking of his own.

She nodded and continued. "I started to make plans to come back, but it seemed that fate had something different for me. I received an offer to be the lead in a play, a big production. It was all that anyone in the acting business wanted, and I felt that I needed to know what it was like, before giving it up for good, otherwise how could I settle myself into a different life? I was still scared though, and might have refused the offer when I met this man, Jerry. He helped me overcome my father's loss and made me foresee the rare opportunity I had in front of me."

Charlie shifted on the sofa.

"He was a good man, Charlie," Georgia continued. "He protected me in all possible ways. You know what people say about actresses. They think that we're available, and accessible, easy prey, willing to do anything for a part. At that time, I was frightened, feeling alone in the world. My father was the last link to our small family."

"Did you get married?" he said with undisguised disappointment.

"No," she said looking tenderly into his eyes. "I would never marry another man."

"Did you love him?"

Georgia thought for a moment before answering. "Yes... but in a different way. He was older than me, in his forties. He taught me how to be a better person." Georgia trailed off, noticing Charlie's annoyance. "At this time I was pessimistic about us. I imagined you married and happy. Then I accepted the acting offer. I really had an amazing experience on stage and finally made good money. For a period of time, I thought that I'd made the right decision. But I soon realized that it wasn't enough to fulfill me. I was still unhappy and feeling guilty. Besides, all the glamour, fawning, countless social meetings, wasn't the life I wanted."

"And what life did you want?"

A faint smile crossed her lips as she gazed tenderly into his eyes. "A normal life, I guess: a home, cuddling with my child at night time, the company of a loving husband, flowers at the window, and a Ford in the garage."

"You're talking about something that happened..." he trailed, "when was it? Ten years ago? It seems quite a long time to make a decision. It doesn't match the girl who needed only three months to leave her newborn son behind."

"That girl had grown up, Charlie," she replied. "Five years

ago I was ready for a turning point in my life, but fate had different plans again. Jerry, my partner, found out that he was ill."

Charlie felt unsettled again, growing impatient this time. He couldn't bear her gaze.

Georgia's voice fell to a whisper. "I could leave him, and he would never stop me because he always knew that my heart wasn't there with him. But he had no family, how could I let someone fight cancer alone? I just couldn't leave him. It was a hardship for both of us. I thought of you and Marty every day, and thinking that you at least had each other gave me relief and helped me to do the right thing." Georgia inhaled deeply. "He died two weeks ago, after a five-year fight. I asked fate what else it wanted from me, and I got no answer, so here I am."

Charlie was silent. Could he trust her? Did he still know this woman in front of him?

"I always believed there must be someone above us taking care of everything," Georgia amended. "Sometimes you don't know what to do, and the only thing that can make you feel better is if you can feel that you're doing the right thing. And I learned that, hurting people or forsaking someone who needs you isn't the right thing to do." She gazed at Marty's picture, anguish choking her heart. "But now, in front of you, I feel like everything I did..." Georgia looked imploringly at Charlie. "Can you please, tell me? Did I do the right thing?"

Raising his eyebrows, Charlie slowly released his breath. "Right or wrong," he said, "it's done. We can't change the past."

Georgia nodded, feeling her anguish grow. Charlie's words sounded like a sentence in which she'd been found guilty.

"What are your plans now?" Charlie asked.

"I have no plans, since nothing that I want depends on me, but I have a dream..." she hesitated. "I say 'a dream' because only in a dream is it possible for a man to forgive a woman and love her again when she least deserves it." Tears filled her eyes.

Charlie's face did not reveal what he was feeling. He looked emotionless. He silently fought the urge to say "yes", and kiss her lips the way he countless times had dreamed of doing, and put *We Belong Together* to play on the Victrola and back her around the room, finally bringing her upstairs and making love in the bed that no other woman had lay in. "I thought of you too, many times," he said, after a moment of silent reflection, "and many times I considered that being with you was like riding a horse bareback. It was fun, but challenging and unsafe." He paused. "I can't answer this now. If you stay around, we can see how things will go."

Georgia was relieved. At least he didn't say "no". "I'll stay," she said.

Charlie was silent for a moment, staring at her face, falling for her humbleness. But when he opened his mouth, what came out wasn't any less defensive. "I wonder if you have come back the first time if you hadn't got pregnant," he said, striving against the magnetism of her eyes.

"I can't answer that, but I think this is the way fate works."

"You always rely on fate..."

"What else is there to rely on? My heart? I did that once..."

Charlie felt that his strength was fading with every word she was saying, and was glad that a noise, coming from the back door, interrupted the conversation. Soon a big, clumsy, old dog with brownish fur and a goofy face came to meet them. He went straight to Georgia and smelled her feet, her knees, and the hand she offered with a friendly smile. "Hi, big boy; who are you?"

"C'mon, Mr. Bogart, leave her alone." Charlie scolded the dog.

"Mr. Bogart?" Georgia repeated holding a laugh. "The actor?"

The dog stepped back, and shook the water off his drenched body, which splashed all over the place.

"Whoa, whoa, whoa!" Charlie was ashamed.

Georgia laughed and protected her face from the splashes. What a blast! She hadn't laughed so spontaneously for a long time. Charlie's house was sounding, feeling, and smelling like home, like family, and normal life.

Charlie laughed too, because Georgia's light was sparkling all over the room, and her dimples were flashing. He saw the same girl he had met long ago, and was glad that she was still there. When the laughter faded, they stared at each other without words for a moment, and then Charlie went to check on the weather at the window. "It's raining heavily," he said. "I hope it doesn't last long. We had problems enough two months ago. We had flooding in some areas and damage and lots of mud to clean up."

"The hurricanes were in the news. I worried about you and your family."

"My mom had no major problems. Her house is on the hill. At the factory though, we had a considerable loss, and a lot of cleanup to do."

"You still work at the hat factory?" she was surprised.

"Yes. After college, I began working full-time, and after few months, Mr. Clear hired me to run the office. Through the years, he kept putting more and more on my plate, and now I'm running almost the entire place."

"It sounds like you've been very busy."

"Things aren't as good as they were in the past. After the war, since cars became affordable, hats aren't as essential as they used to be."

"For a town that grew around its hat factories, it's really sad."

"We'll survive."

"What about your dreams? You wanted to be a scientist."

"I wanted to be a botanist," he amended. "But when I

finished college, I had a roof over my head, a child, my mother, my sister...I couldn't only pursue dreams."

Georgia flushed, and lowered her eyes.

Restless, Charlie went to check on the rain once more. "The way it's pouring, it doesn't seem that will stop soon. Maybe it's time to think about dinner."

The dog, lying in the middle of the room, seemed to catch what Charlie meant. He got up instantly and came close to Charlie as cheerful as an old dog could be. He trotted into the kitchen.

"You know how to cook?" Georgia was curious.

"I'm not the best, but I can make my own food. The time in the army had its values."

The phone rang in the dining room. Charlie apologized, and left her to answer it. A minute later, he came back looking disappointed.

"I'm sorry; I completely forgot that I promised Marty I'd help him with his school science project tonight. He's a sophomore in high school now."

"That's okay, I think I'd better go," Georgia said, standing up.

Charlie raised his hands in agreement: "At least in the hotel you can have something better for dinner."

Georgia smiled. "I'll be happy to come back for dinner any day."

"I don't cook every day. Tomorrow for instance, I'll go for dinner at Roy's Diner. It has been my Friday routine for years now. You can join me there at 6:00, if you want."

"It'll be a pleasure! May I ask you something?" Georgia said with pleading eyes. "I'd like to see Marty."

The tension returned to Charlie's face. He was still striving to foresee what her return would represent to his life. He had more experience now, and his heart had developed some endurance. He believed he could manage it as long as it regarded himself. After all, when he looked back on his life, he was forced to admit that he had done nothing else but wait for her. Marty though, was a higher level of concern. It would change his life, and Charlie wasn't sure if it was worth the price. "I'll see what I can do," Charlie said, hiding his thoughts.

"Will you tell me tomorrow?"

He nodded, but thought otherwise. He needed more from her than words. They needed to spend more time together until he figured out her sincerity.

She kissed his cheek goodbye, and he smelled her perfume, which triggered sweet feelings and a chemical reaction in his body. He stayed frozen, lost in the sensation, as she headed to the front door.

"Wait a second," Charlie finally reacted. He disappeared inside the house again, and this time he came back handing her an old, black men's umbrella. "It's not feminine, but will keep you dry, more or less."

She thanked him for his kindness with a smile and left. From the door, Charlie watched Georgia struggling with the umbrella to get inside the car. He waved his hand slightly when the car moved away.

Chapter 22

The rain continued into the following day and Georgia did not leave the hotel until the afternoon. The previous night, she could not shut off her mind or ease her tensions. She had had a glass of wine, tried to read a book, and relaxed at the window, watching the rain come down in waves by the light of the street lamps. Ultimately, she lay awake in bed. In the morning though, she prolonged her time in bed. The falling rain was a relaxing soundtrack and an irresistible invitation to stay toasty and cozy under the sheets, since she had no schedule to fulfill. The rain was heavy in some moments then receded into drizzle, but never stopped.

After lunch, dressed in warmer clothes and carrying the umbrella, she had in mind to buy a present for Marty, but had no clue about what he liked or disliked. Taking him as an average boy could be a blunder, and blunders were something that she had had enough of. After visiting a few stores and finding nothing that suited her, she decided not to take the risk. Maybe, later she could get Charlie's opinion on this.

The rainfall was heavy and steady in the middle of the afternoon, making the streets inadequate for pedestrians. The curbs on the corners had disappeared under the water, and streams were running alongside the streets, making it hard to cross from one side to the other.

Georgia took refuge under the awning of a luncheonette to rest her arm from the umbrella. "What a wet day!" she mumbled, wishing she could take her shoes off and wring out her hose. She gazed inside the luncheonette searching for a comfortable place to sit and perhaps to enjoy a cup of coffee to warm up her body, preventing her from getting a cold. A boy, savoring a humongous dish of ice cream and talking to a girl at one of the tables, caught her attention. She stared at him for a moment, recognizing her son, older than the picture she saw the day before, but her heart couldn't be wrong. "It's him!" she whispered in astonishment.

Georgia entered the luncheonette, and found a stool at the counter that offered a clear view of the young couple. She gazed at him. He resembled his father in his youth, especially when he smiled and his eyes sparkled—something that she had not caught in the pictures. He looked older for his age, maybe because of the way he dressed, more mature than other kids his age. The girl had a spontaneous smile, and they seemed to enjoy each other.

Georgia's heart melted as she leaned the umbrella against the counter, and grabbed the menu to disguise her curiosity. The attendant was busy with three gabby kids on the other end of the counter. She tried to even her breath and calm her trembling hands. How she desired to approach him and introduce herself, but fear paralyzed her, and she was helpless to think of something reasonable to do. Looking at her son, she realized how much she had missed of his life. Not only had she missed the normal parenting milestones such as his first steps, first tooth, first word, she also had no idea what his personality was, what he thought about life, about girls, even about his ghost mother, if he still did think about her. Was he a rebellious teenager like almost all the kids his age? No, she had caught the pride in Charlie's face when she asked about him. What about school, was he doing well? What did he want to be? A botanist like his father had dreamed of or the administrator he became? When the attendant came to help her, Georgia was striving to hear the sound of her son's voice.

She ordered a cup of coffee with cream, still catching Marty out of the corner of her eyes. The gabby boys at the other end left the counter and passed behind her toward Marty's table. Georgia watched them over her shoulder with a bad feeling. The tallest one, a flattop bull, wearing blue jeans and a red jacket with the collar up, seemed to be the leader of that small gang. He walked with a swagger. "He thinks he's James Dean," the attendant commented to Georgia, with a disgusted face.

The boy approached Marty and the girl, followed by his friends. His first words to Marty confirmed Georgia's suspicions. "Hey nosebleed, what're you doing here? Shouldn't you be with granny doing your homework?" he said with a sarcastic smile, moving his malicious gaze to the girl.

Georgia grew uncomfortable. Marty was a good size for his age, but looked smaller compared to the provocative boy, who seemed older, maybe eighteen. Marty seemed familiar with his threatening approach though.

"What do you want, Ray?" he said, without removing his eyes from his ice cream.

Ray felt motivated to keep teasing him, always watching the girl. "C'mon, Diane, why d'ya waste your time with this loser? Don't you wanna know what a real man is?"

"Why are you asking, Ray? Have you met one?" Marty replied ironically.

Ray seemed surprised. "Of course you can't recognize one when you see one, because you have no idea what that means," he said, "but I'll clue you in, Mickey Mouse. A real man drives a car not a bike. A real man takes his sophie for a backseat bingo not a banana split. A real man knows exactly what girls want."

"Wow!" Marty was sarcastic. "Thanks for sharing. Where did you learn this? I guess you might've been watching *Betty Boop*, otherwise how'd you know what girls want? I've never seen you with a girl. You're always busy with boys."

Diane smiled at Marty with admiration. Ray's eyes widened, and his hands clenched into a fist. He leaned over the table, his narrowed eyes aflame.

"C'mon Ray, let's go," one of his friends said, pulling his arm.

"Cool it, Bruce. I just wanna check if this unborn is as brave as he thinks he is smart," Ray said, pushing his friend's hand away, without taking his eyes from Marty.

Georgia was proud of her son's cleverness. *He is like his father*, she thought, *smart, centered, and fearless.* But if a fight broke out, it would be between a small David and a giant Goliath.

Fearing for her son, Georgia looked around, checking amongst the small number of kids scattered at the luncheonette tables, for anyone who could offer help if needed, but none of them seemed to be paying attention. They probably were used to Ray's bullying.

Ray was leaning towards Marty, practically lying on the table, and Georgia spotted his finger deepening in Marty's ice cream bowl, provoking Marty's reaction. She could no longer control her instincts, and in less than a second, she was on her feet, and rapidly walked toward them.

"Excuse me," she said, jabbing her finger into Ray's rib. "I think you should leave these kids alone." It sounded like an order and was supported by the serious expression on her face.

Ray turned his broad shoulders towards Georgia, surprised by her audacity. "Whatcha want, lady?" he said, licking the ice cream on his finger. "Mommy came to protect his baby?" He laughed for the other boys, unaware of how his words affected Georgia.

Georgia froze with his malice and glanced at Marty, who gazed back at her with surprised eyes.

"Of course, you can't be his mommy." Ray kept the same sarcastic attitude. "Mommy put the baby Moses in a basket long ago and sent him down the river."

The other boys stepped back. Ray was going too far with

his disrespectful behavior. Georgia grew angry, but managed to hold back the fire in her stomach. Words were the only possible effective weapon against that ill-bred kid.

"I'm sorry that I interrupted your spectacle," she said with a hint of the same sarcasm he had used. "But I was right there enjoying my coffee…" she pointed at the counter, "when I heard your conversation. I know it's not polite to listen to somebody else's conversation, but it was very loud. You're wrong about girls."

She blinked at Marty, who was still surprised with her interference, though curious about how she was going to deal with his bully.

"Whoa," Ray mocked. "And what's your concept? Razz my berries, lady. I have to warn you, though, I can take older girls, but you're out of my range"

Georgia gave him a wry smile. "First of all, you're not totally wrong. Indeed, there are girls who like cruisin' for a bruisin' boys, but they have a misguided sense of self-criticism."

"What is this? Ray raised his eyebrow, making a horseshoe-shaped mouth. "Have you come from another plan—?"

"Hang loose, kid," Georgia cut him off, with a stern look. Ray quieted, surprised with the tone of her voice. Then she continued. "I'll make it easier for you: not all girls are equal, as well as boys. I believe that this girl is one of those who equally value brain, heart, and muscles. And, according to what they say, muscled boys usually are lacking in other respects. It explains why they prefer to kiss a girl in the darkness of a car, where they can hide their disproportional 'gifts', which they certainly have no reasons to be proud of."

Ray's face was flushed, showing his shame and the internal volcano about to erupt. He stared at her for a moment then released the air from his lungs in an abrupt exhale. He grumbled something to Marty like: "We'll finish this later," and made his way out of the luncheonette and into the rain, followed by his friends.

Marty gave Georgia an open smile. Diane, his girlfriend, was more expansive. "You really put him down!"

Georgia resumed breathing. Words had left her, and she stared at Marty for a moment in silence. "You should not monkey with this kid," she finally said.

"Barking dogs seldom bite," Marty replied.

Georgia smiled, sensing Marty's confidence, and figured it was best to go back to her coffee, instead of delivering a mother's speech. She headed to the counter, her heart was pounding fast, and her hands could hardly hold the handle of the cup.

She reached for some coins in her purse and spread twenty cents on the counter. "Keep the change," she said, standing up, trying not to show her nervousness.

When she reached the sidewalk, she was still in shock. She turned towards the hotel but had only taken a few steps when she heard a voice calling her from behind.

"Excuse me, ma'am." She stopped and turned around to see Marty coming in her direction.

"You forgot this," he said gently, handing her the umbrella.

She thanked him with a smile, and he went back to the luncheonette.

Chapter 23

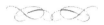

At 6:00 p.m. sharp, Georgia arrived at the diner. She spotted Charlie at a table as soon as she entered the front door. Charlie stood up when she approached and greeted her with a smile. He had been nervous while waiting, but she couldn't tell by looking at his serene face. He looked confident.

She offered a cheek for a kiss, and the scent of her perfume went straight to Charlie's heart.

"I wasn't expecting you to be so punctual," he said. "You never were."

"Well, I'm working on my bad habits," she replied, taking her coat off with his help. "But not all of them. I still procrastinate before going to bed at night, as well as getting up in the morning."

They sat down, and a waiter approached. "Hello Charlie, my friend. Good evening, Miss," the man said politely.

"Hello, Nick. How're you doing?" Charlie replied.

"Oh boy, I'm sick of this rain."

"I know. Who's not?"

"I have bad feelings about it. It has been pouring for almost forty-eight hours now. Four point five inches so far."

"Don't be depressed. The weather reports are calling for a clear sky tomorrow afternoon. The storm is moving off the coast."

"It better be; otherwise we'll be in trouble again. You know, the ground is still saturated from August's rain."

"Well, what can we do besides pray?" Charlie said. "By the way, Nick, this is Georgia," he introduced her. "Nick is an old fellow from Army," he explained.

"Georgia?" Nick said with startled eyes. "You mean Georgia-Georgia?"

Charlie nodded, under Georgia's curious gaze.

"Pleased to meet you, Georgia!" Nick offered his hand to shake as if looking at a celebrity. "This man has talked quite a bit about you."

"I hope not only bad things," she replied with a smile, her eyes catching Charlie.

"If he had bad things to tell, he kept them secret," Nick amended.

"Well, maybe he's not a good friend," Georgia teased Charlie, without removing her gaze from him. "Friends don't hide secrets from each other."

"I've seen Charlie sitting alone at this table for years now, and now I can see why he never replaced you."

"Okay, Nick," Charlie cut him off. "Why don't you bring us some wine?"

Nick became businesslike. "Any preference?"

"Do you have Charles Krug, a Cabernet from California, by chance?" Georgia asked.

"I'm sorry, only Cabernet Sauvignon from Connecticut. We have a limited wine list, you know. This is a diner. People don't order often."

"Sounds good to me," she agreed while looking at Charlie for approval.

"All right, I'll be back in a minute." Nick disappeared behind the counter.

"I'm sorry. He's a big mouth," Charlie said.

Georgia noticed that Charlie was half-embarrassed, and she liked that. "Should I expect anyone else to know about me?" She teased, trying to bring some relief to his frowned eyebrows.

"Are you kidding me? In a town like this? You can't keep many secrets," he said, avoiding her gaze.

She took off her gloves and put them on the table, near

Charlie's hat, a gray Homburg. "Is that the reason you didn't sound surprised when I called you yesterday?" she said.

"Well, you'd been walking in town. People saw you..."

"Huh... Small town. Was it a good surprise?" she probed hesitantly.

"I don't know yet. But I guess I'll figure it out."

Georgia lowered her gaze. "What about this hat?" Georgia grabbed it and turned it around to take a careful look. "It looks familiar."

"I bought it fifteen years ago."

"Right! You were wearing it the day I left, I remember."

"I'm surprised. I thought you never noticed." He had not worn the hat for a long time and it was still in good shape. But he was afraid that it smelled of mold.

Georgia did not seem to notice. "I have a clear picture of that day in my mind. I can tell the clothing everyone was wearing, even the cab driver. I can see my baby in your mother's arms, sleeping like an angel... I replayed this scene in my mind thousands of times."

"So you remember what else I bought, besides the hat?"

Georgia held her answer for a moment, her gaze deepened into his eyes. "You wanted to know if I'd ever forget you," she said.

"You were going to be an actress, I needed to protect myself."

"What?" she was puzzled.

"If you lied to me I'd never know," he said with a sly smile.

Georgia gave him a dirty look. "Seriously? You think I would lie to you?"

He shrugged, and she didn't know if he was just teasing her.

"You know what?" she said revengefully, keeping the mood. "You'll never know if I brought that glass slipper necklace back to you or not."

"I'll take it as a confession that you didn't," he provoked

her. "But, I'm glad that you at least remembered it."

"You'll need to be better than that. I won't tell you, unless you beg my apology."

Nick came back with two glasses and a bottle of wine. "This is on the house," he said.

"Thank you Nick," Charlie said. "But it isn't necessary."

"C'mon Charlie, enjoy it. Life is too short." Nick opened the bottle, and poured the ruby-red wine into the glasses. "I'll give you more time before you order." He winked at Georgia and left.

Charlie raised his glass in front of him. "What can we toast to?"

Georgia squinted, trying to find the best reason. "How about hope?"

"Umm... hope?" Charlie was unsure. He knew very well what hope was; that he could tell backwards. But he felt stupid waiting so long for someone who never treated him as a priority. "Let's toast to our health, a good life, your return..." he proposed.

"It sounds like a package; this is not the way toast works," she teased. "One thing at a time. We'll have many occasions to celebrate."

"All right," Charlie agreed, offering his glass for a clink. "To hope!" he surrendered, and completed the sentence in his mind: "To the hope that we'll have many reasons to celebrate."

They took a sip and rested their glasses on the table, staring at each other silently.

"I'm thinking about what Nick said," Georgia said. "I mean...why did you wait for me Charlie? You could've found a nice woman, got married..."

Charlie lowered his gaze to his glass and played with it for a moment, uncomfortable with her question. "I could, but I didn't."

"Why?" She insisted, with a loving tone.

"What do you want to hear? I had a couple of girlfriends, but no one worked out." He sounded impatient. In fact, he had never gotten into a relationship, had never allowed himself to fall for another woman. He was in part cautious with women, afraid of heartbreak, and on the other hand, he still loved Georgia so much that he couldn't help comparing her to every woman who came into his life. Although he had met interesting girls who had different virtues and beauty, Georgia was still all-in-one, funny, intelligent, and beautiful; a perfect combo. He learned that love is not one's choice. Love, actually, choose you, and after you fall, you are in hopeless trouble.

Sensing his discomfort, Georgia changed the subject. "I saw Marty today."

Charlie frowned. "Where was it? Did you talk to him?"

"Not exactly, I'd rather say that I helped him with some bullies."

"But, did you..."

"He had no clue about who I was. It happened that we were at the same place, and I recognized him from the picture you showed me. This enormous kid came to bug him and his girlfriend, and I just couldn't stand that. Don't worry, Charlie. I'll respect your will, and I accept your guidance on the best way to tell him."

Charlie seemed relieved. "I spoke to my mother about you." He paused. "She wants to see you. I told her I can bring you over tomorrow afternoon. Marty will be there too. I'll introduce you and let you have a private conversation with him. We'll be around, just in case. We don't know how he'll react."

"I understand; it sounds good to me. I don't know how I'm going to react either. I appreciate your kindness, Charlie." She paused. "I wanted to buy something for him but I realized that I don't know what he likes."

"Not necessary; Marty is not the type of kid that gets impressed with presents. He's not a child anymore."

"He's smart, intelligent..." Georgia shared her first impresssion. "Just like you. I hope he has the same kindness and will allow me to compensate him for all these years."

"He's a good kid, with a good heart, but this is something that's up to him."

"I bet he is," her eyes lit up. "Tell me, what does he like? What have you done together?"

"Besides his girlfriend..." Charlie's face contorted.

"Isn't he too young?"

"Well, he's a teenager now; you know, the hormones changing his body, his voice, all that stuff. Why are you so surprised? We started dating in high school."

"Well, we were seventeen...sixteen if we consider the period before our first kiss." Georgia recalled.

"If he accepted my advice, he's been cautious with girls." Charlie rubbed his chin.

Georgia caught his intention. "What else does he like?"

"His new guitar, his bike...and recently he's been interested in social justice, racism, all that stuff."

"He's growing too fast!"

"Yes, he is," Charlie agreed.

"It's so cute. How many kids his age worry about social problems?"

"White kids, you mean," Charlie said. "That's what he complains about. He thinks that we live in an unreal world, where we whites only see our kind."

"Perhaps he's going to be someone engaged in changing the world, maybe a president of the United States."

"Well, he definitely is a great kid, but I'd rather that he focus on his studies and leave the social justice for politicians." Charlie took a sip of his wine. "I need to add that he has an adventurous spirit. I guess he got that from you."

Feeling proud, Georgia took another sip of her wine. "And, what have you fellows done?"

"Well, nothing extraordinary. We used to play baseball, go fishing, and grow vegetables in my backyard. In the fall, we spent lots of time at the fair, and in the winter, we hibernated like bears. But now that he's fifteen, we don't spend much time together. He has his friends, his new girlfriend..."

"You still grow vegetables!"

"Yep, you should see my garden," Charlie was proud. "I've been busy lately with a new method of growing plants using mineral nutrient solutions in water, without soil."

"Did you invent it? How does it work?"

"It's not new, maybe older than this wine," he said humbly. "You know that plants absorb essential mineral nutrients in water? In natural conditions, soil acts as a mineral nutrient reservoir but the soil itself is not essential to plant growth. Plant roots, actually, absorb mineral nutrients in the soil when they dissolve in water, so if you introduce the required mineral nutrients into a plant's water supply artificially, you don't need soil to make them grow. You can grow vegetables, for instance, indoors..."

Charlie trailed off, and the light on his face faded. "Speak of the devil," he said, gazing at the front door. Georgia turned her head and saw Marty walking into the diner, and then stared back at Charlie.

This is not supposed to happen. Can you please contain your anxiety? Charlie thought, looking into her eyes.

Don't worry, Charlie; he doesn't know, Georgia thought in response.

During this silent conversation, Marty traveled from the front door to their table. "Hi, Dad." Marty looked surprised to see the strange woman who had helped him earlier. "Hey, I guess I should thank you for what you did," he said to Georgia, "though I could've handled it."

Georgia gave him a friendly smile. "No problem."

"Why did you do that?" Marty inquired.

"That kid owed me." She shrugged.

"She is awesome, Dad. You should see how she put Ray down."

"Who's Ray?" Charlie gave Georgia a curious look.

"Doesn't matter," Marty said, fidgeting. "Can you lend me a dollar or two, Dad? I'm going to hang out with my friends. You can take it out of my allowance."

Charlie stretched his neck to see the friends inside a car in the parking lot. He reached his pocket, took a couple of dollars from his wallet, and handed to Marty. "I'll see you tomorrow at 3:00 at your Grandma's," he reminded his son.

"Grandma told me," Marty said. "What's it about?"

"I'll let you know. But it's very important that you'll be there okay?"

"Okay," Marty agreed suspicious. He glanced at his friends through the window signaling him to hurry. "I gotta split now." He said a brief goodbye, and sprinted out.

"It seems that you're getting along well with him," Charlie commented.

"It's just fate working." Georgia took another sip of wine.

Fate again! Charlie wondered how she could be so confident. What if Marty didn't want to have a mother? What if he didn't forgive her? Did she ever have a plan B?

"You were telling me about your garden."

"I told you many things already. It's your turn now."

"Okaaay. What do you want to know?"

"Well, anything, about acting, about living in LA. You can tell me your best moment, your worst..."

Georgia took a moment to find something newsworthy in the pages of her story. "I think that my best moment was when I first stepped on an empty stage and clearly felt like it was for me; I can tell you the story, but I can't describe in words the sensation I had. If there's such a thing as reincarnation, I'd say I had a reencounter with my past life on that stage. It was clear for me that I'd been there before. I could feel the whole place pulsing, alive, and I was there only standing in the middle of an empty theater."

"I don't know much about reincarnation; I don't believe in

it. I rather believe that maybe it was just your calling."

"Maybe, but I like the idea of living different lives. Let's make a deal: If I die before you, I'll come back to tell you whether it exists."

"Okay," Charlie smiled at her fantasy. "And what was the worst moment?"

Georgia smiled with the memories that came across her mind. "Okay," she said, getting settled. "It wasn't a comedy, just a regular drama from the nineteenth century. I had a long scene with the main character, a grouchy old man who could not handle it if things did not go exactly as rehearsed. When I entered the scene one evening, something inside my right shoe was stabbing the back of my sole. As I walked, it worsened. Then I had the idea to drop my folding fan, so I'd have an excuse to crouch and remove whatever it was."

"Uh, Very smart," Charlie praised.

"Thanks," she said, holding her laugh. "But here's the best part: when I crouched, the man was in the middle of his longest line. He stopped to see what I was doing with my index finger inside my shoe trying to fish out the little thing. He signaled me to stand up, and I signaled him back to keep saying his line. The audience started to whisper. I finally reached a tinny piece of nut that probably got stuck in my hose when I was changing my outfit in the dressing room. The man was impatient, and came closer to me, and pulled my arm to stand me up. My glove got stuck in my shoe. I had to finish the scene without my right glove which was hanging on my right shoe."

Georgia laughed broadly, showing her dimples. Charlie laughed too, thinking how much he missed moments like this with her. She hadn't changed a bit.

He wished that it could be simple like that, like the joy they share together, the words that never were so easy to say, the easy laugh...

The conversation shifted from one subject to another. They

ordered food, and enjoyed the rest of the night around memories from the school days, his days in college, her's in LA. All bad memories seemed to disappear for a moment.

When they left the diner, rain was still pouring. Charlie offered to take her to her car parked fifty feet away. He put his arm around her shoulder to hold her closer, underneath the umbrella.

A man, trying to open the door of his car across the street, recognized Charlie. "Hello, Charlie," the man waved.

"Hello, Dan," Charlie responded without much affection.

"I told you. It's her, isn't it?" the man said with an open smile.

Georgia was curious. Was he the one who told Charlie that she was in town? Then she recognized an old friend from high school. "Danny, is that you? Oh golly, you became a man," she said.

"Hello, Georgia. Nice to see you again," the man said. "Hey, Charlie, why don't you bring Georgia to Concordia tomorrow night?"

"I'll see you, Dan. Keep yourself dry," Charlie said, dismissing him.

"Great! I'll see you, Charlie. It'll be a superb night."

"I didn't say 'I'll see you then,'" Charlie corrected him. "I said 'I'll see you, Dan.'"

The man didn't seem to mind. "If he doesn't want to go, just let me know where to find you, Georgia."

"Bye, Dan," Charlie insisted.

The man entered his car and left with the same open smile.

"He just wanted to be nice," Georgia said.

"He was always a gossip. I don't like him."

"But it is a good idea. I'd like to see the Concordia again. I don't remember the last time I went to a dance."

"This is a bad idea..."

They reached the car. Georgia motioned to him to open the

passenger door so she did not have to go around the car and get her shoes soaked in the water. After Charlie opened the door, instead of getting into the car, she stopped and turned to Charlie, her face close to his. She stared at him for a moment, and he tried to avoid her gaze, but she touched his cheek gently, and turned his face right to her then kissed him.

The sweetness of her lips took from Charlie the will to resist. He became still. He had wanted this kiss for so long, but he wasn't ready yet. He wanted to save it for the right moment, when all doubts and concerns were gone, and he could kiss not only her lips, but also her soul.

She removed her lips from his, scanning his face for his emotions.

"You'd better go," Charlie said, in contrast to her expectations.

She nodded, lowering her gaze, and started to get into the car. But, once again, she stopped and turned back to him. "I'll never leave you again, Charlie," her voice was pleading, "only if I die."

Charlie stared at her. "You're not good at keeping promises."

"I'm not good at many things, Charlie, but I'm willing to learn by your side," she said. "All I'm asking is a chance, and I'll prove to you that I mean every word I'm saying. We can start over. We can even have another child, and I'll never skip one sunset without giving thanks to God for having a family with you."

Charlie seemed disturbed with her unexpected proposal, her voice raising, pleading and persuasive. "You had good reasons, fifteen years ago. Why should I believe you now?" Resentment rose in his voice.

"Because I never lied to you, Charlie," she replied in the same persuasive tone. "I could not tell you at the time when I found out I was pregnant, but I came back because I knew how happy you'd be. And I had no plans to leave Marty; I just did it because I knew he'd be safer here with you. I never meant to have another man in my life, either. It just happened, but I was never really with him, because all I could think and see and feel was you. And that poor man was trying to move the earth to make me happy." She paused. "I wanted to come back—oh gosh, how I wanted to! I was afraid of making more mistakes; I had to do the right thing." Her voice softened, "I couldn't foresee how long it would take."

Charlie was silent and angry. All he wanted was to believe in her and be able to say it to her. He turned his head and gazed vaguely through the raindrops. His heart tightened with the memories of the days when he had to overcome sadness and anger to be a good father, a good man, and not utter a curse against God. He didn't want to open his mouth to his resentment because bad things would be said, and it would hurt her badly. "You'd better go," he repeated. It sounded more like advice.

The expectation on her face faded. "You're right," she said with sadness shading her expression.

Charlie eyes were wet as she drove off. "Easy come, easy go," he repeated to himself on his way back to his car. *Gosh, it would be easier if she'd never come back*, he thought, feeling the same deadly sensation he had on the day she left; the day when he cried like a heartbroken child, and got drunk for the first time in his life.

When he reached his car, he threw the umbrella inside the vehicle, and raised his face to catch the rain. Releasing the distress of fifteen years of silent and agonizing waiting, he screamed at the top of his lungs.

Chapter 24

Rain was falling in a drizzle the next afternoon, when Georgia left the hotel. She cursed the weather, realizing that her feet had not been dry since she arrived in Connecticut. She grabbed an extra pair of shoes to match her navy blue dress.

On her way to Mrs. Baker's house, she took deep breaths to cast out the butterflies fluttering in her stomach. She drove under the train tracks, past the Mallory Hat Factory, and the hill to number 100. She parked in front of the house, behind Charlie's Ford. Looking closer now, she noticed that the house had been well kept up, if not modernized. She rested her soaked umbrella on the new wooden rocking chair on the porch.

Charlie came out to welcome her. He was wearing a dark gray suit. Georgia had no idea what the occasion might be but she liked to see him in a suit; he'd become a very attractive man.

"Hi," he said with a glow in his eyes, noticing her ability to highlight her beauty in hairstyle and makeup.

"Hi," she forced a smile, hoping that his mood had changed overnight.

"Nervous?"

"About to die."

"Don't worry; she's in a good mood."

"Can someone be in a good mood in this weather?"

He raised his brow. "I'm sorry about last night."

She shook her head slightly. "No, I'm sorry. I should be more…smart."

Charlie nodded. "Let's get this over with."

As soon as Georgia crossed the threshold, she met Mrs. Baker's gaze. She was standing in the living room with Ellie by her side.

"How're you doing Mrs. Baker?" Georgia said. Charlie's mom had aged considerably. She was in her sixties now, her hair thinning to gray, and her lips cracking. Wrinkles had started to deepen around her mouth. But her eyes were still two vivid chestnuts, signaling her unbeatable spirit.

"Living day by day," Mrs. Baker answered, and her voice sounded enigmatic.

Ellie had become a pretty, grown up woman, resembling Charlie. She gave a broader smile to Georgia and pulled her into a warming hug that caused Georgia's nerves to relax.

Georgia scanned the house, noticing the changes. A new sofa set covered in mustard yellow fabric surrounded a twenty-one inch Admiral television. The curtains were the same, though sun-faded now. Framed pictures hung all over the wall, above the piano, and on top of the china cabinet. Small decorative wooden birds on the windowsill and some plants here and there completed the decorations. Georgia thought that if Mrs. Baker cared about Marty's education as much as she cared for the house, her son couldn't be in better hands.

"So, you came to bring us rain?" Mrs. Baker joked, trying to fill the silence after the greetings.

"I wish I had the power," Georgia replied. "The paper says the area is safe from the water now," she added. "Thank God! It seems to be the topic of the day in town."

"I don't trust the paper," Charlie declared. "They say that, but it's still raining. According to them, it was supposed to be a clear sky by now. I don't see any sign that it will clear soon."

"Maybe they just want to give hope to people," Ellie said.

"Hope." Charlie snorted. "They may be just wrong this time." Charlie was nervous with the endless rain, afraid with the possibility of another August.

"Why don't we have a seat?" Mrs. Baker invited.

They settled on the sofa set.

Georgia looked around. Mrs. Baker sensed her concern and gave Charlie a look, as if asking him to take the lead.

"He was supposed to be here by now," Charlie said, showing signs of impatience. "It seems that he didn't take me seriously."

"He left the house this morning. He's probably with his girlfriend; she's the only thing he cares about now." Ellie sounded jealous, just like Charlie the night before.

"What about you, Ellie?" Georgia probed. "No boyfriend? Look at you, so grown up, and so pretty! How old are you now, twenty, twenty-one?"

Ellie thanked her with a shy smile. "I'll be twenty-one in the spring."

"Oh my gosh! I'm getting old," Georgia said, glad that Ellie hadn't forgotten her, which might be expected from the five-year-old girl she had been the last time she saw Georgia.

"I still have the teddy bear," Ellie said.

"Aw... I wanted to bring you another one, but I realized that it would no longer be appropriate."

"I guess it wouldn't," Ellie smiled, her eyes shining with admiration.

"So, what have you been doing, Georgia? Done with pursuing your dreams?" Mrs. Baker said, not as kindly as Ellie. "Charlie told me about your father, I'm sorry."

"Thank you, Mrs. Baker. I've been through a lot, and now, I guess I just want to settle down."

"It sounds like you need a vacation." Mrs. Baker sniffed.

"I know what you mean, but it's more than that," Georgia replied in a calm tone. "I don't expect forgiveness for what I did, Mrs. Baker. All I want is a chance to prove that my perspective on life is different now."

"Are you famous?" Ellie couldn't contain her curiosity.

Georgia smiled. "No, Ellie; I jumped ship before fame caught me."

"But you're an artist now?" Mrs. Baker insisted. "Once an artist, always an artist! How can you give up your dream?"

"My dream charged me a price that I can't afford," Georgia replied serenely and changed the subject. "Marty looks great! I want to thank you for all that you have done for my son."

"I did it all for my grandson," Mrs. Baker replied promptly. "He had all the love a child needs, but if thanks need to be given, it should come from both sides. Marty is the best thing that happened to this house."

"I'm sure that Marty had the best from you. You have a beautiful family, and I hope I can learn from you," Georgia replied.

Mrs. Baker glanced at Charlie. "Marty is in this period of life they call 'the teenage years'," she raised her eyebrows in annoyance. "You know, a time of questioning and rebellion. Despite this, he's doing great so far. But the last thing he needs now is a mom who cannot handle his demands. I hope you have more to offer than a short stay."

"You can rest easy, Mrs. Baker. I have no reasons to leave again. Even if I had, I accomplished all that fate required of me."

"Are you rich?" Ellie interfered once again.

Georgia smiled in response to Ellie's innocence.

"Why don't you go to check on the laundry?" Mrs. Baker rebuked Ellie.

"What's wrong, Mom? People from Hollywood are rich."

"Well, I've been there once. For a tour only," Georgia answered patiently. "But all that I have is a reasonable amount in my savings and that car outside."

Ellie seemed disappointed. Mrs. Baker's dirty look prevented her from asking further.

"Would you like something to drink? Coffee, juice..." Mrs. Baker offered politely.

"Maybe you want to try the pumpkin pie I just made," Ellie jumped up.

"That'll be great," Georgia answered, with a grateful look at Ellie.

While the women were talking about recipe secrets over the pie, Charlie was impatient, going to check out the window several times, in hope that he would see Marty arriving. Rain was still falling uninterrupted.

A few minutes later, Charlie reached his limit, and asked Ellie to join him to search the town.

"You know the places he usually hangs out," he said.

Ellie made her way to the car in disappointment; she wanted to stay and enjoy Georgia's presence. Marty hadn't told the family about his girlfriend. They had no clue about where she lived, her parent's phone number, or how serious their relationship was.

Georgia stayed with Charlie's mom in the living room, enjoying her last piece of pie under Mrs. Baker gaze.

"I'm glad you're here," Mrs. Baker confided, surprising Georgia. "I'm not going to hide from you that if it was only for me, I would have things the way they are. But I'm a mother too, and I understand that some things in life need to be settled. I'm not saying that it'll be easy for you or for Marty. I can't tell whether he no longer thinks about you or if he's just trying to put you out of his mind. He doesn't talk about you. You've been nothing else but a ghost mother to him."

Georgia nodded, this time she did not know what to say.

"With Charlie it won't be any easier," Mrs. Baker continued. "You hurt my son badly, more than once, and I hated you for that. But as time went on, I saw Charlie building his life around his hope. He bought a house expecting that at any time soon you'd come back. He never said that, but it was always clear to me by the way he decorated the house, his care with the flowers. Charlie is a man with a big heart, but stubborn. He's still young, but not young enough to be alone.

He never loved any other woman, and I can tell you that many girls attempted to win his heart, but he chose rather to focus on college, and then on work."

Georgia strived not to grin. Charlie was an amazing man, and a man with that kind of love was rare. She felt honored that all that love was for her. Anything required to win his heart and his confidence again she was ready to do.

"Many times I wished you'd come back," Mrs. Baker continued, "not because I believed you could make my son happy—of that I'm not sure—but I wanted him to see who you are." She paused. "Who are you, Georgia?" Mrs. Baker's voice sounded challenging. "You don't have to tell me, but you have the opportunity to show Charlie who you are. You'd better do good things this time, or you may lose him forever."

Georgia's joy faded from her face, and she swallowed hard. She thought of saying things in her defense, exposing her plans, telling how much she had suffered at a distance, and how much she wanted to be with Charlie. She admired Charlie's mom, her sincerity, her authenticity, and above all, her broad view of all situations. Her words provide a road map you can rely to reach your destiny.

The conversation went on, now in a different direction. Mrs. Baker shared some memories from Marty's childhood. Then she left the living room for a minute, and brought with her a photo album that caused Georgia's eyes to shine. The photos were an illustration of the stories she just heard from Charlie's mom, precious moments of her son's life, that Georgia had irrevocably missed. Charlie in the pictures made her sigh more them once, and she wished she could go back in time to take that sadness from his gaze.

"Be patient with Charlie. A wounded man needs time to work out his resentment," Mrs. Baker advised. "My suggestion is that you take it slowly. Try to bring back the joy you had together in the past. Bring back the memories of your first date, and talk about things you both said and believed, and why you chose each other. Talk about what makes you a strong couple and how being together, now as parents, will make you even stronger. Good memories need to overlap the bad ones in order to repair the foundation of your relationship."

Georgia smiled, relieved, feeling Charlie's mom to be an ally.

Charlie and Ellie came back after an hour of unsuccessful searching. Charlie was visibly unsettled, and, as evening approached, he told Georgia that they decided to postpone the meeting to the next day. He wanted to go out, breathe fresh air, and cool off before he lost his temper. He told his mom to keep Marty in the house when he came back.

At nightfall, he asked Georgia if she wanted to go somewhere. She was disappointed that they were leaving without her seeing and talking to her son, but she still had plenty of stamina to enjoy a night with him, hoping that it potentially could turn into a romantic date.

"Aren't you worried that something happened to him?" Georgia expressed her concern.

"If I did, I'd have gray hair at this point," he said, quite upset. "Marty is an independent kid; he makes decisions on his own and lets us know later."

"But a kid his age, who doesn't bother anyone to wake him up for school and fixes his own breakfast, deserves credit," Mrs. Baker intervened.

"That's so cute!" Georgia was surprised. "Does he do it well? I mean, does he know the importance of a healthy meal in the morning?"

Charlie gave her a curious look. "Yes, Mom."

Chapter 25

"Of course I want to go," said Georgia, after Charlie mentioned the Concordia as an option for their night. "I'm excited to see if it's still the same."

"Really? What do you know about that place?" Charlie asked, without taking his attention from the wet road.

"Well, I know that it's a German Renaissance-style edifice, built in 1914, and cost about fifty thousand dollars, and it is equipped with the latest and most improved sanitary plumbing."

"Wow! I'm impressed. Have you been there before?"

"Just once, with a friend in..." She turned up her gaze, reaching out her memories. "...1938, I think. I like the history behind old buildings, and this one is very unique in town."

"Yes, it really is."

"By the way, how can you get access? Concordia is only for people of German descent."

"Not any more. Five years ago, they opened their doors to everyone in the community. I have my membership, and I still go there, once in a while, to play shuffleboard with my fellows. I used to like the downstairs barroom, but not since I quit smoking. I got sick of people smoking on my nose."

"I didn't know you smoked. But I'm glad that you quit," she praised.

"Oh boy, I started it in the army and smoked for a few years."

They reached the two story golden brick building with "Concordia" in gold lettering above the front entrance. The music could be heard from the parking lot adjacent to the building.

"I'm afraid that I'm not dressed properly," Georgia said.

"You're beautiful," he said, making her eyes shine like diamonds. But she couldn't find joy in his face.

"What is it?" Georgia said, noticing that he was reluctant.

"Not sure if this is a good idea." He looked at the rain, resting his hands on the steering wheel. "We're going to see people that we met before. Maybe it's too soon…"

Georgia sensed his concerns. "I understand if you don't want to go there." She was sad. "But I want you to know that it'd be very special for me. Maybe we can have one single dance and leave."

Her voice was soft, as irresistible as her Marilyn Monroe melting eyes.

"One single dance and we leave," Charlie stipulated.

Charlie checked his wristwatch. It was almost 8:00 p.m. and rain was pouring harder. He opened the car door followed by her, and rushed out to the club, holding Georgia tight under the umbrella.

A good number of people attended the party, considering the bad weather. When they got into the building, the small band on the stage was playing the Glenn Miller big hit "In the Mood" when they approached the dance floor.

"Would you like a drink?" he asked settling at a table.

"Yes, please, A Martini."

Charlie gave her a curious look. "What's the thing with Martinis?"

"Well, if I tell you what I saw people up to after only two Martinis you wouldn't believe."

"Uh, I will never be surprised with human madness, not after the Nazis."

"This is different. They don't make war when they drink; they only get silly and spontaneous."

"Have you been…'spontaneous' before or silly?"

"Just once. You know, drinking is part of the social game,

and some people judge your talent by the way you hold your glass. You have to be 'cool' or at least pretend that you are; otherwise you're out."

"I can't picture you in this scenario."

"Me neither now. Life in LA feels like it was on another planet, different from the rest of the country. That's why I'm here; I belong to this planet."

Charlie smiled, glad that, after all, she had found her way back to him, and she smiled back.

Charlie waved for the waiter and placed the order, deciding on a Martini, as well.

The music was inviting, and the dancers glided by, as if floating on clouds.

"Well, here we are," Georgia said, with an undisguised ulterior motive.

"Yes, here we are," Charlie assented, pretending he didn't notice, though he couldn't wait to have her in his arms on the dance floor. He thought that it'd be better to have a drink first; he hadn't danced for a long time now, but the band was playing "Unforgettable", so he stood up and offered a hand to Georgia. "C'mon snake, let's rattle!" He said with a wink.

They slid on the dance floor. Charlie held Georgia's waist with confidence, and soon, they were whirling gracefully, just like old times.

Her body moving sensually and so close, the warmth of her sweaty palms, her perfume filling his lungs and becoming part of his breath, and her heart pounding against his chest, was trance inducing. Charlie knew that one single dance wouldn't be enough to satisfy fifteen years of longing.

Georgia surrendered in his arms, feeling that this dance was a metaphor for the way she was picturing her life with him: safe, free, and with joy in every movement. His hand on her waist lit a flame that soon spread through her whole body.

When the song was finished, they had no desire to be

separate again. But the musicians announced a break, promising a rock-n-roll sequence afterwards.

Charlie kept Georgia's hand in his, and guided her through the couples on the dance floor. Someone tapped his shoulder. "Hey, Charlie! Good to see you again," said a voice from behind. He turned, and saw Danny, the man who told him about Georgia's arrival. Charlie's expression was one of annoyance, and he didn't make any effort to disguise it. "Hey, Dan, what's up?"

The man looked at their hands in a loving clasp and nodded knowingly. "Hi Georgia," he said. "This is a very special night for this town." He was excited.

"Okay, Dan, I'll see you later." Charlie turned away.

"C'mon, Charlie, you'll want to listen to this," Dan insisted, holding Charlie by his shoulder. "We're going to have an unexpected high school reunion tonight."

"Not interested." Charlie started to leave again, but this time Georgia held him back.

"Wait a minute, Charlie," she said. "What is it, Danny?"

The man had a mysterious expression. "Well," he said, "I knew you fellows could possibly be here tonight, and I made a few calls."

Georgia's eyes sparkled. "Seriously? And who's coming?"

The man listed names that brought more excitement to Georgia's face. Charlie though, didn't seem to be in the same mood.

"If you follow me to my table," Dan said, "we can check if I forgot someone."

Charlie and Georgia had a brief silent conversation. Her pleading eyes won out.

They made a quick stop at their table to grab their Martinis, and followed Dan to his table. Georgia instantly recognized five old fellows in their thirties: Frank Taylor, the football player; Barbara Thompson; her best friends Betty Stuart, and Marie Lan; and Bob Marinaro, the comedian.

The girls greeted Georgia with cheer, and they exchanged compliments over their looks, while the men invited Charlie to pull up a chair.

"We, in fact, had our ten-year reunion six years ago," Danny said to Georgia. "But, for this special night, I decided to get rid of the squares, and only include the coolest cats."

The others exchanged looks, knowing that they were the only ones who had patience with Danny's goofy ways. Thanks to their tolerance and acceptance of him in the group, Danny got rid of the bullies, and safely made his way through his high school years.

"You look gorgeous, Georgia," Frank said. "I bet you have a lot to tell as an actress in LA."

"Be careful with what you say," Betty warned Georgia. "Frank is now a writer for *The News-Times*."

"Don't worry, Betty," Georgia replied in the same tone. "I know how to deal with his kind."

"So, you might consider an interview," Frank teased.

"I'll give you my agent's card," Georgia joked. She was happy to see them again; they were on the bright side of her memories. "I want the updates, folks. Who married who, how many kids...? Betty, did you marry Rick?

"I got married to a decent man, and I have two kids," Betty answered, "Rick and I broke up after high school. He was a cheater."

Betty's answer made Barbara uncomfortable. Georgia knew she had always had a crush on Rick.

"Well," Marie Lan said. "I got married, and I also have two kids. And my husband is..."

"Chuck Solomen!" the girls completed with one voice.

"No! Our biology teacher?" Georgia was astonished.

"C'mon, girls," Bob intervened, "let's talk about something less girlish."

"Like what, Mr. Comedian?" Betty challenged him.

"Well, what about Eisenhower's plans for the highways?"

he suggested.

"Politics?" Barbara rejected. "You're joking as always."

Charlie showed little interest in the conversation. The unexpected reunion wasn't in tune with his plans for this night. He looked around, trying to find a convincing excuse to drag Georgia out of that place, and noticed unusual commotion by the entrance. He got Frank's attention and discreetly pointed to a rain coated, helmeted fireman trying to make his way through the crowd. Both men went to check on the entrance. The fireman headed to the barroom located in the basement, causing rumor amongst the parties in the main hall.

The brick walled, low ceiling barroom was packed with a group of formally dressed ladies and gentlemen who gave no credit to the bad weather and decided to enjoy this Saturday night. It looked like some sort of private party.

The bartender told the fireman that the water from the storm sewer was backing onto the floor in the boiler room, threatening the heating unit. The fireman's presence made the people at the bar uncomfortable. One of them called out: "Hey, these people are traumatized by the last flood. Do you want to scare them again?" The fireman looked around to identify the arguing gentleman, and replied in a scary tone: "I wouldn't be here if it wasn't necessary, believe me. And if I were you, I'd consider getting out of here."

Charlie gazed at Frank in disbelief. They visually followed the fireman entering the boiler room and immediately coming back with a shadow over his expression: "The flood water needs to be pumped immediately. And everyone in this basement needs to leave," he told the bartender.

"These gentlemen are always too cautious and dramatic. We're not in a mood for a hero." A man at the counter grumbled.

Charlie and Frank approached the boiler room entrance. The fireman asked them to make room as he started to pull the suction hose through the basement window from the driveway. Charlie started to offer help, but the frantic voice of another fireman on the pumper outside, on the driveway, urged them to leave. "Fast!" he yelled, but they had no time to react. The suction hose was hauled up, and dirty water cascaded through the basement window, flooding the entire barroom floor in the blink of an eye, soaking the parties' slippers and long dresses in the muddy water. The parties finally splashed out of the bar.

Charlie sprinted back to the ballroom and pulled Georgia by her hands. "What is it, Charlie?" she asked frightened, as Charlie walked fast, pulling her with him. "Another flood! We have to leave now." His voice was full of tension. He rushed with her through the ballroom, and when they reached the stair at the front door, he saw what he already had foreseen. The little Still River channel across the street had overflowed its banks, turning the street into a stream. The parties from the bar found their cars already awash over the hubcaps. The water was rising fast.

Their high school friends joined them at the front door.

"It seems that we have something to talk about at our next reunion," Bob said.

"This is not a time for joking, Bob," Betty scolded.

"I'm leaving," Frank stated. "I've got to go to the *News-Times*. Who's with me?"

Everyone decided to join Frank in an attempt to reach their cars. Charlie grasped Georgia's hand to hold her back. "Wait," he said. "My car can't make it through this water. We'll have to soak our feet a bit."

Georgia gazed him, with fear growing inside.

"Don't be afraid," he said. "This is the lowest area of the town; we can easily reach the corner, and go around the block, where surely it is dry and safe."

Charlie knew from the August flood how the river would behave. "The two branches of the river meet there," he pointed to the left corner of the street, "so we want to go the opposite way."

He was the first to step into the water that now reached over his knees. He offered a hand to Georgia, who stepped gingerly into the icy cold water.

Charlie held her hand tight, feeling the pressure of the water against his legs, and they began to walk. A few cars were making it through the water. Most were stranded.

When they reached the corner, Charlie watched stores and houses on Main Street by Wooster Square under the water. The water had risen to the level of his thighbone now. The rain was still pouring and the ever-widening river had turned the cold night into an end of the world scene.

Georgia was tired and shivering, and Charlie took off his coat and gave it to her to put over her jacket. One more block of strenuous effort and they reached a dry area. Charlie took time to look back, while Georgia was catching her breath.

"Oh, boy!" he said perplexed. "This cannot be happening again."

Georgia embraced him, leaning her head on his chest, trying to comfort him, and at the same time getting some heat from his body.

"You okay?" He asked, feeling her shiver.

"Yes, just tired."

Charlie squeezed her against his chest gently, watching the river running powerfully in the darkness, widening through the town as an intruder that came back to steal the remained wealthy of the merchants, and to mercilessly hit their stricken souls. He silently cursed the weather forecasters and the newspaper, which had reported they were safe and free of serious damage. "They were just wrong this time," he mumbled.

They walked around the block towards Charlie's house, Georgia in bare feet, hanging her high heels over her shoulder. They had to step again into the shallow water in the front yard to enter the house. Charlie turned the lights on (the electrical main service panel was out of reach of the water), and Mr. Bogart came to greet him and lick his hands. He told Georgia they needed to carry every possible thing in the house upstairs: the food from the pantry and from the fridge, the rugs from the living room, and the pillows from the sofa set. He took special care with the Victrola and his records. They put the china on the top of the buffet and the cushioned chairs on top of the dining table. As the water began to come in the front door, Georgia tied up the curtains at a height the water hopefully wouldn't reach. Charlie seemed to know exactly what to expect, and they worked efficiently to save as much as they could in the house.

After they had done all they could, Charlie ran his hand through his hair in disbelief. Standing in the middle of the living room, he cursed the water that reached a foot inside the house.

Upstairs, with the dog, Georgia took time to visit Marty's room, to learn a little more about her son. She opened the door and turned the lights on, noticing that he was as organized as his father. She stared at every detail. His bed was carefully made. Posters of James Dean and Space Patrol were glued side by side on the wall over his pillow. She smiled, sharing his admiration for the recently deceased actor. At the foot of the bed, leaning against the wall, were a baseball bat and his guitar. She stood still for a moment, feeling the vibration of the teenage decorations, her heart full with the hope that soon they'd be together as a family.

Charlie came after her, and when he came closer, she turned, hearing the creaking floor underneath his steps behind her. "You should change your wet clothes," he said, handing her a towel and a warm sweater. "I have some pants that you can try. At least they are dry and clean."

"Are we staying?"

"We're safe in here."

"Aren't you worried about Marty?"

"He's fine. He's probably backed home at this time."

"What about your mom? Is she safe?"

"The water will never go that high. There isn't much we can do for now."

Charlie barely finished his words, and Georgia took him by surprise with an ardent kiss. This time he embraced her waist without hesitation and accepted the kiss, relaxing into her arms, her warm body giving him the forgotten comfort of a woman's love.

The steady falling rain pelting the glass window reassured them that nothing else could be done at this moment in regards to the damage in the house, and they had no reason to fight the desire spreading through their bodies. Charlie brought Georgia in his arms to his bed and slowly freed her from the wet dress. Lightning had no time to crack the sky before he was inside of her, feeling the softness of her burning skin against his, and her body shaking with pleasure. Feeling the power of their love, Charlie finally understood that the past should definitely stay behind, and that keeping his defensive attitude any longer was only a waste of time.

When they finally came to stillness, Georgia rested her head on his chest, silently enjoying the relaxing sensation throughout her body. No words were said. Charlie's hand slowly massaged her neck.

Maybe one hour had past when the lights in the house flickered announcing that they were about to lose power, which in fact happened just few seconds later.

They got up and put on dry clothes. Charlie found a flashlight, and they went downstairs to assess the situation.

"I guess we have to get our feet wet again," Charlie said, standing on the last step above the water. "We'll freeze here over night."

"You should call your mom. She might be worried."

Charlie nodded, and soaked his feet in the cold water to

reach the telephone in the kitchen. He came back only few seconds later to report that the telephone was dead. He sat by her side on the steps in disappointment. Mr. Bogart came to join them and sat quietly by their side. Georgia leaned her head on Charlie's shoulder, watching the muddy water in the living room and the firewood floating around the fireplace.

"I'm so sorry for your house, Charlie."

"I feel sorry for my garden," he forced a smile. "I saw my neighbors going through this, and I guess it's my turn now. They got a foot last August, and I just had my floor wet. This time it seems even worse. What the hell have we done to God?"

"Tragic events happen all the time around the world," she pointed out. "Some randomly caused by nature, others by human insanity, like that stupid war. This is not about God."

He nodded and kissed her eyes tenderly, tightening her against his chest. Despite the tragic situation, Georgia felt fortunate for the special moment they unexpectedly had. She felt safe, as if the world outside could perform the worst catastrophe, and still nothing could take away the safety of Charlie's arms.

"Life is a joke," Charlie said. "I kept this house for all these years the way I promised you. The neighbors were surprised every spring by the new arrangement of bushes and flowers in the front yard. They said I should be a gardener; that as a gardener, I'd be a rich man."

Georgia gazed at him tenderly, noticing that Charlie's stricken soul had finally emerged.

"Oh boy, I became obsessed with cleaning the house and keeping everything organized, to the point that Marty felt more comfortable at his grandma's. He said: 'I don't want to live in a military barrack, Dad'." Charlie paused, his voice echoing the dismay of his soul. "I scared my son."

"What you did was great, Charlie. Only a man with a special soul is able to do what you did." Georgia tried to show the brighter side.

"But you took so long, and this is all that I have to offer you now: a flooded, stinky house."

"What do you mean? Is this an invitation?" Her eyes glowed.

Charlie gazed around the water in the darkness. *Who on earth would consider this mess an offer? Only a woman with a true love for him would cheer with that,* he thought.

"No," he said. "But I guess you don't want to live in a hotel forever." He paused and stared deep into her eyes, as she shook her head in expectation. "What I mean is...I want to marry you. I want you to help me to bring our son back into this house."

In Georgia's eyes tears welled in bliss, and she kissed him, repeating between each kiss: "Yes... yes..."

Outside, the rain receded in celebration, promising an open sky with stars, and hope to the devastated town.

Chapter 26

Charlie and Georgia were astonished when they left the house in the middle of the night. People, stuck in their houses, were boarding dump trucks. A canoe, full of people, was sailing through the dark streets. Charlie was called by a friend and joined the rescue effort, while Georgia joined a group of women at a shelter the Red Cross had improvised at the Knights of Columbus Hall to provide food, hot coffee, and a warm bed to those who were homeless.

By daybreak, the whole town was awake, and the river was at its peak, running powerfully through the streets. The National Guard sent a rescue team and a helicopter, which hovered over the affected central area. Charlie went to meet Georgia at the shelter and watched the helicopter rescue a young boy, airlifting him from his apartment to the roof of another building.

Georgia came to meet Charlie at the entrance of the shelter.

"How are things going here?" He asked, looking at the people on the cots, and the white capped ladies from Red Cross performing their jobs efficiently.

"Under control," Georgia replied.

"You must be tired. Did you sleep at all?"

"Couple of hours, maybe. But I'm not tired. I'm afraid to sleep and find that what we had last night was only a dream."

"It was a dream," he smiled. "A good one!"

She smiled back. "Why don't you have a cup of coffee?"

"I'll take it. Then I'm going to check on the factory; would you come to my mom's? You need some rest."

Georgia took a moment and gazed around. "Okay. Have some bread too, while I tell them I'm leaving."

Charlie grabbed a cup of coffee and a piece of bread and in less than a minute, Georgia was back and ready. Charlie had borrowed a car from a friend; he drove the long way around to avoid the flooded streets. The area around the Mallory Hat factory was completely flooded, and the water had reached the first floor of the buildings.

Mrs. Baker's house was above the damaged area, as Charlie predicted, and Georgia's car was safely parked in front of the house.

"Go inside and rest," Charlie said. "There is something that I need to do at the factory." He squinted, taking account of the situation. "Last flood, Mr. Clear told me that it's one thing to lose some hats, and another to lose the accounts receivable. I'll see if I can save them."

Charlie kissed her, and began to walk down the hill to the factory.

"Charlie, Wait!" Georgia said with a bad feeling growing inside.

"What is it?" he turned, curious.

She had the desire to go with him or to make him to stay. They should not be away from each other, she thought. But maybe, it was only fatigue after the sleepless night. Maybe it was the whole tragedy proving how fragile life could be and how precious the moments of being safe with loved ones were. She could not identify the unexpected feeling growing in the shadows. But all she said was "Good luck!"

Charlie waved his hand, and Georgia stayed in the front of the house watching him walking down the street, until Marty came out of the house, pulling his bicycle.

"Good morning," Georgia said.

"Good morning," Marty replied surprised. "You're all over the place."

"I guess so..."

"Did you see that?" He referred to the flood at the factory.

"Yeah, that's sad. In town, things are even worse," she replied. "Where are you going so early?"

"I need to see someone... my girlfriend. She's home alone, her parents went on a trip for their anniversary. I'm worried that she may be in trouble."

"Does she live in town?"

"No, her parents moved to Georgetown."

"And you think you can reach there on a bike?"

"I have no choice; the damn telephone is dead."

Georgia gazed at him for a moment, amazed at his courage. The ride would take thirty minutes by car, but on that bike, he'd spend at least half of his morning. It could be an excellent opportunity to spend time with him and take a better look at the girl he was hiding from his family. "I can offer you a ride," she said, gesturing towards her car. "It's safer and faster."

"Is this car yours?" Marty was surprised. "It's a man's car...but it's cool." Marty hesitated. He wished he could go around to take a close look at the vehicle, but he needed to rush out. "I don't mean to bother you."

"Not at all," she replied, not minding the comment. "Put your bike back in the house, and give me the opportunity to do something nice for you, okay?"

Marty smiled and accepted her offer.

Georgia drove downtown to find a way to cross the river and to reach Route 7 safely. She had the feeling that the roads wouldn't be drivable, and she was glad that she didn't let Marty go alone on this adventure. When they crossed the town, she had a better view of the extent of the flood. Trucks were still engaged in the work of rescuing people from their flooded houses, as well as the helicopter overflying the area. The sleepless town had plenty of people on each of its corners by the edge of the water, curious and astonished. The once small and invisible Still River was still running powerfully through the streets.

Marty was silent, and Georgia noticed that he was a little nervous, probably because it took several minutes for them to hit the road toward Georgetown, after a long zigzag through the streets. "Don't worry, we'll get there," Georgia said, disguising her disbelief.

"I never had a ride with a woman before," Marty confessed.

"Really? And how does it feel?"

"Safe, I guess."

Georgia smiled. Marty became silent, and seemed unsettled in the seat.

"So, your father was waiting for you yesterday," she probed. "He told me you were going to a have a family meeting..."

"I know," he sounded disappointed. "I couldn't make it."

"I bet you had a good reason."

"Diane is staying at her uncle's in Danbury while her parents are on the trip, but yesterday she asked me to go with her to check on her parents' house because people were afraid of a new flood. I couldn't take her on my bike, so we took a bus, and when I got back home, it was too late. Dad had gone." He turned his gaze to her. "Is he mad?"

"I think so. It seemed important to him." Georgia was worried, but afraid that she would sound like a parent. But she couldn't keep herself from asking, "And you stayed there alone with her until late?"

"I wanted to bring her back to Danbury, but she wanted to stay there. She's sixteen already. Her uncle and her aunt treat her like a little girl."

They became silent. Georgia wanted to go farther to satisfy her curiosity, but was unsure that she should. After a minute though, she couldn't contain herself any longer. "Do you know how babies are born?"

Marty gave her a wry look. "I know what you're thinking. Don't worry, I'm sixteen too."

"Not yet. You'll only turn sixteen this January," she said

before she could stop herself .

"January is in three months... How do you know that?"

"Your father..." She was embarrassed. "He told me." The last thing she wanted was to sound like a frightened judgmental parent. She wanted to be the one who he could totally rely on, so when the moment to reveal her identity arrived, he would accept her with no hesitation. But now she was feeling stupid; the blunder was catastrophic in her mind.

But Marty seemed unaffected. "Can I ask you a question?"

"Of course, you can," she answered quickly, in hope that it could be an opportunity to redeem herself.

"I trust you," he said, looking embarrassed at first. "You're hip, and..." he was hesitant. "I want to ask you something, but you can't tell my dad that I asked you."

"I can handle that." She was puzzled, but glad that she still had credit with him.

"Can a girl miss her period even if she isn't pregnant?" He said earnestly.

Georgia stopped breathing for a moment. Marty's words were practically a confession.

"Well... it can come late, but it eventually comes, if she isn't pregnant," she said, catching him from the corner of her eyes.

"Always?" he insisted.

Georgia gave him a compassionate look. His question triggered an uncomfortable feeling, and she knew that every time her son made a mistake in life, it would send her back to the guilt for her long absence. Being in the shadow at this moment, when Marty was trying to express his fears of a premature jump to such an adult responsibility was a punishment for her. "Are you in trouble, Marty?"

"No, just curious," he coldly disguised his concerns.

Georgia sensed that she could never be successful acting as someone she wasn't. She wasn't his best friend; she was his mother!

"You never told me your name," Marty said, dragging her out of her thoughts.

"You can call me Gigi..." she said hesitantly, recovering from the surprise.

"Are you dating my dad?"

"I guess so," she said, noticing that he didn't seem suspicious.

"You're cool. I hope my dad doesn't dump you."

Georgia gave him a curious look. He was chatty and smart. "What do you mean?" she asked.

"Well, I never get to know his girlfriends before they're gone. They never last more than a month or a few weeks..."

"So that's why you don't introduce your girlfriend to him either?"

Marty thought for a moment. "I will. It's just not the right time yet."

They became silent again, and Marty grew anxious with the safe pace Georgia maintained on the wet road. "Can you wail?" he demanded. "We'll never get there with this speed."

"You mean, speed up?" She translated his slang just to make sure she understood. "I don't think so..." she motioned at the road ahead.

The next stretch of the road was flooded, making it impossible to move forward. The water was still. It was only the expansion of a brook in the area, but it was widespread and of an undetermined depth.

They got out of the car. Marty looked around in search of a possible way to make it through the water. Georgia leaned against the hood of the car, feeling the fatigue of the sleepless night. "It seems that it won't be any better from this point," she said, discouraged by the obstacle.

"We can go back and take the next right. It seems to take us back to the water, but it goes up the hill instead. From there, we can come out the other side." Marty sounded skilled.

"You look so confident. How'd you know that?"

"I was a Boy Scout. You learn that when the obstacle is ahead you can get around or go over it."

"That's smart. How long were you a Boy Scout?"

"Five years. My dad was the leader of the troop. He was cool. He was trained by the army, but he never really went to the war."

"It sounds like you and he had lots of good times together."

"We did." Marty wandered through his childhood days. "But I guess I grew up. Things are different now."

"What things?"

"I don't know... He's obsessed with silly things like keeping the house clean, the care of the garden, his car, which has to always be shining... He always told me that people are more important than things, but I doubt he remembers it. When I was living with him, he was always tracking my steps to check if I put stuff away behind me." He paused. "Ellie said he's still waiting for my mom."

"What about you? Would you like it if she came back?"

Marty gazed the muddy water on the road. "I don't know. I don't think she ever will. I won't waste my life waiting."

Georgia felt her chest tighten, and anxiety spread through her. She'd promised Charlie she wouldn't reveal her identity yet, but fate had brought them together and the moment seemed so right for the conversation she'd dreaming about for such a long time. Charlie was the perfectionist who always created perfect situations for things to happen; she was the one who believed in fate. She opened her mouth to say something, but felt her energy low, after working all night. Maybe it was time to consider Charlie's perspective and be clever, she had to admit. Besides, Marty was focused on his girlfriend's safety.

She followed Marty's lead, and drove around through the back roads, eventually returning to the main road. "If I remember," she said, "soon we'll cross the Norwalk River. I have a bad feeling about it."

"I know," Marty agreed. "Yesterday, when I came home, it was almost up to the bridge and the firefighters were there."

She drove less than a quarter of a mile, and when they went down the hill, she had to slam on the brakes again.

"Holy cow!" Georgia mouthed.

This time the situation required more than a Scout's experience to overcome. The Norwalk River was furious and scary. The road totally disappeared under its wide, threatening bed. Bunches of bushes and debris were going by. A wooden fence by the side of the road was no more than five inches out of the water. From where they were, they had a wide view of the area, and not too far away, they saw an empty bus near a barn in the middle of a vortex. They got out of the car to watch the spectacle the river was performing against the rocks and trees on its way.

"This is it," Georgia said. "We have to go back; it's not safe to be on these roads."

"I guess so," Marty was disappointed, staring astonished at the water. "Diane is smart. She'll get to a safe place if needed," he said, trying to convince himself.

Georgia motioned to go back to the car, but Marty called her attention to something. "Jesus Christ!" Do you see that?" He pointed a small two-story house in the distance.

Georgia came closer and saw the house in its resistance against the current. "God, I hope there's nobody inside," she said.

Marty scanned the property in the distance. "I think I see something…" he grew anxious, "It looks like a person."

Georgia came closer, and followed his finger pointing into the property. "No," she said in disbelief. "Maybe it is just a poor dog… or a deer."

"We should check it out," Marty said decisively, frightening her.

Georgia took a closer look at the scene, and finally agreed that it could possibly be a person, and they couldn't leave without figuring that out. They got back into the car and she drove down the hill toward the flooded area. She carefully entered the driveway of the property and parked in a safe spot near the edge of the water. The house, twenty feet ahead, looked like it was built in the eighteenth-century. Small and fragile, surrounded by four feet of water, it was bending as if resisting bravely the power of the current.

Beyond the north side of the house, they saw what they were looking for. An old woman, frightened and shivering, was clinging to a tree. They waved to her, shouting words of encouragement.

"We should go to find help," Georgia said to Marty.

"It'll be too late till anyone gets here," he said gazing around. He saw a detached garage to the south of the house, and thought that he could find something there to help him reach the woman. Inside the garage, the water was high enough only to wet Marty's feet. He saw a wooden canoe hanging on a wall, and rushed back to Georgia to get her help to move it to the water. They put the canoe down and pulled it to the water.

"Have you paddled one before?" Georgia was visibly terrified.

Marty was shaking with nervous anticipation, but didn't want to tell her that he'd never been good at water sports. In his Boy Scout days, he always slipped away from the water activities. But, now was different. It wasn't a matter of choice; it was a real demand, a life-threatening situation. He was ready to overcome his fears and offer at least a little hope to this helpless woman.

"I have a plan," he said, running back to the garage to grab a thick-coiled rope he saw on a shelf.

Marty tied the rope to one end of the canoe and asked Georgia to tie the other end to the bumper of the car. He finished his side first and anxiously watched Georgia struggle to accomplish her task. For the first time he noticed the license plate of the vehicle, and a suspicious thought crossed his mind. He stared at her for a moment, and she could not understand the expression on his face, which, from a distance, seemed inappropriate for that situation.

"The rope isn't long enough to get there," Georgia said, after finishing her task.

"I'll use the canoe to reach the front door." Snapping out of it, he explained his plan. "You see that?" he pointed to the north side of the house. "Through the second floor, if I reach the roof of the back porch, I'll be very close to her."

Georgia considered it a crazy strategy, but fatigue and fear were sucking her capacity to measure things up fairly. She looked deep into his eyes and hugged him.

"Please, be careful," she pleaded. "I'll be here for anything you need."

"I know," he replied, and kissed her cheek. She touched her face puzzled, and they exchanged a meaningful look.

Marty pushed the canoe into the water with her help, and quickly paddled the twenty feet that separated him from the front door. He easily reached the door and pulled himself into the flooded house, the water reaching his chest. Georgia kept shouting for the woman, who did not answer back. "If Marty doesn't get there soon, it'll be too late for her," she thought.

A few seconds after Marty entered the house, Georgia heard a cracking noise coming from its frame. The house was collapsing from the level of water arising inside. The roof twisted with a scary sound, and she grew terrified. Why had she allowed Marty to attempt this crazy rescue?

The house was shaking under the pressure of the water. Georgia pulled the rope, bringing the canoe back to the edge. Getting into it, she rowed to the north side of the house where Marty would soon emerge. Her goal was to prevent him from going back inside. The current helped her reach the point where the rope stretched fully behind her, but this was still far from the point she wanted to reach. She had a closer look at the woman clinging to the tree, nearly giving up with exhaustion. Georgia shouted to encourage her, although, at this point, she was afraid that they wouldn't be able to reach her. A new cracking noise came from the twisting house and Georgia feared that even for her son, hope was questionable.

The house seemed to move as if announcing its collapse. She held the oars firmly, trying to bring the canoe back to the edge, but a big bush floating in the water made a barrier behind her. She grabbed the rope and tried hard to pull the canoe back, but her arms were shaking, and exhaustion hit her quickly. Georgia mouth was dry, a terrifying fear growing within her. The situation was out of control, and she knew that she was in irreversible trouble.

The house finally took off from its foundation, breaking its last attachment to the ground beneath the water. It began to move and collapse at the same time. The dead electrical wires whipped in the air, and a few short trees came down in the edge of the river, stricken by the movement of everything around the house. Georgia shouted to Marty in despair. The last thing she saw was the tree where the old woman had been, and she understood that her own destiny was going to be that of the woman. A tree fell over the canoe striking Georgia with deadly force.

The rising water invaded the driveway and Georgia's car floated away. The fallen trees, pulled by the house, sank the canoe and dragged the car together, leaving behind no traces that those two heroes, confronting their own limits, unsuccessfully attempted to save the life of a stranger, only to lose their own.

Chapter 27

The car was submerged half way in the water when the firefighters removed Anna and Marvin from inside the car. Ana's injuries weren't as bad as the damage to the vehicle. She had only a bump on the left side of her head and a small cut on her scalp. The blood on her face led the paramedics to the regular emergency procedures, immobilizing her neck and making her body steady on the stretcher. She came back to consciousness right when the firefighters reached her in the seat, and felt safe in those experienced arms, though she was worried because she couldn't feel her feet after they got immersed in the cold water, God knows how for long. For her, it felt like hours, but the firemen reached her no more than twenty-five minutes after the water began to rise slowly through the damaged doors of the vehicle.

She couldn't recall what happened immediately. Even Marvin hadn't come to her mind yet. Only when her body became warmer, did fragmented memories begin to pop up in flashes. The first thing that came to her mind was the therapy session she was rushing to make in time, and she lamented that she'd missed it. Then she remembered vaguely the strange presence of Ralph in the passenger seat, which came with the conclusion that it had only been a dream or a sort of delirium caused by the head injury. She tried to hold this memory and link it to the next, but all that came were confusing and disconnected.

Lying on the ambulance stretcher, she could see the stars in the sky up above and the lights of the fire trucks and the police cars spinning up like luminescent butterflies at a steady fast speed. She closed her eyes, blinded by the excessive brightness, and felt a smooth touch on her right arm. She opened her eyes again. A tall man in his red firefighter outfit and yellow helmet was standing by her side. She couldn't turn her head, but he wasn't the one who had touched her.

A child's voice close to her ear sounded like a warming breeze. "You're going to be okay, Mom."

She smiled, feeling Marvin's soft hand stroking her face. Marvin's presence finally came to her confused mind and she was relieved that he was safe.

"I saw you, Mom," Marvin said. "I wasn't alone, you were there with me."

His voice caused memories to cascade in her mind. Past and present were so blended that she couldn't tell in which she currently was. She understood she had just been rescued from the flooded river, and by some miracle, her son was safe despite the collapse of the house. The images were interchanging; she began to talk in a confused way, and when the paramedic asked her name in a regular procedure to assure that she was in her mind, she answered without hesitation: "Georgia Cordeiro."

At the hospital, her mind settled down. The consciousness of the present came back gradually, but during the medical procedures she was still absent, now purposely immersed in the vibrant detailed memories of the events in her past. Doctors couldn't get much information from her. They considered that she was in shock and sedated her. Then, they called the last call on her cell phone, and Lisa came right over.

Lisa called Larry, and he got in his car immediately, with Anna's parents in tow. When they arrived it was late at night, and Anna was sleeping deeply. Lisa told them all the details she heard from the doctors, but Larry only relaxed after talking to the doctor on duty. Dr. Lynch gave him a full report and managed to sound as if it was anything but serious. She wanted to check on Anna in the morning though, just to be sure.

While Anna's parents took Marvin home, Larry stayed, sitting beside Anna's bed. He fought against sleep until morning.

When the first morning lights crossed through the window, Anna opened her eyes and saw Larry by her side with a pale face. He held her hand gently, and made a sign that she didn't need to talk.

"Where's Marvin?" she whispered, with a bitter taste in her mouth.

"At home with your parents," Larry replied, pouring water in a glass and offering it to her. He held her head gently to help her to reach the precious liquid.

"My parents?" she asked after a sip.

"They came with me last night."

"How am I? Is everything okay?"

"Everything is okay. You just got few stitches on your head." He stared at her for a moment. His expression was a mix of compassion and guilt. "I'm sorry. I shouldn't have gone without you."

"It's okay. I've been busy, anyway."

"You never stop."

She cocked her eye as if to say that was just the way she was.

"I feel bad," Larry continued. "I mean, I had enough time to think about us, and I realized that I've been selfish and could've done more for you, for Marvin..."

Anna gazed at Larry with compassion. "What you've done is very special," she said, comforting him.

"What?" he was surprised. "What have I done that's special besides being skeptical and selfish?"

She took a moment to have a good look at him, trying to see through his lives. She was taken by the remembrance that he had been her supportive partner before, as if he was a sort of angel that kept coming to earth only to protect her, truly dedicating his life to provide her with comfort and safety.

She was intrigued that they never had a "perfect connection," the kind of connection that led to easiness in life. "Maybe he hasn't always been an angel," she thought. She could now play with possibilities; life was a complex and amazing network. What if Larry had had an unconscious commitment to compensate for some damage he did to her in the forgotten past? Wasn't that the way things worked? Maybe, what brought them together wasn't necessarily "love." Love had never been as natural for them as love was supposed to be for lovers. Maybe there were other reasons behind their lives, their reencounter as partners.

What mattered, she thought, was a sentiment beyond gratitude that she noticed growing inside at this moment. It was something so unexpectedly intense and, at the same time, so light. Then, she concluded, that if for whatever reason two souls found each other again like they did, love would also find its way to tie their hearts together, if only they would allow it. She admired him because he had chosen to love through a heroic life commitment, and it was about sacrifice and time spent together, not necessarily in romantic adventures, but mainly in support and companionship. Seeing life from this perspective, she thought, anything became possible. For no matter what reason they were together again, the kind of love Larry had for her could certainly perform major improvements in her own feelings as time went by.

The unexpected reflection brought back the images she had accessed during her first session with Ralph, about her life in France, in the nineteenth century, with Lisa and her cheater husband. She tried to grasp the connection of it all, but the images dissipated instantly, as if it wasn't for her to know.

"Are you okay?" Larry asked, noticing the change on her face.

"Yes..." She tried to shake off the sensation and be present.

"I know. My question is not easy to answer," he said.

"Yes, it is. You gave me the best thing I have. You gave me Marvin," she finally said in response. "And you're still here with me."

"Of course I am." He relaxed into a smile. "I will always be here; you're my wife."

She smiled back. "When can we go home?"

"Soon, I guess. The doctor said you were confused when they rescued you, and she wants to make sure that you're okay, you know, for safety, all that stuff they do when you hit your head." He paused. "What exactly happened there? They said that a driver behind you said you chose to avoid killing a deer; that was noble!" he spoke in jest.

"I know it sounds stupid. I guess I didn't want Marvin to witness his mother killing a deer. Mother's instinct. And it seems that it worked out. I'm still here, and the deer is with his family."

They exchanged a deep look, and though for different reasons, both were saying in their minds words of gratitude for Anna still being alive and for having each other. They still had an hour or so of private time before Lisa showed up for a visit. She had gone to get some sleep. "The Sleeping Beauty woke up," she said coming into the room.

Larry took advantage of Lisa's presence to go get something to eat.

"I doubt you'll find anything vegetarian for you in the cafeteria," Lisa warned. "I can ask them to bring you some fruit."

"Thanks, but I need something hot, and coffee, at least, they might have," he said heading out of the room. Although he was grateful for her help, he never felt comfortable in her presence.

Anna moved to the head of the bed to sit. Her head still felt a little heavy, but her body responded well. "Hey, thank you for your help last night."

"No problem. It's just one more thing you owe me," Lisa replied wryly.

"What do you mean?" Anna was surprised. "You sounded mad in the message you left on my phone."

"Mad? You lied to me for no reason, almost killed yourself and Marvin... I feel like I don't know you anymore."

"Why are you saying that? I never lied to you." Lisa was supposed to be familiar with accident stress, and have a more reasonable behavior, Anna was surprised.

"You lied about the therapist," Lisa replied quite upset. "What are you hiding from me? Are you having an affair?"

"You mean, about Doctor Stevenson?" Anna was puzzled. It was true she had never mentioned the crush she had on Ralph, but why would that make Lisa so mad?

"You should be smarter next time, and find someone still alive," Lisa said, meeting Anna's gaze. "I knew that I had heard his name before," she said to herself. "You made me feel like the most stupid person in the world. How could I not remember? He's Doctor Lynch's ex-husband, who died in a car accident a year ago with his son and his niece."

"What?" Anna was completely lost. "You must be wrong. It has to be someone else."

Lisa pulled a piece of paper out of her purse and handed to Anna. It was an article about a car accident with a photo. "I don't think that there are two therapists called Ralph Stevenson in a small town like Bethel."

Anna took the article and could not prevent tears from flooding her eyes. She grew pale, and was shocked looking at the man in the photo. *How can it be possible?* She kept repeating in her mind. Although the article explained his presence in her car, how it could explain his presence on all other occasions? In a fraction of second, Anna recalled his approach at the library and the things he had said to her since then: "We're never alone."

"How can it be possible?" she finally released her thoughts for Lisa.

"You're right," Lisa kept the same mood. "How can you possibly think that a silly lie—"

"This is him!" Anna cut her off.

"What???"

"You don't understand; it is him!" Anna repeated with startled eyes. "He might have a twin brother, or...wait a minute." She paused collecting her thoughts. "You said his son and his niece were in the car?"

Lisa nodded mutely, sensing that Anna's reaction was quite authentic. "Both died too."

Anna sobbed, as if that accident had just happened, and that man, who became more than her friend, had just passed away. She remembered when he told her about his life, things that he could not achieve with his wife, and it made her cry even harder, feeling his pain, in a mix of grief and compassion. She felt like she was grieving for someone she would never see again. "I spoke to him, just like I'm speaking to you now. He guided me through all this; he knew that my accident was going to happen and just appeared inside the car to lead me to what was probably our last session." She paused as her mind got caught up in a flash. "He must've guided Marvin through the trance the night Marvin told us about his own death..."

"You're saying that this dead doctor helped you? That is just..."

"Crazy! I know."

"It's amazing!" Lisa concluded with a surprising glow on her face.

Anna shrugged, and they stared at each other sharing how strange and amazing and surreal and unbelievable such an experience was.

"He said his ex-wife works here. I'd like to meet her," Anna finally said.

"Well, it's not that hard, since currently you're her patient."

Anna had the opportunity to meet Sara Lynch, when she came to check on her. In spite of the scrubs she wore, her face was attractive with a mixture of maturity and grace. She was smart and a good conversationalist, probably in her early forties.

Anna remembered Ralph's advice not to tell people what they were not prepared to hear. But she couldn't help mentioning Ralph, if only to asses Sara's willingness to talk about him.

"I met you ex-husband," she said when Sara sounded like leaving. "He was my therapist."

Sara gazed at Anna for a moment, and from her eyes, it was clear that what she was remembering was painful. She tried to disguise it with a faint smile. "Was he a good therapist? Did he help you?"

Anna nodded. "He couldn't be better; he changed my life."

"Good for you." Unable to contain her emotions, Sara left the room.

Later that morning, Anna was discharged, and once back home, she enjoyed the company of her parents, her son, and her husband. During the day though, she couldn't shake off Sara's gaze. She knew how precious family was, and imagined how devastating it would be losing them all together, even as a divorced woman. Ralph never sounded like all was finished between them. Sara still seemed lost, just like Anna was before meeting Ralph. Anna felt that the difference between them was that Sara chose to fight alone, while she, Anna, was open to grabbing the opportunity when Ralph offered it.

Chapter 28

Except with Lisa, Anna chose to be silent about what she had learned from Georgia's life. With her parents around, rare were the moments when she could retreat into a shell to review the vivid images in her mind and write them down in her diary. She knew she had accessed information about her past life that was not always available to a regular mortal—maybe for the monks from the Himalayas or for the masters of ancient cultures, but not for her, a regular housewife in the midst of a personal and a marital crisis. Ralph had opened a doorway to a reality that she never expected to experience in life, though she still was amazed that she could call it "reality". However, telling people about it and dealing with their skepticism was another thing. Moreover, it wasn't about the past anymore; it was now about what she would do with her future and the future of those who were a part of her life.

"Maybe someday I'll tell Larry and everyone else," she told Lisa one afternoon. "But I have no desire to do it now. Those are my memories, they belong to me, and sometimes I wonder if the day will come when I will doubt that it really happened."

"You could write a book," Lisa replied.

"You're kidding me, right? This is my life! Would you expose your personal problems and marriage issues in a book?"

"Well, you spent time researching, you pursued answers, and you ended up with a terrific story to tell. That's what people do, they write books about things that matter. And they make lots of money, baby!"

Anna sighed. "Yes, I pursued answers, I got them; but I still don't know what to do with them. I mean, what did I find? That I have a husband who returned to this life to support me yet again in reaching my goals? That he loves me truly and unconditionally and that makes me feel so guilty because I still can't love him back the same way? Instead, I'm stuck on this love or at least a memory of this love, that attracts me in a strange way?"

"A love for an arrogant elderly man?" Lisa smile wryly.

"C'mon, Lisa, I'm serious. I know it sounds weird, but this is not about age, or physical appearance, or romance; this goes beyond. We have an unfinished business, and it affects our lives in one way or another. Besides, it came to me for a reason."

"Which was to help Marvin with his problems. By the way, how's he doing?"

"I don't know. It hasn't rained lately, but the accident on the water didn't seem traumatic for him. Maybe something changed..."

Lisa stared at Anna for a moment, sensing her anguish. "Okay, what do you intend to do about it? Keep all this a secret to tell your grandchildren in the dusk of your senility?"

"I don't know yet. Charlie has so much hope that his son is still alive. It's not right to take it from him." She trailed off and her gaze became vague. A smile played at the corner of her lips while an idea crossed her mind. "Maybe I'll get inspiration from the same angel that guided me up here," she said, thinking of Ralph.

Anna's parents stayed for few days, and while Marvin had plenty of attention, Anna took the time to do some more work with her past. She took a tour of the town, revisiting the most remarkable places from her past. The Hotel Green had been transformed into senior housing called Ives Manor. The facade had changed and the four giant columns removed. The

Concordia Society was still there, but the main hall was transformed into offices. Only the barroom was still running in the basement, exclusively for members. Across the street, the Still River was flowing through a concrete flood control channel, a project that definitely saved the town from further flood problems.

Anna drove up to Bethel, curious about what she would find if she got access to Ralph's office. Deep inside, she hoped to meet him once again, to listen to his wise words, and to expose herself to the cleverness of his unique personality. For that, where else could she go? She missed him, how could she hide this from herself? Although she still needed one more answer, she knew that he already had given her more than she expected, and lit a bright spotlight to guide her on her journey of self-knowledge. She could never again ignore the reality he had unveiled. Life had now a new meaning for her. She had tried to express it in her diary: *One's life on Earth is just one of many tiny periods of time in a soul's journey, and all these periods are connected as opportunities to heal souls from bad choices made, from the wounds some experiences can cause, and to make them free from what went wrong. It is an opportunity to progress, to heal relationships, and repair damages, and if one follows his fate and sticks to love as a safe beacon, he'll never get lost.*

Ralph had changed her life forever, and now that she was going to meet him again—at least through memories—she realized that she'd be satisfied if she could only say "thank you".

The front door of his building was locked, and like the previous time, she went around the parking lot to the back door, which was unlocked as expected. She entered the building, which was backlighted by the morning sun crossing the window, and reached the waiting room upstairs. The place looked as it had before: the chairs, the frames on the wall, the cabinet with reading material. But now it was sad and dusty.

The bonsai, on the top of the cabinet, was dry and lifeless. The clock hanging on the wall still showed ten minutes before three, and its minute hand was not moving.

She felt a breeze running inside the room though all windows were closed. It reassured her somehow that she was welcome there. She felt as if she had been there before in a different dimension, full of life and light. She turned to Ralph's office and saw his nametag on the door. Then she approached, her heart pounding with expectation. She opened the door slowly. The room was plunged into darkness, and she groped along the wall by the left side of the door, where she remembered seeing the switch. To her surprise, the place still had power.

She took a moment to catch her breath. Then, she moved hesitantly toward Ralph's desk, near the shelf where the picture of his son still rested in a frame. She took the picture in her hands. The dust on it assured her that nobody else had been there for a while. A year had passed since Ralph's death, and the place was preserved as if waiting for him to return. Maybe Sara couldn't cope with her grief and could not bear to dismantle the last piece of hope the office represented.

Anna saw the lounge chair, and couldn't resist sitting on it once more. She leaned back, closed her eyes, and in her mind, she could hear Ralph's voice inviting her for a trip in a slow and steady countdown. His voice sounded like a distant song in her memories, and she knew that whenever she wanted to hear it again, she had only to close her eyes, and it'd be there, just like now, whispering in her ears. She could feel the warmth of his breath and the wisdom of his words spreading a pleasant sensation inside her brain, so relax that she felt like falling asleep. Some images began to pop up as if in a dream, and she instinctively decided to allow them to come.

Anna saw herself by the side of a mature man during the time when she lived in Brazil as Lucia, the daughter of the lame man. She recognized the mature man as that special one she had seen in her first regression, the one who never forced her to do anything she didn't want to, the only one that asked questions and made her feel loved, the one she dreamed of running away with. He was a married man though, and had left his devoted wife and his child, seduced by Lucia's youth. They found love and happiness together. He freed her from her father's exploitation, but he had to cope with the misfortune that befell the life of his wife and his child. The agony expressed in his eyes showed his inability to abdicate his happiness with Lucia and go back home and repair the disgrace he caused to his family. He was Charlie! It was the life when they first found each other and shared love and passion together.

Anna sensed that her last question had been just answered, and it was about who Charlie was, and when all between them had started. She heard a message, like a whisper in her ear, before the images faded to black. *Those who find the secret path into our hearts never leave it. Love is the essence of the soul, and similar to a soul, once it is born, it never dies. But, it can't be rushed to be claimed over someone else's misfortune, for it has its own time to ripen. Like any fruit, it needs to reach maturity to reach its fullest potential... in its right time.*

Anna stayed quiet for a moment until she felt that all the magic was gone. She went to Ralph's desk, sat down on his chair, and took a pen from a penholder to write down the message on a notepad while it was fresh in her mind. She closed her eyes for a moment with a sensation of having Ralph again close to her. Her hand started to move over the paper against her will. She opened her eyes and read on the notepad: "I will watch over you. You are never alone." She felt her hands being released and heard Ralph voice whispering in her ears. "Leave it on the desk."

Anna understood that it was a message for Sara. She closed her eyes, only to find that there weren't words to translate her feelings at that moment. She just sighed and released her emotions in a single happy tear.

After her visit to Ralph's office, she felt that she had brought closure to the grief she had felt on hearing about Ralph's death. Now, she could focus on Charlie. She started to plan a new visit. Not wanting to feel naïve and speechless in the face of his stubborn skepticism again, she decided to do some research and gather information to provide the proof Charlie required as evidence to validate her story.

She wasn't sure though, if she should tell him all that she knew or what would be appropriate to tell without hurting him badly. What she had witnessed at his house on her previous visit, told her that he was still waiting for his son to come back, and not only him. He was clearly waiting for Georgia, for love, for happiness. She repeatedly asked herself if it was fair to take it from him, and was disappointed that no answers echoed back. How he would bear life after knowing that he had nothing else to wait for? She had nothing to offer in exchange. Hope was the only thing left for him to cling to in his effort to survive the tragedy of his life.

In the meantime, she visited Georgetown in hopes of finding Marty's Diane. It took her a lot of time and hard work since she didn't know Diane's last name. First time there, she found only frustration. When she came back for a second try, she brought Marvin along. He led her straight to Diane's parents' house and from there, to Diane. Marty's first love received them with an open heart, and she held back tears while listening to their story. Marvin recognized her and shared some memories. For Diane, the reencounter provided closure, healing decades of quiet sorrow and longing for her sweetheart. The visit lasted a couple of hours and when Anna and Marvin left Georgetown, Anna realized that she had just found something to offer Charlie. She decided that it was time for another visit.

The next morning, following her intuition, Anna knocked on Ellen's door. She invited Anna in with the same friendly smile, and they settled on the couch in the living room. As Anna shared her memories, Ellen frowned, Anna's words squeezing her heart while the images were revealed. When Anna was finished, Ellen was in tears.

"I'm happy that Georgia didn't do anything stupid," Ellen said in confession. "I always loved her, and I hated that I had to be mad at her."

"So, do you believe me?"

Ellen nodded. "Marty's disappearance affected me greatly. I never believed that my nephew would ever be away from his family for so long without a word, unless he no longer belonged to this world. I intuitively knew it, even before you came to visit us, but I never had sufficient evidence that could close the door on hope."

Anna gave her a long and warming hug, allowing Ellen to release all the old pain she had stored up.

They spent time over a cup of tea, and Anna saw a glow slowly coming back to Ellen's eyes while she was telling stories from her youth.

"I want to see Charlie again," Anna said afterwards. "Can you please help me?"

Ellen stared at her for a moment with a grin. "More than anyone, I want to see my brother free of all hatred and pain this untold story has left. I'll call him. You can trust me; he'll want to see you again."

Anna smiled. "I can't find words to thank you."

"You already did."

"Can I ask you one more thing? You said you have Georgia's belongings in your attic. I'd like to spend time with them."

Ellen gave her a curious look, but agreed. "Come with me," she said. "I'll get you a flashlight."

Piled in a dark area in the attic, the cases that once belonged to Georgia were covered with dust. Anna turned on the flashlight, and the vision of them next to Marty's guitar case and his baseball bat felt like time travel. Her mind went back to the memories of her last day with Charlie, but she strived to be present and focus on what she came for. She reached for the train case lying in the back of the pile, as if the secret inside it still needed to be hidden from the world. She took it and slowly dusted the top before opening it. She removed the makeup to clear out the bottom, and found that the false compartment had never been uncovered. She opened it, and what she found was exactly what she expected.

From Ellen's house, Anna went straight to Charlie. She had a peaceful feeling inside, confident that it was the right moment and that she had the right words to say.

She grabbed her purse and left her car. The house seemed quiet as usual. She inhaled deeply before ringing the doorbell. A couple of seconds without an answer seemed an eternity, and she was going to ring the doorbell again when she heard the door being unlocked from inside.

Most of her anxiety was centered on how Charlie would react to her presence, which turned out to be surprisingly quite civilized. Ellen had called him and begged him for another chance for Anna to apologize. Ellen thought this excuse was the only way her stubborn brother would open his door for Anna again.

Wordlessly, he looked straight into her eyes. He opened the door widely and motioned her to enter. Once in the living room, she noticed, with surprise, that the three records, with which Charlie had challenged her, were still on the coffee table, which seemed unlikely for a man so obsessed with organization.

"Thank you for having me again," she said.

He nodded, this time avoiding her gaze. "Ellie begged me to. If you came for my apology—."

"May I have a seat? It won't take much time," she cut him

off, glancing at the couch where they once chatted.

He motioned for her to sit and moved toward the sofa visibly thwarted. Anna, instead, approached the old Victrola and grabbed Marty's picture. It was the same picture Georgia saw on her first visit to Charlie after she arrived back in town—the one Charlie took of Marty in LA, on that frustrating trip to find his mother.

"I wonder how it would be if you had found her in LA," she said, handing the picture frame to Charlie.

His expression was one of surprise, as he didn't remember mentioning to her about that picture. "This we'll never know," he replied.

"It wasn't your fault, Charlie. She had moved, after her father died." She trailed off, noticing the anxiety growing on his face. "I can give you her address, but I guess it's too late."

"You know nothing." He responded with an ironic smile then frowned, annoyed.

"But you wish I knew."

Charlie's expression changed. "Listen lady, I've had e-nough of your lies. If you aren't here to apologize, you should leave now."

"I'm sorry that our last conversation ended up that way," she said. "But I have more than apologies to offer." She was confident, and Charlie could not bear her gaze. "You've told me that anger gives you strength, but I guess I'm not the liar here."

Charlie finally looked at her.

"It's hope," she said fondly, bearing his gaze. "Why does a man never get married and keep the house organized, if it's not for the vision of the woman he loved more than anything else coming through that door and begging for his forgiveness?"

Charlie seemed transfixed by the irresistible magnetism in Anna's voice.

"You left these records here because you couldn't let go of

the hope that I could tell you what song you last danced with her. Am I right?"

Charlie's face contorted.

"Do you want to listen to a song?" she boldly challenged him.

A flame lit up in his eyes. He watched, astonished, as Anna picked up the Nat King Cole album and turned it over to read the list of songs on the back. Then, she brought it to the Victrola, and slipping the vinyl out of the cover, she placed it on the turntable. She rested the needle on the track she had chosen as if she had done it many times before, and then gazed back at Charlie. She waited until the first notes of *Unforgettable* filled the air. A smile played at the corner of Charlie's mouth. He felt lost in his disbelief when Anna offered him a hand.

"C'mon snake, let's rattle!" Anna gently took Charlie by his hand and pulled him up. Charlie responded as if a strange force was in charge of his emotions. He held her right hand on the level of his shoulder, embracing her by the waist, gently pulling her closer. She closed her eyes and rested her head on his chest. He was hesitant for a moment, and finally closed his eyes, moving his feet in time to the music. The connection to their past, their love, and their days together was palpable, a magical bond as they touched each other's hands.

Unforgettable, that's what you are... The song filled the air as the living room became the Concordia Society dance hall, and they were back on the night of October 15, 1955.

Unforgettable in every way... He kept his eyes closed and smiled with joy—the joy he had dreamed of for so long. And he surrendered to the mirage of being young again, and having Georgia in his arms.

That's why, darling, it's incredible that someone so unforgettable thinks that I am unforgettable, too... He was so taken by the moment, that he felt as if his classmate, Danny, would come at any time to tap on his shoulder.

When the song faded out on the vinyl, Charlie let go of her hand and sat back on the couch, feeling physically instable. Georgia went to remove the needle from the vinyl and came back to the couch.

"What is this?" Charlie finally said, this time unable to disguise his joy. "Are you a psychic?"

She grinned. "It wasn't that hard to guess, wasn't it?"

Charlie stared at her and nodded. "It was a good shot, though." He said that, but he wanted to hear that it wasn't a guess. He wanted to hold the image of Georgia in his arms and hang on to the marvelous sensation the dance had left.

"I will gladly tell you more, when you're ready," she said without removing her gaze from his. "I can tell you what happened on the last night at your flooded house after you proposed to her. I can tell you that you worked hard that night while she volunteered at the Red Cross." She stopped.

Charlie's expression had grown pale and his eyes startled.

"I can tell you what happened next, to her and Marty, after they left your mom's house in her yellow Chevrolet." She kept talking in a steady rhythm. "I can tell you that the last page of her diary was accidentally torn out by Georgia, after she wrote your phone number on it. What she wrote wasn't anything threatening. She only wanted so much to have a family with you, Charlie. If you had taken a good look at that hotel room, you would have found it somewhere." She trailed off, giving space for him to decide. "When you're ready…"

"How could you know about these things? Have you met her? Where is she?" Charlie still tried a skeptical reaction, not exactly because he was still refusing to believe; he was confused and dizzy, struck by Anna's revelation.

"She's dead, Charlie," Anna said gently. "She died only few minutes after the last time you saw her."

Charlie was unable to say a word. Before his astonished eyes, Anna described the details she could remember of the tragic last moments of Georgia and Marty's lives, and how she discovered it. She told about the regression and the accident. Her words finally seemed to have an impact on Charlie's skepticism. Then, she reached for an envelope from her purse and handed it to him. He opened it slowly, with his hands shaking from the expectation, and slid a paper from its nest.

"What is it?" he was hardly holding on to his emotions.

"A copy of a statement I got from the archives of Danbury Savings Bank. It took a lot of diplomacy for me to get it. As you can see, all the money Georgia had is still on the bank records as silent evidence that she never planned to leave the town."

Charlie wept like a child, releasing almost fifty years of sorrow. Anna couldn't say another word, taken by Charlie's emotion.

"How is it possible?" Charlie finally said when his emotions subsided. "Their bodies would have been washed up somewhere. I bothered the police almost every day. They'd have called me if they'd ever found the bodies."

"I don't know. Maybe the power of the water dragged them to the ocean. We aren't that far. The car maybe was found, but it wasn't in her name, as you know."

Charlie thought about all the time he has spent believing that Georgia had betrayed him, and he felt like a horrible person. "How unjust I am! She only wanted to be loved," he said, echoing Georgia's words.

His comment melted Anna's heart, and a bright smile of relief broke out on her face.

Charlie gazed at her, almost with veneration, as if trying to see the woman he loved behind the traces of her face. "So, you are Georgia," he concluded.

She shook her head. "No. I'm Anna, a married woman, mother of a boy, who, out of the blue, began to unveil our past lives and brought us together. Georgia and Marty are a mutual part of our past, and I guess we need to work together to move on."

Charlie sobbed once again. "Move on..." he repeated after her.

"I believe that it's what all this came back for," she said, fondly holding his hand. "We needed closure. You need to forgive me—it wasn't my fault—and accept what, for some reason, is your fate," she deepened into his eyes. "Everything in life has a reason, Charlie. My son and I came back to this life to help you. You're not alone, we can do this together. My son would love to have you around. I don't know how long his memories will last; they say that they fade away as he grows, but you can be the grandpa he can't have often by his side because my parents live far away." She trailed off, as she kept the best part for the last. "Besides, I think you will be very busy with your own grandchildren, teaching them how to grow vegetables and how to be organized."

Charlie's gaze turned into dismay. "I don't have grandchildren. It seems that you have it all, and nothing is left for me," he said, sliding his hand from hers to wipe his face.

"I didn't come here only to take from you all that you have, Charlie. If it was the case, I would keep all this to myself."

Charlie shook his head mutely.

"The day before the flood," she continued, "Marty spent at Diane's house, and that's why he never came to our meeting. But it wasn't the first time he did that. Diane got pregnant. You are a grandfather of a forty-six year old man, and a great grandfather of four kids that would love to meet you."

Charlie got lost in past memories, he could not believe in it. "Diane..." Charlie forced his mind to remember. "She came to me once, after Marty was gone, but I scared her away."

"You have so much love, Charlie," she continued. "You're a unique man, you could make any woman the happiest; but this is a time for you to hold off on your dreams and share your love in a different way."

"Why?" Charlie was thwarted. "Why did it happen to me? What have I done to God?"

"It's not about punishment, Charlie. We make mistakes in life, and sometimes we carry the burden from one life to the next. You and I have been together before, and we hurt people in our past life. We built our happiness over somebody else's disgrace. This life now is for us to learn to wait and trust; to respect, and to make better choices."

"Learn to wait..." Charlie was despondent. "I haven't done anything but wait my whole life."

"You need to wait no more; now you have the answers."

Charlie's expression changed. Anna looked at him with expectation, unable to read his emotions He stood up and took some steps, as if lost in his own house. Then he gazed away through the window. The wind was playing with the leaves on the ground.

"None of this is possible," he finally said. "None of this is possible," he repeated, his gaze focused anywhere but on the present moment.

Anna's heart tightened, and she strived to hold back her tears, watching Charlie cross the living room with a total absence of emotion on his face. He left the house and went into the backyard. Through the window, she saw him grabbing his tools and entering his garden, ignoring the cold wind. A deep compassion grew inside Anna's broken heart, and she hoped that time could help him digest all the information she had given him.

She glanced around the house, imagining how it would be if they had never been apart. This would be her home, and she'd be an old well-settled woman now, who had had the fulfilling experience of having the love of her life always around. But life had claimed its compensation, as she had learned. Maybe the future would reward them for bearing it bravely and doing the right thing. Maybe they would come back together once more, this time without the burden that bad choices and ignorance had created in their past.

She fished in her purse for the glass slipper necklace she

found inside the false bottom of Georgia's train case at Ellen's attic. She held it in her hands for a moment, thinking that the promise this piece of crystal once represented still stood: she never forgot him, and she never would.

She hung the glass slipper necklace on Marty's picture frame and left the house.

Chapter 29

The day was sad, gray, and cloudy, though a little warmer than the season had been. Scattered rain fell as expected after the warm days of fall.

Anna's anxiety had gone and she felt settled into life as she had never felt before. She was focused on turning her home into her haven; her family was her priority now. She had begun to consider Lisa's suggestion to write a memoir, but still was unsure if she should. Would anyone be interested in her story? Wouldn't it sound too surreal? She wondered about how many stories could be told by billions of souls coming and going to and from this planet, experiencing life in all possible perspectives as they journeyed toward their often-unclear desire of eternal freedom. She thought that many sorrows could be avoided if they could understand the way things work beyond the illusion of the material world, the love and perfection that exist behind the laws that orchestrate destiny as she had witnessed herself. Maybe they'd think less of war, hatred, separation, and more about love, solidarity, and the gift of being here at this moment, knowing that every soul connected to our own is a co-writer of our story, which certainly did not start at birth and will not end after our physical lungs stop breathing.

This day, Anna wrote in her diary:
"Life
"Life is a mystery when we live in the dark place of ignorance about spiritual life.

"The present is for us to live wisely. All movements we make reflect on somebody else's life and on the whole as well, just

like a wave on a lake. We don't have to be perfect; we're only apprentices. But we do need to learn from our mistakes. The past is a powerful force, and it will always reach us, so it's better to strive to make better decisions now, because, sooner or later, we might face the aftermath.

"Happiness

"Everyone looks for happiness, but I found that happiness is about events that make our heartbeats speed up. Joy is something bigger. True joy comes from truth and faith. Truth sets us free from ignorance and a false perception of life, and faith gives us the certainty that, above our human fragility, there is a powerful force watching over us and ruling the universe. All that's right and good will fall into place eventually, in perfect order, as perfect as the mathematics of life, providing answers for all questions and solutions for all equations. We only need to be ready to listen to the silence within us with a humble attitude and an open heart."

Charlie represented the only part of her life that Anna hadn't yet found peace. It had been almost a month since that day. After leaving his house, she called Ellen and told her to take good care of him. Since then, Anna hadn't heard from her. Many times, she worried about Charlie and about how he was managing to live after all that she told him. Was he able to just ignore all the evidence he had and to keep his stubborn attitude of denial or was he managing to rebuild his life around the truth? She had decided to respect his pace, and if he ever wanted to see her again, it would be on him. She couldn't think of anything else she could do about it, besides wait and hope for a miracle.

This day, Anna settled on the couch in the living room to work on plans for Thanksgiving dinner. She had made plans to include her parents and also Lisa. She had begun to make some notes, when she got caught up with Marvin, distracted by the raindrops pelting on the window. She was surprisingly glad, noticing the relaxing pleasure sparkling on his face, and wondered whether he was healed from his phobia or if it was only a moment of distraction.

The phone rang, awakening Anna from her thoughts, and she moved to answer it. She was excited when she recognized Ellen's number. "Hello, this is Anna."

"Hi, Anna. This is Ellen. How are you doing?" Ellen's voice sounded smooth.

"I'm doing great."

"And Marvin?"

"He couldn't be better." Anna glanced at her son tracing something with his finger on the blurry window. "What about you...and Charlie?"

"We're doing well. Listen, I'm calling because I'll have some guests for Thanksgiving, and I wonder if you and Marvin—and your husband, of course—want to come over or at least stop by."

"Guests?" Anna's heartbeat sped up, as she guessed the hidden intention behind Ellen's invitation.

"Diane and her son will come with the kids, and I thought you'd like to join us."

Anna was speechless for a moment, grinning with relief. "Will Charlie be there?" she asked.

"Actually, it was his idea."

Anna closed her eyes in silent celebration. The miracle she hoped for came sooner than she expected. "You can count on us," she said without hesitation.

After hanging up, Anna stayed lost in her thoughts for a moment, visualizing the reencounter with all of them, and especially with Charlie. Surreal, amazing and...unforgettable! Those were the words she found to express her expectations.

She sent out a prayer of gratitude. When she opened her eyes, she joined Marvin who was standing on the sofa, leaning forward to press his nose against the windowpane. She kneeled by his side, sharing his joy with the wet day. "Do you like to see the rain?"

"Yeah. God's watering the plants."

"Yes, he is." She disguised her cheer.

A deer came out of the woods and trailed across the front yard, catching Marvin's attention. "Mom, where do deer stay in the winter? I mean, where do they go when they have no food, or when the ground is covered by snow?"

"They stay around. It's challenging, but they survive. Nature is wise."

"Do they feel cold?"

"They have their natural 'winter coats'."

"Maybe we can feed them, so they won't be starving."

"That's a nice thought, but our food is harmful for them."

"But there's nothing out there for them to eat."

"Well, there are nuts and woody plants. They also take some nourishment from the fat they build through the spring and summer."

Marvin became silent, as if she had satisfied his curiosity. "Mom, do you think that Charlie will come to visit us some day?"

Anna gazed at Marvin, surprised by his unexpected question, wondering if he had heard her conversation with Ellen. "Would you like it if he would?" she asked back.

"I guess so. I miss him," he answered.

"Well, maybe someday…we can't rush life. God's time has its own pace."

It wasn't only a hope; after Ellen's unexpected invitation, it became a possibility. Anna's heart seemed to take off to a different reality. In her mind, she pictured the old man straightening his gray Homburg in front of his 1948 green Ford parked in her driveway. She felt that, somehow, Georgia was still alive within her, with her unique life perspective, as if neither death nor rebirth had power to clear out from one's spirit what is true. A birth is always a new beginning for a soul, but what you conquered is yours to keep, she thought. This is all you can really take with you.

Her vision faded, as if washed away by the rain that had picked up outside.

Marvin gazed at her, and Anna frowned in response, trying to grasp the glare of excitement in his eyes. She looked at the pouring rain outside and back to him. "Are you ready?" She asked, reading his mind.

As he nodded, she took him off of the couch and flung open the front door. Marvin ran cheerfully into the front yard and she followed after him.

Connect with the author at:
www.robertocabral-author.com

Made in the USA
Middletown, DE
18 November 2015